The Mother I Could Have Been

BOOKS BY KERRY FISHER

The Island Escape
After the Lie
The Silent Wife
The Secret Child
The Not So Perfect Mother
The Woman I Was Before

The Mother I Could Have Been

KERRY FISHER

bookouture

Published by Bookouture in 2019

An imprint of Storyfire Ltd.
Carmelite House
50 Victoria Embankment
London EC4Y 0DZ

www.bookouture.com

ISBN: 978-1-83888-028-6
eBook ISBN: 978-1-83888-027-9

PART ONE

2018

Patience. Patience. Patience. He kept saying that to me, as though I lacked understanding about how these things work. I did. I'd never needed to find someone who'd disappeared before. Naively, I'd assumed that if you did it for a living, it would be a few hours fiddling about on the internet before hitting the jackpot. But it appeared that there were a lot of Vicky Halls in the world and even a private detective who proclaimed himself 'the expert at finding the haystack needle' required more time than I'd expected. I bristled when he asked why I wanted to find her. I hadn't told anyone the real purpose. When other members of the family asked, I just said I'd been thinking about building bridges for a long time. I wasn't about to explain the exact reasons to anyone. I couldn't risk letting her find out the truth. I played the emotional mother card, said we'd lost touch and I felt it was time to have her back with us, where she belonged. He looked sceptical. Kept saying that it was usually easier to get a better 'outcome' if he knew the whole story. But I couldn't let him loose with that. He'd have a hard job persuading her to come back as it was, without frightening her with the facts. Like us, she'd be shocked at how much had changed since I saw her last.

I smiled and brushed off his comment. 'Do any of us recognise the whole story? Or do we just offer up the best version of ourselves?'

Then I started to cry, telling him my heart was completely broken. Which was true, though not for the motives he thought.

I suggested doubling his money if he found her within a month.

He put his head on one side. 'Is there a reason you're in such a hurry?'

'I don't want to waste any more time.' It wasn't just that I didn't want to. I couldn't afford to.

VICKY

July 2009

The day after I graduated from university – the event my mother was 'so looking forward to' but failed to turn up at – I had brunch with my flatmate, Liv, at her parents' posh hotel. Her mother, Fiona, was over-the-top jolly, as though her saying, 'Celebration breakfast on us, Vicky. Buck's Fizz?' would make up for the fact that the previous day I'd been the odd one out again, the weirdo with no parents to see me receive my degree in English.

Mum's number had flashed up on my phone, twenty-five minutes before the ceremony.

'Mum? Where are you?'

And there it was, all in the sigh. The sudden and unwelcome knowledge that Mum wasn't speaking to me from outside the university library, her head swivelling round trying to understand whether she should walk right or left to reach me. Her words weren't coming to me from a few hundred metres away.

'Darling, I'm so sorry. I'm ringing from the hospital.'

I turned my back on the merry little group. 'Why? Have you had an accident?' Fright surged through me, making me press the phone harder into my ear, as though I'd be able to touch her.

'It's Emily. Just as I was leaving, she ran to say goodbye to me and fell down the stairs. She's broken her wrist and had a nasty crack to the head.'

I should ask if my stepsister was going to be okay. But the words that came out were, 'So you're not coming today then?'

'I'm really sorry, Vicky. I tried to phone earlier but there was no signal in the hospital and Emily was crying and I couldn't leave her. I've only just got out now. I feel so bad letting you down. I really, really wanted to be there.'

I didn't say anything.

Mum's voice took on a tinge of weariness, a hint of irritation that I wasn't rushing to make it easy for her when Emily was hurt. 'I'll make it up to you, I promise. Take lots of photos for me. Get one of your friends to take a picture when you're on stage.'

My eyes filled. 'What about getting all my stuff home?'

'Can you bring some of it on the train? Ian's going to need the car for work for the rest of this week.'

I was pretty sure he'd find a way to manage without it for one day if Mum needed to take Joey or Emily somewhere.

'But we have to give the keys back tomorrow night.' Panic was making my voice sharper, snappier than I ever allowed myself to be.

'Could you find somewhere to store everything and we can drive back at the weekend? Sorry, Vicky, I've got to go, the nurse is calling me back in. Have a lovely day. Look forward to hearing all about it.' The last sentence was muffled, fading, as though she'd already taken the phone away from her ear, ready to shove it back into her handbag and be a good mother elsewhere.

I'd stood to one side, anger boiling around my body, desperate to find an outlet. I'd watched the mums pointing out their offspring to each other, dads doing those complicit smiles as they dodged past other parents balancing three glasses of champagne in a precarious fashion, the common ground of children to be proud of uniting them. And my fellow students, their faces reflected all around in older, wrinkled versions of themselves. The protruding teeth they inherited from their mothers. Those dark, thick eyebrows from their fathers. And the thing that made me most envious of all, those familial gestures, a vivaciousness perhaps, maybe a way of flinging out a hand to emphasise a point. All the signals that defined them as being from the same pack, the people they'd find their way back to wherever they were in the world. Where they would recognise themselves and where they would fit without having to change their shape to suit the slot.

But me, I had to borrow a tribe. Which was why I was here now, not picking over the details of the previous day's ceremony with my own mother but with Liv and her parents who not only had managed to turn up on the right day but had stayed on to help her pack.

Liv paused with a piece of bacon halfway to her mouth when her mother announced that I'd be joining them for 'a week or two' in Corfu over the summer. I pushed back the flutter of fear: I'd understood the night before that Fiona had invited me for however long it took me to get a job. Instead I said thank you and that I hoped that was okay with Liv, that I wouldn't get in the way or live in her pocket. Liv did one of those shrugs that always left me wondering whether I'd imagined the evenings when we'd tottered back from town in the early hours, the music still pulsating in my ears, my feet hot with the beat of the dance floor, with her weaving about, saying, 'I always have such a laugh with you.' The nights she'd wept in my arms when Pete the pianist – 'Oh my God, Vicky, you should hear him play' – turned out to be Pete the prick. 'He didn't even look my way. Just carried on kissing her as though we'd never even slept together.' The times I'd missed lectures to help her with her essays. 'Thanks, Vick, you're a star. I don't know why I let myself get so behind.'

But despite Liv's lukewarm response, I wasn't going home. I'd stay away until they were sorry. Until they understood what it was like to be me. I wondered whether Mum had even given any further thought to what would happen to my stuff. She'd assume, just as she always did, that I'd work it out, come up with a plan that didn't involve her. I couldn't wait to hear the catch in her voice, the intake of breath when I told her I'd given everything to a homeless charity, including the ancient TV Ian had reluctantly allowed me to take, terrified that Emily and Joey might somehow miss out on something because, for once, I had benefitted. The defiance was both liberating and terrifying. I didn't know I had it in me to be brave.

Less than a week later, I found myself at Gatwick Airport with one suitcase and a rucksack I just managed to cram into the easyJet holder to the disappointment of the check-in desk employee.

I didn't want to trigger a whole missing person enquiry, so I just messaged Mum with, *Change of plan, going travelling this summer, will be in touch.*

I took a perverse pleasure in not responding to her panicky texts. *Where are you going, Vicky? Ring me.* Every time I pressed the 'reject call' button, I had the competing sensation of power and a desire to hear her reassure me that Emily and Joey needed her more because they were still so little, but she didn't love me less.

And when I got to Corfu, to the villa with its flagstone floor, whitewashed walls and circular veranda overlooking a beach straight out of the Greek cliché of bobbing fishing boats on sparkling sea, I didn't think about it much.

Liv seemed happy for me to be there, though her excitement about her upcoming job on a graduate accountancy programme wounded me. 'The company flat's got a balcony with a view of the river!' The last two years of sharing a flat with me was already passé, as inconsequential as some of the boys who'd resided briefly in Liv's bed, throwing up in our bathroom and leaving a pong in our loo.

I wanted to say, 'What about me? Will you forget all about me now?' Because I knew I wouldn't forget her. I loved her confidence, the way she sat cross-legged on the floor in the middle of the common room at university if there weren't any seats, making people step around her, never once looking up to see if she was in the way, not feeling the need to tuck her bags under her knees, to make herself small. To me, she was family. But Liv was scornful, almost hurtful, in her desire to move onto the next stage of her life, as though complete security at home resulted in an obscene haste to rush forwards, away from what she had into adventures that were clearly more thrilling beyond.

As I settled into the drumbeat of a different household, I noticed her family seemed to thrive on benign neglect underpinned by unconditional love. Her parents, as far as I could see, were much more interested in making sure the fridge was stocked with rosé than bothering about where we were and what time we came in. Liv and I would often be walking along the coastal path when it was already light, back from clubbing under the stars in Kassiopi. I never heard her phone ping once with her mother fussing about where she was, yet Liv was so certain of her place in the world. If I ever stayed out later than midnight, Mum would be messaging, asking me where I was, but the subtext was always 'Don't wake us up when you come in.' I thought Mum would be glad that I wasn't at home this summer disturbing them all, but she kept pestering me, 'Mum' flashing up on my phone on a regular basis. In the end, I told her I was with Liv's family in Corfu, just to stop the embarrassment of her name coming up when we were chatting to boys in bars.

About two weeks after I'd arrived in Corfu, Liv mentioned they were all going out for a 'family meal'. I couldn't tell from her tone whether that included me or not, so I played it safe. 'Great, no worries, I'll just hang out here or go for a walk.'

Liv frowned. 'God, don't play the victim over one night. My family have given you a free holiday for *two weeks*, I don't think it's that much to expect that we can all go out without you now and again.'

I sat up, fastening my bikini top, that lurch of feeling that I didn't belong, that I'd mistakenly thought people were happy to have me around. 'I wasn't complaining. Your family has been really generous. I can amuse myself. I don't need looking after.'

Liv did a bad-tempered sigh and jumped into the pool with a huge splash, drops landing on my sizzling skin. She clambered onto the inflatable armchair floating around the pool and lay there, her face tilted to the sun. I nearly asked her if she wanted me to leave, but I was scared to hear the answer. Her mother was always waving airily towards the fridge, 'Help yourself to anything you want to eat, Vicky, try some of that yoghurt – food of the gods!' but, in reality, was she whispering to Liv's dad about how she didn't realise I'd be here *all* summer? Liv flicked her hand in the water, like a cat signalling its intention to pounce. Despite the heat, I felt the chill of being the person that everyone tolerated, felt sorry for – maybe – but no one really liked.

That evening, Liv's mother seemed puzzled I wasn't going out with them. I smiled. 'I'm fine, honestly, I could do with a night in. I don't want to intrude on your family time.'

She shrugged. 'You'd be very welcome.'

But I wasn't.

As soon as they'd gone, I sat by the pool, spraying myself with mozzie repellent and trying to read a psychological thriller Liv's mum had lent me. That panic from earlier, the sense that I'd overstayed my welcome, that I was a drag on the Simmonds, spoiling their summer, churned inside me. It was so long since I'd taken for granted my right to be anywhere, since before Mum married Ian in fact.

The music of the bars drifted up the coastline, luring me from my sunlounger. I got dressed in a white shirt with a deep neckline and more make-up than usual, then strode down the hill to the crescent of bars, shoulders back, feeling daring and rebellious, somehow more confident without Liv's shadow beside me. I waved to a couple of the waiters we'd got to know, feeling their eyes on me long after I'd walked past. I made my way to Freddie's Bar down by the harbour. The drinks were cheap and there was always a TV, so I'd have somewhere to focus my gaze. I'd often seen people come in on their own and sit chatting to the staff, who were young and friendly, mainly English or Irish.

I took a seat at the bar. Freddie, the owner, appeared opposite me immediately.

'What can I get you?' I ordered a beer. 'On your own tonight? Where's that friend of yours? Liv, is it?'

My heart dropped. The story of my life. Seeing me just reminded everyone of the person they'd rather be talking to. 'She's gone out with her mum and dad.'

'Not your thing?' Freddie said, passing me a beer.

'No, I don't really do family… I'm not that welcome at home.' My voice trailed off, the half-truth dangling in front of me like a fork in the road.

The statement that seemed such an extreme take on something that was more of a lie than a truth didn't ruffle Freddie at all. He shrugged. 'Hardly see mine either. They're not big on travelling and I've not got much interest in going back to Blighty. There's such a good expat community out here anyway. You staying long?'

I aimed for 'I'll see where the music takes me' nonchalance. 'Not sure what my plans are. Might get the ferry over to Italy at some point. See how the money goes.' The money I'd earned waitressing in my final year at uni would keep me going for a few more weeks if I could stay at Liv's, but she was going back to the UK in a fortnight to start her accountancy job.

Freddie indicated the bar with a nod of his head. 'You want a job here? There's a room up the top. It's only a box room, nothing fancy. I could do with an extra pair of hands.'

He went on to explain the hours to me, what I'd have to do, the money. But I wasn't listening. Without even trying, I didn't have to be that daughter that was somehow in the way, the friend who was all right to go out with but a bit of a pain on a permanent basis. With a surge of excitement, I realised that I, Vicky Hall, could be that sun-kissed girl, behind the bar, pulling pints with an air of authority, dancing a little shimmy as I moved between the optics, with everyone wishing they had the guts to swap their hard-fought-for two weeks in the sun for a carefree life out here.

I moved out the next day. I gave Liv a hug, the dynamics already changing – 'You'll come clubbing with me on your night off, won't you?' 'Let me know when you can pop up for a swim.'

Her mother hugged me tightly, making a show of thanking me for the plant I'd bought for her. 'We're here until September, so don't be a stranger.'

It was funny how I needed to leave to be welcome to stay.

I settled in quickly at Freddie's, becoming more and more entrenched in my bohemian persona. Whenever there was time to chat to punters at the bar, I felt as though I was juggling the lies of my life until they arced up into a circle of truth. 'Yeah, I'm hanging out here, just finished my degree. Prefer it that way, can't stand being tied down. Who knows what will come next? Maybe head off to France for a ski season?' I said it as though I'd be zipping down the black runs, jumping over moguls, no poles required, when the closest I'd got to skiing was barrier-clinging at the local ice-skating rink.

But I'd see the faces of those holidaymakers in their early twenties flash with envy as they counted down the days before their commute started again. And admiration that I'd had the courage to cling onto the sunshine without worrying about the future. Of course, they didn't know I had nothing to go back to.

If the conversation ever turned to family, whether I missed them, I'd just say, 'I'm not that big on family' with a strange pride that at twenty-one I was already ploughing my own furrow. Even when Freddie tried to delve deeper, I'd wrinkle my nose and say, 'They sort of chucked me out. Did me a favour really.' And I'd laugh, revelling in my newfound rebelliousness, conveniently ignoring the texts sitting unanswered on my phone from Mum. I meant to answer, really I did. But the conversation was so big, it was too hard to see what the opening line would be. Anyway, I knew if I let her off the hook, she'd stop trying and forget about me again.

Then one evening, when Freddie and I had finished clearing up after everyone had been in to watch a football match and the bar was even messier than normal, he said, 'Stay up for a bit.'

We sat sipping cocktails, watching the stragglers leave the nightclubs, the occasional drunken scuffle, the arguments between boyfriends and girlfriends, alcohol turning the dial up to 'You always…' 'I saw you…' 'I'm sick of you…' It was incredible that anyone got or stayed married.

Freddie leaned towards me. 'You're a complete enigma to me.'

My God, the man had me at enigma. I'd never felt so fascinating in my life. When he kissed me, the person he thought I was responded, playful, teasing and in charge.

'Come to bed with me?' he asked, his tone uncertain as though he thought he was punching above his weight.

I couldn't find the shy and stumbling words to tell him I'd only had one long-term boyfriend throughout most of university, that I didn't do casual sex. Freddie was so impressed by me – 'I've never met someone like you before. You don't seem to need anyone else at all' – I didn't want to let him down. I marched up to his glorious whitewashed room with the dawn sun creeping through the shutters as though I was used to men falling over themselves to have sex with me.

After that night, I never moved back to the box room. I became the barmaid whose boyfriend owned the bar. Who was sometimes late to work because I'd just stepped out of the shower and he'd lie back on the bed and say, 'I can't go down there thinking of you up here. It would be such a waste.' And I'd pretend to refuse and he'd beg and, for the first time in forever, I had power. Over a man who was eight years older than me. Nearly thirty. With his scruff of dark hair and a sleeve of tattoos, I'd be embarrassed if my mum saw me with him. But with a jolt, I realised I'd never have to introduce him. At some point, I'd probably go home, get a job my mum could boast to her friends about and spend weekends putting together flat-packed furniture with a bloke named Sam.

Liv was all agog when she came to the bar. 'You've fallen on your feet. Free booze and free lodgings. Is it serious? What will you do when you come back to England after the summer?'

'I'm not coming back.'

'What? You're not going to just stay here and be a barmaid for the rest of your life? What about your career?'

'Plenty of ways from A to B,' I said, parroting Freddie's favourite refrain.

I detected envy beneath her bemusement, a slight draining away of her superiority at landing a job for £25k a year when the rest of us weren't yet out of the starting blocks.

We partied till the early hours the night before she left and I walked her to the bottom of the hill that led to her villa. She hugged me. 'You will pop over and see me, even if you stay out here?'

I couldn't envisage banging on the door of her London apartment with its river view. She'd no doubt be sharing with posh girls, with high blonde ponytails, long eyelashes and slightly quizzical expressions, wondering why Liv was friendly with this girl with a big bum and wooden beads. It would be like turning up to a party just as someone had thrown the last paper plate into a bin bag. There'd be a brief flurry of greeting, then an awkward silence as everyone wondered what to do with me. 'I'll see you next time you come out here. Hope the job goes brilliantly.'

She started up the hill, blowing kisses and waving. Tears prickled at my eyes as I wandered back to the bar.

Freddie was already in bed when I got upstairs. 'Everything okay?'

My voice sounded brittle even though I laughed as I spoke. 'Yep. Just waved off another person who doesn't realise they'll never see me again.'

'I'm going to nickname you Scorched Earth. I hope you don't do that to me.'

I forced some levity into my words. 'You'd better watch yourself then.' I wished I could explain I'd discovered that breaking off contact with people I cared about was less painful than living with them loving me less.

I snuggled up to him, facing away, while tears dripped into my pillow.

By September, the novelty of being the girl making cocktails for the kids having their last hurrah before starting university was fading. They just seemed so young, talking about how they were going to be out clubbing every night and that they only had eight hours of lectures a week. 'Eight hours!' I was finding it harder to put on my smiley face for them all, especially when they were drunk and took forever to tell me what they wanted, then had a go at me for getting the order wrong.

Freddie shrugged. 'Yeah, it gets a bit wearing after a while. Why don't you take a couple of days off? Go to the beach and top up your tan before the winter comes? It's not sunshine every day then.'

I was knackered from all the three a.m. finishes and the idea of lying in the sunshine was very appealing. 'Are you sure?'

'Course. I can manage.'

I grabbed a bottle of water, my swim stuff and headed off. 'Ring me if it gets busy.'

It was the first time in weeks that I'd been on my own. I kept catching glimpses of myself in the shop windows. I searched for that people-pleasing me, the girl who never had to ask for an essay extension, the one who needed several glasses of wine to get on the dance floor. With my big Jackie O sunglasses, tie-dye wrap and battered straw hat, I could have been one of those girls whose name buzzed above all the others in the crowd, who was used to men competing to buy her a Sex on the Beach cocktail.

I wasn't that person, though Freddie thought I was. And the notion that I could be made me reckless.

I walked to a cove that the locals frequented where there was just one little beach shack that served fantastic pitta stuffed with fresh calamari and a barbecue where they grilled whichever fish they'd caught that day. It was never crowded, unless the sailing fraternity turned up. And, as Sod's Law would have it, just as I made my way down the rocky path to claim my place among some rocks that provided a bit of shade at the height of the day, a small yacht anchored in the shallows. With any luck, they'd grab their food and disappear.

With a lot of yahooing, five or six young men leapt over the side of the boat, dive-bombing and swearing at each other in that casual way that denotes both belonging and a sense of entitlement, rendering them oblivious to the sensitivity of anyone around them.

I flapped out my towel, and lay face down, listening to snatches of conversation.

'Leave the boat here and go into Kassiopi?'

'Nah, prefer a barbecue on the beach – I've had enough of drinking for a bit.'

'Can't handle the pace?'

'Just want to give it a rest.'

I lifted my head slightly so I could see who was speaking. The bloke who was all 'count me out, I'm chilling at the beach' was tall, with curly dark hair, wearing a pair of faded swim shorts. Even from where I was lying, I could see he had the most amazing eyes, the sort that had really thick lashes and such bright whites against his tanned skin. He bought a pitta while the rest of them raced up the beach, pushing and messing about, shouting about burning the soles of their feet. I watched him settle on a rock a few metres away, so at ease with himself. He didn't look the slightest bit bothered that no one from his group had stayed to keep him company. I'd have worried about what my friends were saying behind my back.

A Greek family nearby gestured at him, asking whether the calamari was good. He made all the right noises and they laughed as their little girl wandered over to him with her bucket and spade. He helped her make a castle, which was no easy task given that the beach was mainly pebbles rather than sand. She kept asking him something and he was trying to understand, glancing over at her parents for clarification. They were trying to explain with their hands but didn't speak English and the girl shouted in frustration: 'Ochi! Pyrgos!' at him.

I sat up. 'She wants you to build a tower.'

He grinned, his face brightening as he appeared to notice me for the first time. 'Thank you! Thought I was going to cause an international incident there.'

He obliged, patiently balancing stones on top of one another. The little girl clapped her hands in delight, rushing off to find shells to decorate it. Eventually she got bored and went off with her parents to get an ice cream.

The bloke came over to me. 'You're English, right?'

I nodded.

'Do you speak Greek?'

'Not really. I'm living here at the moment, so I've picked up the odd thing.'

'I'm here for a while as well, just till real life catches up. I'm William, William Cottingdale. Do you want a drink? It's bloody hot out here.'

I asked for a Coke and offered him the money.

'Don't be silly. I'll get it.'

It was ages since I'd had a proper conversation with someone from home that hadn't revolved around which cocktail had the most alcohol in it. Freddie talked about the football and the rugby, but he wasn't interested in reading, which I simply couldn't understand. When I tried to explain to Freddie what he was missing, he just said, 'Can never get into books. I prefer telly.' And he'd been away from England for so long that he'd become part of a little group of expats who moaned about what didn't work properly in Corfu without having a clue how bad things were at home. He never trusted any of the local tradesmen, always getting in 'Frank's mate' to fix the electrics or 'that bloke who used to run the plumbing business in Bognor'. I couldn't see the point of moving to Corfu if you just wanted to create the England you remembered, not even the actual one that existed.

I loved hearing William talk about where he lived in the Surrey Hills. I was reassured by the fact that I wasn't the only one who'd left England under a bit of a cloud. Apparently his parents were very keen for him to get started on a career but he wanted to have a bit of time out. 'I just feel like I worked really hard to get my GCSEs, then there was no let-up for A levels, bust my arse to get into Durham, managed to get a decent degree and then all that lies ahead is endless job applications, loads of bloody rejections and, if I'm really lucky, I'll be commuting into London for years without ever being able to afford anywhere to live.'

'So what is the plan? Can you find some work to keep you going?' I asked.

'Christ, don't turn into my mother on the first meeting!'

'Sorry, sorry, I don't mean you have to have a plan, I just wondered what you might do next.'

Liv would have handled this conversation so much better. Known all the cool things to say rather than sounding like a pensions adviser on her day off.

He laughed. 'It's a fair question, I'm only joking. I really like it here. It's pretty cheap to live too. One of the lads has got a house here, so it's just beer money and food really.' He juggled a couple of pebbles. 'And you, what's your story?'

I allowed the truth to become the truth as I saw it, the version most likely to make me interesting to a boy way out of my league. 'I'm just working out what comes next really. There's a lot of world out there to see. I don't really have anything to go back for, no real ties.' I hoped I sounded mysterious.

'Don't you have any family in the UK?'

'Don't know my dad. My mum got married again. She's got a new family, that I'm not really part of.'

William's eyebrows shot up. 'That's hard. Where do you stay when you're in England?'

'Good question,' I said. 'I've just graduated, so I've been in Bristol for the last three years. Gave all my stuff away to charity when I left. So just me and a rucksack now. Wherever I lay my hat and all that.'

'Makes my family look boringly normal.'

I could tell by his face that for all his poise and confidence, he couldn't visualise life without a parental safety net. I bet he had a car sitting on the drive for him at home, a father with plenty of 'chaps' he could call to organise an internship, a mother who cooked his favourite food and reminded him about dental appointments. I let him believe that I was alone in the world, damaged, daring and up for an adventure. I quite liked that new version of myself.

I omitted to mention that my last text from Mum asked when I was coming home and went on to say that if I gave her a bit of notice, she'd try and pick me up from the airport. I didn't bother to reply. I wasn't going to put myself in a position where I'd be all hopeful that she'd be waiting for me in the arrivals hall, and then there'd be some drama and I'd end up fighting to get a last-minute ticket for the National Express.

Eventually, the sun started to drop, his friends came back with bread and cheese and a massive watermelon they smashed open on a rock. William introduced me and some were more charming and interested than others, but no one seemed to mind me being there. I kept making murmurs about heading off, and was still mumbling about it later when the Greek families were long gone and we kept running in and out of the water, swimming out to the boat, then clambering on board for a beer. I couldn't relax. I was either terrified that my bikini would somehow slide to one side and they'd all laugh at a great expanse of pubic hair hanging out or I was dreading that William would say, 'Right, we're going to get off now.' I sagged with relief every time they engaged in a boisterous race back to the shore.

I kept squinting guiltily at my phone, to see if Freddie needed me at the bar. At nine, he texted me: *You OK? Been a long day without you!*

I replied, *All good, just chilling out, enjoying the quiet of the beach now everyone's gone and fancy going to get a bit of dinner if you can manage without me?*

No rush! Not that busy! Missing you!

I didn't know why Freddie's exclamation marks annoyed me.

About ten-thirty, the boys made noises about nipping up the coast in the boat to go clubbing and I started packing up my towel and book, determined to look like I wasn't hanging around waiting for an invitation. William shrugged and said, 'I'm going to head back to the house. Not really feeling the party vibe tonight.'

The other blokes did an exaggerated stare at me, then at each other. The stocky one with a crew cut that did not flatter him winked at William. 'See you later then. Or not.' And with that they all splashed off back to the boat.

I sat on the rock clutching my bag to me. The waves were rolling in and out. I couldn't look at William, though I was aware of him, to the left of me, running his fingers through his hair.

'Hey.'

I forced myself to meet his eyes.

I don't know what answer I gave to the silent question he was asking, but he came to sit by my feet, and leaned against my legs. I didn't move, though I was desperately hoping my leg hair wasn't prickling his arm.

'So, Little Vick, what have you got to say?'

I felt under pressure to come up with something witty, something that all the girls who'd attended his posh school might come out with, to show that they weren't taking all this being left alone together on a deserted beach seriously.

All I could manage was, 'About what?'

'Life. The universe.'

I felt like the thick girl in class, frowning over a maths equation that everyone else had solved in seconds. I reached for my flip-flops. It was better that I left before he realised that I was nowhere as interesting as he'd hoped.

'Oh bugger it. I'm going to have to make the first move, aren't I? Just come down here and let me kiss you.'

And there we lay, kissing, listening to the waves and talking in a gentle manner, the sort that holds a light and kind teasing tucked inside the tone. I'd never lain on a beach stargazing with anyone. I wasn't even sure people really did that – well, not girls that grew up in a little terraced house in the Fens and spent school holidays working at the local mushroom farm. William actually knew some of the constellations – 'We live on a big hill in the middle of nowhere and on our top floor, we've got a telescope. On a clear night, the stars are amazing.' I rested my head on his arm, lost in the perfection of the moment, of the romance I thought only existed in films. My mind pinged between the gorgeousness of William and the miracle that he'd bothered to speak to me in the first place.

I stayed until way too late. Until I had six or seven increasingly concerned text messages from Freddie. Until I had to tell William that I really had to go.

'I'll walk you back and get a cab from Kassiopi.'

'No, I'll be fine, honestly.' Though I did feel nervous about the mile or so of road with no lights. Not quite so devil-may-care as I made out.

'I'm coming with you.'

In the end, I decided he could walk me to the outskirts of Kassiopi and then I'd make an excuse.

We walked on the road, our feet tapping along in the silence between us. But his hand in mine made words redundant. We'd probably never meet again, but I tried not to let that interfere with the joy of the moment. In fact, I almost started humming Lou Reed's 'It's A Perfect Day', but it reminded me too much of everyone singing it on Mum's last birthday, me mouthing the words so Ian and the kids wouldn't laugh at my out-of-tune voice and underline, yet again, that I didn't share their genes. A splinter of sadness squeezed in.

William turned to me. 'What did you think about just then?'

'Nothing. Why?'

'You loosened your grip as though you're getting ready to run off.'

The lights of Kassiopi were very close. 'I can't walk into town with you. I hate everyone knowing my business. The expat community is pretty gossipy.'

William pulled me to him and leaned his forehead against mine. 'You'll have to do better than that, Little Vick.'

I drew back. 'What do you mean?'

'Took me a while to piece it together, but you work at that bar in the harbour, don't you? I've seen you with the guy who owns it. Your boyfriend, I'm assuming?'

'Sorry. Yes, sort of. It's complicated.'

'I won't make any trouble. Just give me your phone a second.'

I hesitated. 'You can't speak to him.'

'Why would I want to speak to him? Trust me.'

I unlocked my phone. He put in a number and I heard his phone buzz.

'There. You know where I am.' He put his lips to mine and kissed me so gently I wanted to stay up all night, mapping out his face, his body, under my fingertips, going to places that I hadn't known existed but could feel hovering within my reach. Instead, he sighed, 'Go on. Back to your life. Give me a ring if he doesn't turn out to be what you want.'

I walked away, combing through a curious mixture of elation and devastation. Every time I turned round to look, he was standing there with a hand raised. Just before I dipped round the corner, he shouted, 'Call me.'

2018

Where does a young woman with no money go? When he asked me for any contacts, any known acquaintances, I realised I didn't know the names of any of her friends. So when the girl she'd shared with at university turned up, I had a huge surge of hope. Liv. It was her parents who took her off to Corfu after graduation. She was looking for her too. Said she'd got our address by asking a bunch of lads at a bar in Kassiopi where Freddie worked. She mentioned it as though I should know who Freddie was, so I nodded and went along with it. She told me Vicky'd been in touch for a few months after that summer, but she hadn't heard from her since Christmas 2009. It was as though she'd just dropped off the planet. Even I'd had more recent contact than Liv, who told me she'd tried her mobile, but the number no longer worked.

As I wrote her details down, I felt the hot shame of judgement radiating from her, standing there in her smart suit, next to her shiny BMW. She seemed flabbergasted that I didn't know where Vicky was. I didn't bother to defend the indefensible. There were so many things I should have done differently. Or, better still, not done at all. Looking at the tattered remains today, no one would ever believe I did what I did out of love – I found it hard to accept myself.

Liv put up a hand to wave goodbye, no doubt re-evaluating and appreciating her own family in light of ours. I wanted to tell her that she could never judge me anywhere near as harshly as I judged myself.

VICKY

September 2009

William consumed my thoughts. I spent my hours at the bar scanning the people milling around the harbour for his face, my heart quickening if I spotted one of his friends, then dropping down again when I realised William wasn't with them. After a week, I called him. Several furtive meetings later, I made a plan to move in with him. But when it came to telling Freddie I wanted to end things, I dithered. I had no experience of leaving people who were more attached to me than I was to them. In the end, he called it after he'd wanted sex and I couldn't face it for the third night in a row. Not when every tiny bit of me was aching for William.

It was ironic that this man who'd provided a lifeline to me, who'd quietly encouraged me to be my bravest self, had made me confident enough to set my hat at someone like William. When I wriggled out of his arms, he raised his head like a dog sensing danger. 'Not tonight? Or not me?'

I cried, said I was sorry, I'd leave the following day, that I was grateful to him.

He pulled on his boxers, and scratching at the stubble on his chin, he said, 'I wanted you to feel love, not gratitude.'

I heard the door to the little box room click shut and I lay in Freddie's bed for ages, frightened about what I was giving up, whether I was – as my mother frequently used to say – 'leaping from the frying pan into the fire'. I wanted to go through to the other room, to make it right, for him not to think badly of me. I felt an odd sort of disgust for myself, as though, in an effort to find my way in the world, I'd crushed someone who was kinder than me underfoot.

I packed my rucksack, left my key on the pillow, next to a note saying, 'Sorry and thank you' and texted William. Within an hour, I was installed in the villa he was housesitting. Within days, I'd begun to believe my own lie, that Freddie had been fond of me, but in the end I'd been a useful barmaid and a guaranteed summer shag. What I had now, with William, was the sort of love that made me get up early to buy the best tomatoes and fresh oregano at the little market for the sheer joy of hearing him say, 'This is awesome!' in that accent that a lot of the posh boys had, slightly Australian, a touch of American, something that suggested surfboards and drive-in movies. I'd tried it out a few times when I worked at the bar, but I couldn't make it sit naturally in my speech. I was still more Poundland than Prada.

I spent the autumn discovering the joy of herbs, of peppery basil oil, of cheese direct from the farmer. And with it a growing sensation that I might be brave enough to say I didn't really want to work my way round Italy or head off to Australia. That I wanted to anchor myself where other people's time and tide couldn't destabilise me, where I never had to question whether I belonged.

Gradually, William's friends drifted back to the UK, out of money or craving the structure of work rather than the pressure to make their own adventures. Instead of searching out new company, we hunkered down, coasting towards Christmas, with William rejecting calls from his parents to return home for the festivities.

'Have you told them about me?'

He shook his head. 'Nope. My mother will start pestering me for photos and wanting to know what our "plans" are and I just want to do what I want without having to justify it.'

And with the days running into each other without deadlines or decisions, it was mid-December before I realised I hadn't had a period for a while. But I pushed it to the back of my mind, far more interested in making our little Greek Christmas as perfect as possible. So it was after the New Year when I nipped out to the pharmacy for a test kit and discovered I was pregnant.

I walked down to the beach and sat watching the waves, combing my memory for the last time I had a period. Definitely since I moved in with William because I'd been embarrassed about bleeding on a sheet. I thanked heaven for small mercies. If I had to go home – could I even do that, now? – Ian's face didn't bear thinking about if I turned up not only up the duff but with a choice of two fathers. I wracked my brains for dates. End of September? October? A cool wind whipped across the shore, sending me back home, my life teetering on a precipice without knowing which way it would fall when I told William.

I couldn't look at him. Couldn't bear to see his fear of being trapped before he arranged his features into something more neutral. I just handed him the test, aiming for a casual, 'You need to see this', tagging a little laugh onto the end as though it was no big deal, that I wasn't expecting anything from him. An image of Mum handing me Joey when I first saw him in hospital flashed through my mind. His delicate fingernails, his squidgy little feet fascinated me. I felt a protective surge of emotion towards the tiny being inside me. With a rush of something that felt like wonder, I realised I was keeping this baby, however William reacted.

Finally he spoke. 'Holy shit. How did that happen? We've been pretty careful.' Then I reminded him of the times we'd taken a risk when we'd run out of condoms. He frowned. 'But I'd always pulled out in time.'

I sat, frozen, seeing our future crash into a brick wall.

Slowly, a smile crept across his face. 'You, me and a little bean. Wow.'

Those few words were like the dawn breaking across the darkest sky, sending little fingers of orange hope out into the world.

We lay, arms wrapped around each other, discussing how William would find a new housesitting job to take us over the summer. We congratulated ourselves on 'the bean' growing up roaming beaches and poking about in rock pools, rather than fighting over a couple of ride-on cars at a village playgroup. How he or she would be bilingual in English and Greek, how we'd teach our child history not from a textbook but by travelling – to Turkey, to Italy, to Germany.

But in March, I started to bleed. The doctor couldn't explain what had caused it.

William took over. 'We should go home. We don't want to be stuck out here with no one to help us if there's an emergency, and you won't be allowed to fly soon.'

So, within a fortnight, we left the crisp blue skies of Corfu behind and landed at a grey Gatwick.

His father, Derek, was there to greet us, nodding at William as we came through arrivals. They shook hands. It seemed so formal. The sort of thing you'd do with a teacher.

I stuck out my hand too. 'Pleased to meet you.'

'Vicky.'

I waited for him to say something else. 'How are you?' maybe, perhaps ask about the baby, make a quip about becoming a grand-father. But nothing, just that glance, tinged with bemusement as though I was nothing like he expected.

I sat in the back of the black Range Rover while William's dad cursed at the traffic on the M25 as we headed towards their home near Guildford, initially chipping in with innocuous parent-pleasing comments about our time in Corfu. Derek barely acknowledged I'd spoken and eventually I sank back into my seat in silence.

The entrance pillars, the automatic gates and the long tree-lined drive to the house did nothing to reassure me. But I needn't have worried about a chilly reception from his mother, Barbara. She flung herself on us as soon as we got out of the car. 'Willy!

Lovely to see you, darling. And you must be Vicky.' Her hand went straight to my stomach and gave it a good pat, which I tried not to mind. 'Thank goodness you came back. We'll get you registered at my doctor's tomorrow and have you checked over. Let's get you settled in. William, you bring the cases. Vicky is not to carry anything.'

And from then on, I had no doubt about my place in the world, at least as far as Barbara was concerned. Every time anyone walked through the door, she'd call me down. 'You must meet Vicky, mother of my future grandchild.' She knew exactly how many days until my due date at the end of June – 'Sixty-three days today and you'll be a mummy!' 'Forty-four days today and I'll be a grandma. Or a granny. Or perhaps a nanna. Not nan, don't like that.'

I found her excitement overwhelming especially when, helped by his father, William landed a job at an accountancy firm and was no longer around to deflect her scrutiny of what I was eating, drinking and thinking. As she showed me picture after picture of cots and cribs and mobiles, I wondered if I wasn't maternal enough because I couldn't find it within me to care about Winnie the Pooh blankets.

I tried to address it with William. 'Your mum seems very keen on the prospect of being a grandmother. I worried that your parents might disapprove.'

'She probably thought she'd never get a grandchild from me. Anyway, good job she's doing all the legwork because I wouldn't have a clue.'

I tried not to feel ungrateful, tried not to wish that we were in a little flat, quietly scouring charity shops for everything we needed rather than ambushed by Barbara's avalanche of enthusiasm.

'Will your mother come when the baby is born? She's very welcome to stay here. What about your father?' Barbara asked one evening.

Having spent the last year making out that I was a wayward child no one cared about, I now felt peculiarly protective towards my mum. 'I don't know my dad.'

Barbara did an 'Oh', as though that didn't quite fit with the heritage she had in mind. 'But your mother will come, won't she?'

'I haven't told her I'm pregnant yet. She's very busy with my stepbrother and sister and we've lost contact a bit since I've been in Corfu.'

I expected Barbara to insist that I gave her a call, but she said, 'Well, you can tell her in your own time. You've got us as family now. We'll look after you and the baby for as long as you need. William will be a great dad, I know.'

I nodded, paralysed by the thought of ringing Mum after so long without being in touch and announcing I was pregnant. By someone she didn't know anything about. Every night I told myself I'd do it in the morning and every morning I convinced myself it was too early, she'd be getting the kids ready for school, then probably with one of her hairdressing clients, school pick-up time, fighting to get Emily to eat her tea, bath time, she'd be too tired now. To assuage my guilt, I focused on the fact that her efforts to contact me had dwindled dramatically; she probably wasn't that bothered about hearing from me anyway. And so the days passed.

A few weeks before the baby was due, Barbara asked me if I'd invited my mother to be present at the birth.

'No, I haven't. I thought I'd keep it to William and me.'

Her face lit up expectantly. 'I'm very happy to be on standby. William can get a bit squeamish. When you're in pain, it's really good to have someone who's calm.'

Of all the birth scenarios I'd imagined, Barbara peering over the midwife's shoulder to see if the baby was crowning hadn't featured.

I asked William if he thought he'd be okay. 'Yeah, I'm completely chill. I'd better take the head end. I did throw up when the cat had kittens, but I was only about twelve.'

Over the weeks leading up to the birth, Barbara kept talking about the things that might go wrong. 'Let's hope it's a straightforward birth. When I had William, the woman in the next bed had

had an episiotomy. She could barely sit down. Still, not the end of the world. If it does happen, it's just a tiny snip.' She made a little scissoring motion with her fingers. 'I'm sure it will be fine. It's better to be prepared for the worst and then there are no nasty shocks.'

It was so alien to me to discuss everything in such detail. Mum's communication of anything difficult or embarrassing was along the lines of, 'Do I need to talk to you about periods/sex/contraception?' At which point, I'd say 'No', whether or not I needed the information, and we'd spend a day or two avoiding each other's eye just from the awkwardness of her saying the words out loud.

One afternoon when Barbara was putting the breast pump together 'so you can get some sleep and I can feed baby', I blurted out that I was thinking about getting in contact with Mum.

She frowned. 'Of course you should, but you do want to avoid any upset that might stress the baby at this stage. Why not get in touch once everything's settled down? Once the baby's here safe and sound. You've probably got enough to think about at the moment.'

And like a frond of seaweed wafted along by the tide, I immediately agreed with her, taking comfort in someone relieving me of the responsibility of decision-making. I had a half-hearted idea that I might call Mum straight after the birth. In the event, towards the end of June, I started to bleed heavily a week before my due date and the consultants bandied about terrifying phrases such as placenta abruption and placenta previa. An emergency Caesarean put paid to my romantic notion of 'the bean' being born to the relaxing playlist William and I had picked out together. Afterwards I was so exhausted and in so much pain, I could barely manage to sip my tea, let alone face up to a difficult conversation with Mum.

While William cuddled Dimitrios and Barbara photographed them from every angle, she kept saying, 'Poor Vicky. I guess it's just the way you're made. William, you popped out in a matter of hours, like podding a pea. Must be my child-bearing hips.'

I was ashamed of not having the right physique for something that should be so simple. But my failure to squeeze a baby out without a drama was nothing compared to the horror of trying to breastfeed.

'Maybe you should think about getting that baby on a bottle. Something so natural should be so much easier, shouldn't it?' Barbara said as the nurse came to help, squishing my boob this way and that, trying to get Dimitrios to latch on. I had so much milk, he was practically snorkelling in it. Barbara leaned in, offering advice and repeating, 'I stuck William on a bottle straightaway, and he's barely had a day's illness in his life,' as though we hadn't given her enough plaudits the first time she said it.

'What's his name?' the nurse asked, giving me a little wink.

'Dimitrios. It's Greek.'

'I'm going to have to work on my pronunciation of that.'

Barbara nodded. 'I know. I think I'm too old to get my head around a foreign name. I'll probably spend the next twenty years saying my own grandson's name wrong. If you want something Greek, how about something simple, like Theo?'

Just before I left hospital, William mentioned he also thought Theo was a much better name – 'Otherwise he's going to have a lifetime of people misspelling his name.'

'But I thought you liked Dimitrios.'

'I did when we thought we were staying out in Corfu. But I can't see it working down at the tennis club. He'll be known as Dimmy. It's probably a bit silly as we don't live in Greece any more.' He sounded brisk, as though I was making a problem where none existed. The two-hourly feeds through the night had robbed me of my ability to form a coherent argument. Just watching all those other mothers who were latching on their babies with magnetic magic made me cry my eyes out, so my capacity to assess whether I was making a fuss over nothing was a bit impaired.

Within days of getting home, worn down by Barbara's assertion that 'it takes a village to raise a child' and that I might cope better with a bit more sleep, I'd given up breastfeeding. And within a week, my son became Theo and I became a mother who had no trust in her judgement about what was best for her baby.

2018

How hard can it be to find a thirty-year-old woman who must surely be working somewhere to support herself? Thirty. I can't believe how quickly those years have flown by. We won't be the only ones who've changed. Maybe she's married now with a family. That could really put the cat among the pigeons. But I'm not going to give up. I can't think of anything else I could do. If that private investigator tells me one more time he's doing his best, I'm going to explode. We are all doing our best, even me. Or at least I thought I was, but look where that got me. Motherhood is hard. I made so many mistakes. I wish I could go back and do it again, with grace and generosity. Vicky will probably never understand how ferociously a mother loves a child and that primeval desire to protect.

Maybe I should have trusted things to work out, had confidence in everyone making the right choices in the end. But Vicky's reactions were always so unpredictable, I couldn't just leave it to fate. What sort of person finishes university, jaunts off to Corfu and never comes home again? I wanted to spare us the pain of separation, but instead I caused us an agony from which we'll never be free. Despite what I did, I'd nearly phoned her so many times, weighed down with guilt about what she was missing out on. I wish I'd connected those calls now. That's my burden to bear.

Ironically, she'll have to hate me even more before I can attempt to put it right.

Unless he finds her soon, it will be too late for all of us.

VICKY

Valentine's Day February 2011

I thought back to Valentine's Day last year when we expected to stay in Corfu. I must have been about five months pregnant and William ran me a bath, then got in it with me, laughing as the water almost flowed over the sides. 'Must be Junior taking up all the room,' he'd said, even though my bump was still very neat. Despite the luxury of the villa where we were housesitting, all the baths seemed small, almost half-sized. William blew raspberries on my stomach, then got out and made breakfast – eggs, fresh orange juice and really good coffee – which he'd served up on the terrace. He'd put the heater on and we'd sat there looking at the sea, talking about whether we wanted a boy or a girl and which features he or she might inherit. 'I hope it has your little nose rather than my big hooter,' he'd said.

I'd touched my nose. 'I don't care what it looks like. I want it to be sure of its place in the world. To feel loved.'

William had laughed, with the self-assurance of someone who'd never looked at his family and thought, Do I matter to you? 'Of course, it will be loved. How could it not be? We're going to be brilliant parents.'

I let him carry me along with his confidence. I kept telling myself I just had to make our baby feel safe, the most important thing in the world, that I'd never let him or her down.

And a year later, we hadn't let him down. The tiny upside to living with the in-laws was that there was always someone to sing to him, to walk him around the garden, to take him to the park. But William and I were a long way from that couple sitting on the terrace. This year instead of flowers in a jam jar, I had Theo on his changing table by the door, and I was cleaning up his exploding nappy while William was running around our bedroom, flinging about all the clothes I'd folded neatly the night before, swearing about not being able to find his keys. 'I'm going to miss my train!'

His helplessness, the idea that remembering where he put his stuff wasn't really his responsibility had seemed like a cute quirk when we met. It appealed to the persona I'd adopted of someone who 'cared about experiences, not material crap, right?' But now we had a baby, a man who constantly had to go back into the house for the nappy bag and never checked for a dropped mitten or blue bunny just shredded my sleep-destroyed nerves. I already had one little being depending on me full-time, I couldn't take on another. So I carried on with my task of stopping Theo smearing the contents of his nappy everywhere.

'Vicky! Have you seen my keys?'

'No. I haven't. We have this every morning. We need a hook in here for you to hang them on.'

William tutted as though I was somehow the cause of this endless chaos.

Eventually he found the keys under his sweatshirt, which he tossed on the floor and then pushed past us, banging into the end of the changing table and rushing out of the door, shouting, 'See you later, not sure what time.' No kiss. Not even for Theo. And much less a breakfast on a sunny terrace with joy about the future.

I envied William. The luxury of walking through a station, buying a coffee, even popping into WH Smith, to browse the books, to know what was out there, taking delight in discovering new authors to add to the ones I always looked out for. I couldn't remember the last time I'd read a book.

The bedroom door banged, startling Theo and making him cry. A draught blew in from the landing. Living in Barbara and Derek's house had cured me of any illusion that big old houses could be cosy. The air coming in through the windows even when they were closed made the curtains flap. Theo's little chest went all goose pimply. I leaned over to shut the door to stop the cold air blowing on him and in that split second, he rolled over and fell on the floor.

He screamed. I bent down and gathered him up, my heart leaping about with fright. 'Ssshhhh. You're all right. Come to Mummy. You just had a fall. How did you roll over so quickly? Ssshhhh.'

But the great yells pouring out of him showed no sign of abating. I did up his nappy and put him on the bed. I couldn't see anything obvious so I held him to me, my heart pounding. 'Please, please stop crying, Theo. Please.'

Then footsteps running up the stairs. 'Vicky? Vicky?'

Barbara burst through the door, taking in the carnage left by William's hunt for his keys.

'Why's he crying like that?

'He just fell off the changing table, suddenly rolled over,' I said, my voice panicky and defensive.

'Did you leave him up there on his own?' She held out her arms for him. I handed him to her, hoping that she'd have the magical formula of an experienced mother to fix him. I tried to explain what had happened, demonstrating where I was standing, how I hadn't even moved away, just leaned over to pull the door to, but she wasn't listening.

'Did he hit his head?' The alarm in her voice frightened me.

'I don't think so. He sort of half-landed on my foot. That broke his fall a bit.'

She settled him on her hip, one leg either side, and he started screaming again. 'Come here, little man. What's hurting you?'

I felt sick. What if he'd really damaged something? What if there were some internal injuries we couldn't see? I was glad Barbara was there, even though I knew she'd probably tell her friends and they'd all look pityingly at me, and say, 'Accidents happen' to make me feel better about being a completely crap mother.

She laid him on the bed. One foot kicked in the air, but the other leg was flat on the duvet. 'Is it normal for only one leg to be up?' she asked.

I wracked my brains. 'I don't know. It might be. I'm not sure.'

Barbara pushed against the leg that wasn't moving. Theo whimpered. 'We need to take him to hospital and get it checked out.'

I nodded, my eyes filling with the magnitude of being responsible for a tiny person and not keeping him safe. I scrabbled everything into a nappy bag and shot after Barbara, whose panic was igniting a jet of terror within me.

'I'll drive,' she said.

The whole way to Royal Surrey County Hospital she was jumping red lights, switching lanes and hooting at people to hurry up and get out the way as though it was a life or death emergency, even though Theo was sitting calmly in his car seat. I tapped out a quick text to William asking him to ring me as soon as possible but without saying Theo was hurt. The last thing I needed was William in a state when Barbara was being dramatic enough for all of us. At the hospital, I had to run to keep up with her as she unbuckled Theo and steamed off to A&E. I stood next to her feeling like a schoolgirl in front of the headteacher while she told the receptionist what had happened.

I'd have managed not to cry if the nurse who saw us initially hadn't said, 'Oh, bless you. That's such bad luck. Nine times out of ten they bounce. Just to be on the safe side, the doctor will send him for an X-ray, check that nothing's broken.' That little acknowledgement that I wasn't the only woman in the world to let my baby drop off a changing table unravelled me. The nurse passed me some tissues.

Barbara patted my hand and said, 'When you're young like Vicky, you just don't see the dangers in the same way you do when you're a bit older, do you? I'm sure there's no harm done.' The nurse agreed, one mature mother to another, as though this would never have happened if I'd been thirty-five, and sent us back to the waiting room. Barbara rattled up to reception every twenty minutes, her posh voice booming out: 'I know you're terribly busy, but any idea how much longer my baby grandson will have to wait?'

The woman looked completely non-plussed, as though she couldn't believe that there was a person left on the planet who didn't know how stretched NHS resources were.

I sat cuddling a sleeping Theo, thinking about my mum. I'd last had a text from her about a month before Theo was born, saying, *Vicky, I don't understand why you haven't been in touch. We're worried about you. Are you still in Corfu? Love Mum.*

I'd texted back: *I'm fine. In Corfu. No need to worry.* I hadn't been able to shake the image that she'd been sitting cuddled up with Joey and Emily on the sofa, dashing off a quick message to me before they needed something.

While we waited for the doctor, I allowed myself to daydream about nipping outside to phone her and her offering to come, waving everyone else away and saying, 'Today, it's Vicky's turn. The rest of you will just have to cope.' But I simply couldn't withstand the disappointment if she didn't drop everything and went into a long and complicated discussion about how it was half-term and 'next week would be a lot easier'. And before any of that could happen, I'd have to explain that I was back in England and I'd had a baby. That bit of home, tucked away in a village in the flat Fen countryside, seemed like a life raft floating further out to sea, that I'd never be able to reach even if I started swimming right now.

The doctor finally called us in. He was the opposite of the nurse, brusque and matter-of-fact. 'Just take me through how this happened again?'

I stumbled through the story, feeling as though I'd moved from being unlucky to being under investigation.

Barbara smoothed her fur-trimmed gloves on her lap. 'It's not Vicky's fault, Doctor, she doesn't have much experience with babies. They both live with us though, so it's not as if she doesn't have any support.'

He scribbled something on his notes. I felt like he didn't believe me, that he was looking for a loophole in my story. Eventually, after examining Theo, he sent us off for an X-ray. Which showed us that Theo had fractured his femur and would need to stay in hospital in traction until it healed. Approximately two weeks.

I hugged him to me, crying onto his soft head before handing him over to be bandaged up.

Barbara took charge, racing home to fetch things, asking me what I needed. I cringed at the idea of her seeing our room at close quarters. She didn't comment directly, just sometimes shouted that she would leave the Hoover outside the door 'in case you want to give the room a quick do' without ever indicating that she thought cleaning and tidying was William's department. I hated the thought of her poking about in my knicker drawer, seeing the lacy thongs I sometimes wore for William, though a lot less lately.

After she'd gone, I sat on the ward, with Theo's chubby legs suspended in the air, his fingers wrapped around my thumb, and steeled myself to explain to yet another nurse how a little boy who was only eight months old had come to break his leg in my care.

Still no response from William to my panicky text. When I looked carefully, I saw it hadn't gone through. I wandered around the ward pointing my mobile in different directions, but the whole place was the enemy of phone reception. When Barbara returned, she said she'd called him at the office, but he'd been in a meeting. 'I didn't like to say it was urgent. I think at this stage of his career, we don't want to give the impression that his home life is chaotic. We can manage between us, can't we?'

I went along with her, though by now I wanted her to ring back and instruct whoever answered to interrupt whatever bloody meeting William was in. But I didn't feel I could make any demands when it was my fault we were here in the first place.

I held Theo's rainmaker above him, a transparent toy in which beads tipped from one side to the other, making a satisfying shushing noise that fascinated him. Long after he'd lost interest, I carried on, to avoid the silence, which every now and then seemed to goad Barbara into another comment about my being so young to have a baby, as though I'd got pregnant behind the bike sheds at fourteen. I was so tempted to comment that, for her era, having William at thirty-seven would have been considered ancient. I hadn't planned to have a baby at twenty-two, but I'd only be forty when he was eighteen and we'd have so much grown-up life together.

Barbara had never mentioned my age before, never given the impression she was anything other than delighted to have a grandson while she was still active enough to enjoy him. She was quick enough to whip out her phone to show off photos of Theo to those friends of hers who came for coffee, bringing their salted caramels and florist-bought flowers. The murmured questions about me often floated through to the kitchen, and I'd open the cupboard quietly, straining to hear Barbara's reply, yet hoping not to. The worst I ever heard was 'Get married? No. No, I don't think that's on the cards.'

When I told William, he said, 'Well, it would be a bit weird to get married while we're still living with my mum and dad, wouldn't it? She probably meant not at the moment. Be a bit embarrassing to carry you over the threshold into their utility room.' And he kissed me on the nose and made me feel foolish for being so paranoid.

Eventually Theo dropped off to sleep and I had no choice but to sit down on the plastic chair next to Barbara. She took a deep breath as though she was pleased to have found the perfect moment for whatever discussion was coming up.

'We need to put Theo's name down for kindergarten at Bathfield House soon as they are always terribly oversubscribed.'

'William and I thought we'd send him to the outdoor forest nursery until he's five. Then the local primary at least until senior school. We're not in any position to send him to private school.' My priority was ensuring my son had the freedom to get dirty, to climb trees, to use his imagination, rather than working out what would give him an advantage in the job market before he was two. And when we'd first come back from Greece, William was definitely on board with that. I sighed as I realised I was no longer sure what he thought: every day he drifted a little further from the laid back surfer boy I'd met in Corfu towards someone who talked about company cars and tax efficiency.

Barbara smiled. 'Derek and I are more than happy to pay for him to go to Bathfield House and carry on the family tradition. William loved it there.'

'That's really kind, Barbara.' I reminded myself to say thank you. 'However, I didn't go to private school and I still did really well. You've already been so generous with us.'

'Don't be silly! It's our pleasure. And you don't want him ending up at Littlestone.' She said it as though he was in danger of catching an incurable disease. Lack of privilege possibly. 'That's got such a wide catchment area.' I was pretty certain it was ending up with a grandson who said tea instead of supper rather than any geographical consideration bothering Barbara.

With the self-loathing that accompanies the moment when you recognise you've allowed someone whose opinion you oppose to edge closer to their goal, I said, 'Let's talk about it again when we get out of hospital.'

She sighed and, briefly, Freddie popped into my mind. I'd loved the way his face had lit up when I came around the corner. As though just by being there, his whole day had experienced a sudden burst of sunshine. I couldn't recall now why I'd looked beyond him.

Maybe I was as bad as Barbara with my prejudices – the list in my head of who I should end up with once I'd stopped pretending to be the bohemian travelling type hadn't had a slot for a barman with a snake tattoo curling all the way up his bicep. Freddie hadn't matched the picture I had of a guy in chinos and an open-necked shirt doing a creative job – maybe a graphic designer or architect – working from home with mugs of coffee piling up around his desk.

But William didn't either. He was part of a club I'd never unlock the code to. Everyone he knew skied, sailed and played tennis and took it for granted that those pastimes were the norm. When we'd first come back to Britain and his friends had visited, they'd clearly been fascinated that he'd got a girl knocked up. Especially one who actually wanted to keep the baby. They stopped short of flicking their floppy fringes and saying, 'Bad luck, mate,' but the forward motion in William's friendship group seemed to revolve around who was up for Val Thorens at New Year, or going out to Barbados in the summer – 'Same gig as last year, really, take over Tootie's house.' They bandied the names of ski resorts about until I made an excuse to take Theo up to bed. The last family holiday I'd had with Mum, Ian and the kids, we'd gone camping in France. Ian had eaten some dodgy salami and spent the night doing comedy dashes to the toilet. Mosquitoes had such a feast on Emily that her whole body puffed up and Mum had dispatched me to help Joey learn to swim in a pool where we had to dodge the old plasters floating about.

Thankfully, a nurse came in then and suggested that Barbara got some rest as there'd be plenty of time for her to do a shift later on. I had to hold in a burst of laughter when she suggested that Barbara might take a turn sleeping on the put-up bed next to Theo's cot one night. I thought she was going to rummage in her handbag for her tiara and her pea. After she'd gone, I sat watching Theo, his little purple eyelids twitching, his mouth pursing and relaxing in his sleep. I hoped I'd be good enough in the long run.

I heard the nurses chatting in the corridor, laughing about the glamour of swapping a romantic Valentine's dinner for an overnighter at work. Just this morning, I'd been hoping William would get home early, ask his mother to babysit and we could escape down to the pub in the village for a few hours, be a grown-up couple with a future to plan rather than two naughty children who were constantly having to tiptoe around his parents, endlessly grateful for a roof over our heads. And now I was sitting on my own in hospital with my baby, who hadn't even got to one year old without breaking anything. I marvelled at the ability of ordinary days to take such a turn for the worse. Were they mapped out in some plan for the universe? I had an image of a graph with gentle inclines and downward slopes with a date pencilled in for the whole lot dropping down like a company announcing its bankruptcy.

About ten o'clock, the door to the ward banged open, causing the other mothers behind the curtained cubicles to tut loudly. William came in, calling for me. A child in the next bed along started to cry. There was a big flurry of a curtain being gathered back. 'For god's sake, keep it down. All the kids are asleep in here and half of us will be up all night as it is.'

'Sorry, sorry,' William said, 'My mistake.' In situations like this, his poshness embarrassed me. Even if he made the same mistakes as anyone else, they just seemed more thoughtless, more selfish, when accompanied by that accent that suggested a life of hip flasks, shooting and horses in every word. But there was no denying his shock when he saw Theo lying there with his legs in the air. 'Oh, my little boy.' He turned to me. 'I came as soon as I got Mum's message.'

I could smell something on him. Beer? Wine?

'Came from where? The pub? She phoned you hours ago.'

The relief of seeing him was tempered with an inexplicable rage that I'd been here all day, dealing with the doctor's sceptical acceptance of the truth of what happened, while he'd been running his finger down the wine list.

'Because it was Valentine's Day, the managers let us go early.'
He blinked as though he realised he'd just dug a deep, deep hole
for himself.

'So what time was that exactly?'

He sighed. 'About five, but I didn't listen to Mum's message.
She's always calling me with crap about whether I want carrots or
sweetcorn with dinner.'

In his voice I could hear that deliberate articulating of words that
comes with a need to appear sober. I took a moment to accept what
I'd heard. My boyfriend could have been home by six but went to
the pub instead. On the one night a year that was definitely a time
to be home early. Luckily for William, the energy to be angry about
that was buried under a landslide of maternal guilt.

He stepped towards me. 'I would have come immediately if
I'd known Theo was in hospital. Of course I would. If I'd seen a
missed call from you, it would have been totally different.' He tried
to hug me, but I stood totem-poling, sandwiched between a paper
towel dispenser and Theo's cot. He bent his head to kiss my neck.
'Don't be like that.'

And before I could even consider the implication, the words
came out of my mouth. 'I can smell perfume on you.'

William took a step back. 'I've been jammed on an overcrowded
train. Here, smell my arm. It probably stinks of Big Mac and fries.
Smell my shoulder. Sweaty student armpit.' He was hissing, aiming
for a whisper, but his vocal cords only seemed to do the big alpha
male baritone I'd found so sexy. 'Never mind all that, what's the
story with Theo?'

I ran him through it all, hating myself for sounding defensive.

'How did he fall off if you were standing right next to him?'

'He just did. I don't know. I took my eyes off him for a second
while I closed the door.'

William's eyes narrowed, as though he wasn't sure he was getting
the whole truth.

'I'm sorry, I wish I'd done better, I wish it hadn't happened. I wish I could dip in and out of parenthood like you do, and not have the responsibility all the time and feel that there's always this unspoken judgement about what Vicky did or didn't do and whether I'm getting it right. I'd love to get on a bloody train at 7.30 in the morning and rock in at 10 p.m., going "What did I miss?"'

William's shoulders sagged. The expression on his face made the distant alarm in my brain ring a little louder. Until now, we'd laughed about the fact that two grown-ups with their own child were stuck in his parents' spare room, with the dual passion-killer of trying to have sex without waking Theo or squeaking the bed. We'd talked about how, when he was established at work, perhaps next year if he got a bonus, we'd start looking for somewhere of our own to rent. But, in that moment, I didn't see someone who was right beside me battling away in difficult circumstances. I saw someone who was clambering up the ladder and pulling it up behind him. With those wild dark curls now cut into the sensible haircut of office conformity, I had to close my eyes to recall that pivotal moment in Corfu when he'd looked all shy and said, 'I'm going to have to make the first move, aren't I?'

Back then, it had felt like the validation I'd been waiting for, the embodiment of the sliding-doors moment that I mustn't let slip through my fingers, the time to be brave, when I knew my roll of the die would deliver a double six.

A world away from the life we lived now, our fledgling love affair struggling to germinate under the thick blanket of reality. But I still believed it was there, somewhere, in the way he sometimes rolled over onto his elbow, kissed me – he could still kiss me into believing anything was possible – and said, 'I had no idea that hippy chick on the rock that day would make quite such an impression on me.' I clung onto that, because there was no safety net beyond.

After he'd left – 'Better go, Mum's waiting for me outside' – I lay on the thin camp bed mattress and tried to picture turning up at my own mother's with my son in tow. She'd love Theo – she'd always been brilliant with babies. But my fragile heart wouldn't be able to withstand the whispered exchanges with Ian in the kitchen, the snatches of 'made her bed' 'lie in it' seeping out, while Joey and Emily sat watching TV, utterly secure in their place in the world. One of them would probably have moved into my old bedroom by now. Mum had let me paint it lime green before Ian had come to live with us, but he'd decorated it in magnolia as soon as I went to university.

When I'd complained, he'd said, 'You've left home now.'

That was news to me. I'd looked at Mum, who'd avoided my eyes and said, 'It's still your room, love, but we just thought it could do with a lick of paint, tone it down a bit, so when we have people to stay...' She'd trailed off. They never had people to stay. My friends from school had occasionally come for a sleepover, but even then, Ian would peer dramatically into the bread bin in the morning as though it was incredible we'd had a slice of toast each.

No. I couldn't go back. Not with yet 'another mouth to feed'.

VICKY

December 2012

By the end of 2012, Theo was two and a half and I'd been at work for eighteen months. William had encouraged me – 'The sooner we get some money behind us, the sooner we can get our own place.' Eventually I'd plucked up the courage to ask Barbara if she would look after Theo for one day a week, 'Only if you want to, if it's not too big a commitment.'

I'd nearly fallen on the floor with gratitude when she'd told me that she would take him Monday to Thursday, though I did have a little laugh to myself when she said, in all seriousness, that she wouldn't be able to do Friday because her golfing partner relied on her for her exceptional putting. I didn't want to leave Theo for four days a week, but after a year of Barbara making me feel totally inept – 'I think he needs a nap,' 'I wouldn't give him any more banana,' 'Is he going to be warm enough in that?' – the more attractive going to work to speed up moving out seemed.

And, initially, the freedom to leave the house every day unencumbered was like losing two stone overnight and feeling that everything around me had got a little looser. I loved my job as a library assistant. And my manager loved me. She applauded my ability to recommend the right book, to make sure the people who used the service – not just as a conduit to find something to read but as a place to escape their daily lives – felt not only welcome, but cherished. So many of them reminded me of my seventeen-year-old self, pushing open those doors to a refuge from everyone else's expectations, the wrongness of me somehow melting away among the shelves and the quiet and the patchwork of people all needing something only the library could provide.

As always, my life was the perfect seesaw. Silhouetted high up against my success at work came the complementary low at home. Just today I'd run in the door at 5.15, ready to do a roast chicken dinner for Theo, geared up for the exasperation of enticing him to eat a carrot, to find that Barbara had already fed him Nutella sandwiches – 'I thought it would save you a job. We'd had such a busy day. He was so hungry.'

I swallowed down the words I wanted to say, reminding myself that my colleagues who paid a fortune for nursery would have willingly embraced my petty frustrations for free childcare. I smoothed my face out and smiled. 'What did you do today?'

Barbara turned to Theo. 'Tell Vicky where we went.'

I knelt down in front of him. 'Tell *Mummy* what you did. Have you been somewhere lovely?'

He shook his head and carried on running his new tractor up and down the edge of the rug.

'Theo, come on, tell Vicky what a fantastic day we had,' Barbara said.

'Went to the farm,' he said, without looking up.

'Godstone Farm?' The farm that I'd planned to go to on Sunday. That Barbara knew we'd planned to visit.

She blundered on, oblivious to my upset that she'd sequestered my little outing. 'We had an amazing time, didn't we, Theo?' She whipped out her phone: Theo cuddling a rabbit, Theo sitting on a tractor, in the sandpit, Barbara's face squashed up to his little cheek.

I made all the right noises, but my throat was tight with envy and something else that I was afraid to pick at, in case it blindsided the status quo.

Early on, when I tried to discuss my reservations with William and said some, though nowhere near all, of the things I thought about his mother, he would pull me to him. 'It's not ideal, but she's just trying to help. With any luck, by next year, we'll have our own house.' But that evening, well over twelve months later, when we still didn't have enough to pay three months' rent up front at any property with two bedrooms, he just put his hand up. 'I can't listen to this again. It is what it is, Vicky. It's not perfect, but I can't see any of your family stepping into help, so maybe just focus on what you've got rather than what you'd like?'

Over the last year when I was at home with Theo, I'd developed a growing sense of walking into a labyrinth of medieval alleyways where the sun rarely rose high enough to light the way out. A complete contrast to my work life, where I could turn around without intercepting a look that made me feel as though other people's disappointment was engulfing me. It was no wonder I was getting into the habit of curling up to Theo in the little single room he now slept in, breathing in that Johnson's Baby Bath smell, rather than huddling on my side of the bed next to William, hostility and resentment lying like a barrier between us.

Even when I'd tried to have a calm conversation about how grateful I was to Barbara but how I wondered if we could just agree a few guidelines so that Theo didn't get confused, I'd ended up feeling as though I was inventing problems where none existed. 'Of course, Vicky. You know your own son. I'll go along with everything – the last thing we want is for him to be confused.'

Nothing changed though and it became obvious that Theo wasn't confused; he was very clear about whom he loved and wanted to be with. I'd often arrive back and Barbara would be helping him build a tower or Derek would be reading his train book with him. If I tried to join in, he'd scream at me to go away. Barbara would frown and say, 'I think he's just a bit overtired. Why don't you put your feet up for a bit while he calms down?'

And I didn't know how to say, 'No. I'd like to be left alone with my son for a bit so he actually remembers who his mother is.'

I tried to get home earlier by working through my lunch break, bringing little cars as a treat, putting on funny voices as soon as I got through the door, a tactic that made me feel self-conscious and desperate – and didn't work. In fact, the screaming and tantrums got worse until I could no longer shrug it off as 'one of those days'. I began to dread the proof that my own son didn't want to be with me. The terrible sinking pit in my stomach would start as soon as I set foot in the drive and by the time I got into the sitting room, I'd be tense, waiting for a car or a train to fling across the room with an accompanying shriek of 'Go away!'

I told William, tried to make him understand. I flailed about, losing my temper about how late he worked, the Saturdays when he had to go into the office, how it wasn't surprising that Theo had attached himself to his grandparents rather than us. William frowned as though I was being difficult for the sake of it. 'What would you prefer? To pay a fortune for him to be looked after by a nineteen-year-old who couldn't care less about him? Mum and Dad adore him. Of course he's going to form a strong bond with them.'

As Christmas approached, the fourth since I'd seen Mum, I got an overwhelming urge to contact her. She'd always loved Christmas. Until Ian, we'd put up our tree on the first Saturday in December, sometimes even the last one in November. I remembered the feel of her hands around my calves as she held me steady on the ladder to put the fairy on the top. And now, every time I went into a shop, or switched on the radio, I heard 'Hark the Herald Angels Sing' – her favourite carol. It made blocking her from my thoughts almost impossible.

So, a few days before Christmas, after Theo had spilt his juice all over the table and screamed at me when I'd lifted him up to move him out of the mess, I found myself in the den debating whether to ring Mum. I'd deleted all her text messages and without them to re-read, I couldn't trust my memory that the majority had begged me to get in touch.

The last time she'd contacted me was well over a year ago. She'd said something along the lines that she was so worried she was considering involving the police. I'd almost weakened then, desperate to tell her she had a grandson, that I didn't know what I was doing and I was so lost and lonely. But then I'd imagined her voice going flat, that little sigh when she heard my news, the disappointment that I hadn't done things in the proper order before having a baby. 'I'd have thought you'd have learnt from my mistakes.' I knew any relationship with me would be negotiated through the filter of Ian. She'd never be able to say, 'All that matters is that you're okay. You've always got a home with us. Bring Theo.'

In the end, I'd texted, *Don't worry, I'm fine*, just to stop her triggering a police search. After pressing send, I'd sat with my phone in my hand, longing for her to ring, her voice all relieved, insisting that I should come home. But nothing.

That night, I hadn't been able to sleep, picturing Ian slagging me off to Mum, 'She's always been selfish. What daughter disappears without letting you know she's okay?' I visualised Mum doing that little pressing together of her lips when she didn't really agree but wasn't going to argue.

The reply had come the next morning. *Vicky, I don't know what we've done to upset you. I've always loved you and I don't understand why you have decided not to have any contact with us. I am always here for you if you change your mind. Love Mum.*

But she wasn't. And all these months later that wouldn't have changed, so I pulled myself together, dismissed the idea of contacting her now and dragged myself upstairs to see if Theo would tolerate me helping with bath time.

On Christmas Day itself, I forced myself not to think about Joey and Emily and their excitement when they saw their presents. It dawned on me, with a wave of melancholy, that they wouldn't believe in Father Christmas any more. They'd be nine and eleven. Joey would be starting senior school next year. Senior school! I'd like Theo to meet them, to have other kids who were important in his life. Maybe if William and I managed to live somewhere where we could actually have sex without Barbara hoovering outside our bedroom door or Derek suddenly needing to bleed a radiator, Theo might have a brother or a sister of his own one day.

But for now I was stuck navigating the minefield of the Cottingdale festive season.

William looked at the outfit I'd put on. 'Is that what you're wearing for Christmas Day?'

'Why?'

'As you know, we do normally try and dress up a bit. You know, church and that.'

It was like being in the Groundhog conversation I often had with Barbara. I didn't care what Theo wore. I offered him clothes to get dressed in, but if he wanted to go into his drawer and put on a pair of swim shorts with a pyjama top in the middle of summer, I just let him get on with it. Barbara, on the other hand, couldn't relax if his T-shirt and shorts didn't 'go'. I tried to tease her out of it – 'Come on, there's only a limited time before you have to conform. Let him express his creative streak.' But by the time I returned from work, he'd always look like something out of a Boden catalogue. And now William wanted me to do the same.

'The first Christmas you fell in love with me, I wore a bikini top and a pair of tie-dye shorts.'

He closed his eyes, briefly, as though the memory of being those two carefree people, in love and lust, caused physical pain. 'Seems like a long time ago, doesn't it?'

'Do you regret it?' I shouldn't have asked the question.

He didn't quite meet my eye. 'Don't be silly. I wouldn't be without Theo for the world.'

I wasn't brave enough to ask the other question I would have liked an answer to. Instead, I fished out the dress Barbara had bought me for her niece's wedding, all puffy sleeves and frilly hems. In the New Year, I was going to stand up for myself a bit more, but today was about Theo, so I'd just keep the peace. And even I couldn't remain grumpy when I watched Theo's wide-eyed wonder at his stack of presents, mainly from William's parents. I took lots of pictures, encouraging Barbara to be in most of them as a nod to the season of goodwill but my favourite by far was one of Theo pressing his nose into William's cheek. In his excitement, Theo even allowed me to help him put together a racing track instead of thrusting it at William. It was my equivalent of a gift picked out with love and delivered with a big gold bow, which was just as well as William and I hadn't bought each other anything. We'd spent our money on a decent tricycle for Theo. I videoed him as he opened it. His little face lit up with such delight, I felt tears spring to my eyes. He tried to cycle round the kitchen. William picked him up. 'Come on, buddy, let's have a go outside on the terrace.'

He'd barely done one lap of the barbecue area before Barbara appeared round the corner, 'Theo, look what Santa has left for you here…' And as fast as his chubby legs could carry him, he shot over to a miniature bright red Ferrari, charging at the socket by Derek's shed. Derek lifted him in, showed him which button to push and how to turn the steering wheel and he meandered off down the lawn, waving and squealing with glee, the tricycle abandoned on its side by the house.

I reminded myself of what Emily and Joey were like at that age, ripping open presents in a frenzy and only appreciating what they'd received in the days and weeks that followed. But the fury that Barbara had spoilt the first Christmas that Theo could really interact with his presents, when William and I had taken time to research tricycles that could also help him learn to ride a bike, made me want to flounce off like a two-year-old myself. I watched

Barbara running alongside, filming him on her phone with a hard and bitter rage inside me. 'Look at Mamma! Look at Mamma! Wave to Poppa!'

And with a sickening lurch, every time Barbara gave an instruction ending with 'Mamma', I realised Theo was turning to her, not to me. My reaction was so instant, I forgot that I was a guest in someone else's house, forgot that I was in their debt. I stormed over. 'Have you taught him to call you Mamma? You are not his mother! I am!'

She did that bloody face that I'd seen so often. The flick of the eyes towards Derek, the sort of look you might give when confronted with a stranger worse for wear, waving a vodka bottle and shouting about global warming.

Her reply, when it came, oozed rationality and calm. 'Vic—ky, of course you're his mother. His *mummy*. But he started to call me "Mamma", short for *grandma*. I didn't see a problem with it.'

I was too far gone. 'Just like you didn't see a problem with buying an amazing present and not even letting him have five minutes enjoying ours before you came steaming in to get his attention. God forbid his own parents should have a minute with their child.'

William was slow to react, glued to his bloody phone as always. I'd already snapped about it once today and received the reply – 'I have to keep up with the markets and international news' – as though no one in banking celebrated Christmas Day. Out of the corner of my eye, I saw him break into a run. 'Vicky! What's got into you?'

'Nothing has got into me. I just wanted one flaming moment with Theo when your mother wasn't taking over.'

Derek stood by the shed, the need to oil the lock becoming the focus of his festive season, despite his tweed jacket and shirt with cufflinks.

Barbara turned her palms up in a gesture of helplessness. 'It was Theo who chose Mamma. I just went along with it. Does it matter?'

A *glance*. One of those Cottingdale glances that made every nerve ending in my body twitch with the desire to take a large blunt instrument and see what the inside of Barbara's skull looked like.

William had perfected a sideways flicker of his own, which, with a flash of realisation, I recognised as 'I have to keep up the pretence of siding with Vicky but I'll agree with you later.'

I stood there, my head turning from one to the other, an odd sense of power, derived from completely and utterly losing it, coursing through my body.

Before I could say anything else, a scream rang out. Theo had taken his car down the slope towards the rose beds and overturned it. We stopped eyeballing each other and ran. William got there first, lifting the car off him. Theo thrashed about, scratching himself on the woody rose branches, getting more and more hysterical as I tried to get hold of him and pick him up.

'Don't want Vicky! Want Mamma!' He hit me in the face. 'No Vicky! Want Mamma!'

I tried to soothe him, but he was arching his back, landing blows with his feet in the fleshy part of my thighs. Eventually, William reached for him and, after a momentary tussle, I let go.

He still wouldn't calm down, squealing in a way that was almost theatrical, his hands reaching out for Barbara, who had finally picked her way down the paving slabs in her high heels. She took him from William and immediately he settled on her hip, thumb in his mouth.

'Mamma' came the slurred word as he snuggled into her.

William shouted after me half-heartedly as I thundered up the lawn into the house, intending to sulk in the bedroom until someone came to find me.

But as I stormed in, my handbag was sitting on the side with the car keys, promising freedom from Barbara and that sympathetic head tilt she did whenever I got a bit snappy. I knew she'd make out that I was tired – 'Why don't you have a lie down before lunch?

Theo did have you up early this morning.' I ran upstairs and pulled
off my stupid dress, chucked on a T-shirt, jeans and my furry parka
and raced back down.

Let them be the ones to wonder, to work out how to calm the
waters for a change. They could sit debating about where I'd got
to, while simultaneously pontificating about whether the cranberry
sauce from Waitrose was 'up to snuff', or how they were somehow
superior for choosing beef over turkey – I loved my mum's turkey
much more than Barbara's beef, despite Barbara's three meat ther-
mometers to make sure that hers was well done but Derek's was 'so
rare it nearly comes in with horns on'.

Theo didn't care whether I was there or not as long as he had his
electric car and the ever-capable 'Mamma'. It would do them good
to realise that they couldn't assume I'd go along with whatever they
wanted. Right now I'd rather go and live in a bloody tent than be
told again how to dry the bottom of the glasses in the dishwasher
so they didn't leave a ring inside the cupboards. How Theo would
eat his broccoli for 'Mamma', so it was odd that he wouldn't eat
it for me.

I turned my phone off, caught between defiance and the fear
that no one would bother to call. And then I drove, turning left
onto the M25. The motorway was gloriously free-running, the
cars sparse, hardly a red brake light to be seen. I studied the other
vehicles packed to the gills with duvets, kids and dogs, the drivers
peering through a hole in the debris. I imagined them arriving at
their destination with bags of presents, the kids dashing into their
relatives' houses to see what was under the Christmas tree, the
clamour for the loo, the smiles, the hugs. The instant and primeval
sensation of coming home, of fitting in.

I'd reached the M4 before I knew it, and considered turning
round and sloping back in, hands held high in apology. But I
didn't feel sorry, I felt weary. Frightened of admitting that, in the
space of two short years, the fascination that William and I had

had with each other – we'd even studied the shape of each other's fingerprints – had faded. Now, he'd be hard-pressed to notice if I dyed my hair pink.

I continued along the M4, the traffic thinning out even more as everyone raced to their destination for pre-lunch 'drinkies', as Barbara would say. Would William defend me? He'd probably default to what he always did when there was disagreement in the air: find an email he just had to deal with 'quickly'. Or maybe he'd join in and slag me off to his mother? Perhaps he wasn't even thinking about me but running around the garden with Theo instead while Derek poured the champagne, my absence remarkable only for my gall to disappear and leave the clearing up to Barbara.

On I drove, Reading, Swindon, singing at the top of my voice to the Christmas hits on the radio, scared to be silent in case sadness engulfed me. I stopped for petrol at Membury Services, responding automatically to the 'Happy Christmas' on everyone's lips – the cashier at Waitrose, at the petrol station, the woman who caught my eye in the mirror in the Ladies'.

I sat in the car for an hour, eventually turning on my phone to face the music.

Nothing.

Not even from Mum. The second Christmas in a row. Did she ever hope I'd just turn up unannounced? Did she sit through Christmas lunch not even aware she was waiting for a knock on the door but registering a flash of disappointment when it was time to stack the dishwasher and another set of crackers had been pulled without me? Or were they all happier, an easy dynamic of four, two children by one father, with no need to accommodate the odd one out who was too old to be told what to do without question.

I switched off my mobile again. Let them worry that I was in a ditch somewhere, my phone shattered along with my skull.

I sat for a few more hours, crying from sheer loneliness, sick with envy as I watched mothers and daughters of all ages come and go, the tiny little kindnesses between them – holding a handbag, picking up a dropped cardigan, a protective hand out at the kerb of a crossing.

Three-thirty. I needed to go back now. It would be pitch black by the time I got home. Perhaps Theo would already have dropped off, worn out by all the attention. Maybe I'd be in time to read him a story. My heart did a little flip of fear, thinking about him shrieking for Barbara, hurling his books across the room. I resigned myself to the worst Christmas Day evening I'd ever had and drove to the exit. At the last minute though, I indicated left towards Bath, away from London, my foot flat down on the accelerator, watching the day fade and the dull sky go dark.

By the time I got to Bristol, I was starving. I barely registered the familiarity of being back on my student stomping ground. My head was throbbing with the fatigue of too much caffeine and not enough food. I pulled into one of those budget hotels on the outskirts, advertising rooms for £50. I took my phone out of the glovebox and turned it on. Now I had messages. All William. *Are you coming back for lunch? Shall we wait for you? Stop being an idiot and getting offended by a two-year-old having a tantrum.* Then *You're just being really selfish, Vicky, ruining Christmas Day.* Then a couple of hours later. *What the hell are you playing at?* Five minutes ago. *Right, we're really worried now. Are you okay? Where are you? Ring me.*

Not 'we love you and we're sorry', not 'we've really missed you'. I got out of the car. I couldn't face them today. I'd deal with them tomorrow when I'd had something to eat and some sleep.

The receptionist couldn't have been less interested in what a twenty-four-year-old woman was doing checking in with no luggage on Christmas Day. I wondered if anyone had ever died in the hotel and how long it would take for them to be discovered if they put the 'Do Not Disturb' sign on the door. Not exactly the cheery train of thought I'd hoped to celebrate Christmas 2012 with.

I took myself off to the restaurant, intending to scoff down something quickly and watch films in my room. But just as I walked in, a large family encompassing an age range from early teens to twenties and thirties, a baby and a couple in their late fifties came in. I sat in the corner watching the boisterous interaction. Snatches of conversation floated over to me. 'Did you see grandma's face when Aidan said "shit"?' 'How many bloody times is Uncle Richard going to tell us about when he was in the army?' I must have been staring – there was only so long the greasy lasagne or even the book I was reading could hold my interest – when one of the young men caught my eye and grinned. I looked away and ordered another glass of wine, trying to reclaim my Corfu persona of chippy independent woman who'd sat in countless bars and restaurants on her own, with a past so mysterious she couldn't possibly talk about it.

Eventually their table thinned out, with the younger and older members going off to bed. The ones that remained decided to play Trivial Pursuit, arguing over the teams. 'Trish is really good at history, so I'll have her.' 'I'm not having Guy, he thinks Newcastle's in Scotland.' I eavesdropped, the banter and insults fascinating me. No one seemed offended.

Then, suddenly, the man who'd observed me staring earlier, appeared in front of me. 'I don't suppose you fancy joining our game of Trivial Pursuit, do you? If you've got nothing better to do?' He leaned towards me. 'We probably wouldn't win unless you're really clever, because all the others are much smarter than me. Which is why no one wants to be in my team.'

There was something in his manner that reminded me of Freddie. Charming, straightforward, unsophisticated. I meant to say no, I was just going to bed, but he did the whole pleading, 'Come on, I'm going to get absolutely slaughtered if I'm on my own. You look intelligent.' He turned to the others. 'You lot, help me persuade her. She's even reading a book.'

They all waved me over, 'Help him out!' so I picked up my stuff and went to sit with them.

Guy, as he introduced himself, poured me a large glass of wine and when they'd finished arguing over who was going first, the game took off with Guy paying no attention to anyone else's questions and interrogating me whenever it wasn't our turn.

'Why are you in a hotel on your own on Christmas Day?'

'Where do you live normally?'

'You got a boyfriend?'

I gave him some old guff about visiting family in Bristol with a small house and being very happy to stay in a hotel – 'There's only so much of us all being together I can take – good to get out before the excess alcohol kicks in!'

'I like your thinking,' he said. He liked it even more when my answers won us the geography and art and literature cheese.

My phone went. William. I stared at it for a few seconds, then switched it off. I drank some more. The others started to get super competitive – 'Guy, you've got an unfair advantage. Vicky's a librarian... she's going to have read lots of books.'

We won, triumphantly, with my answer of Atacama to which South American desert was one of the driest places on earth. After rowdy bragging from Guy, the other four made noises about going to bed.

'Flaming Boxing Day walk at Cheddar Gorge tomorrow,' Guy's brother said.

I smiled. 'Sounds lovely.'

He shook his head. 'Wouldn't be so bad if we didn't have to worry about the oldies. Odds-on that one of them twists an ankle or has to turn back cos their hip's playing up.'

People who had families took the time with them for granted. My fuzzy brain wanted to preach about making the most of every moment but, luckily, I couldn't find the words, buried as they were under the looming cloud of having to face the music myself tomorrow. If I got an early start, I could get back well before lunch and redeem myself by helping Barbara prepare the 'spread' for us and some of her golfing friends who came every year for the Boxing Day buffet.

Guy put his hand on my forearm. 'Help me finish this bottle of red.'

So I did. And then we ordered another one. I veered between a stab of shame every time I thought about storming out that morning and the relief of talking to someone who wasn't waiting to find fault in me. Eventually, just after midnight, we headed upstairs. I was careering off the corridor walls but managed to shake my head at his suggestion that the perfect end to Christmas Day might be going back to his room. Even weaving along with one eye closed to keep focused, self-preservation dictated that casual sex, even with a nice and kind man, would only add another layer of complexity to something I already didn't understand. He didn't push it, just pecked me on the cheek and said, 'Room 115 if you change your mind,' before staggering off.

I woke up several hours later, my stomach churning, the acid notes of cheap red wine an inferno of stench. I made it to the bathroom with seconds to spare, pausing between retches to push the door shut. I stared into the toilet bowl, at the pink of my vomit, and struggled to remember a time when I'd hated myself more. Thank God my last remaining sliver of sense had seen me into my own bedroom.

I stayed holed up in the hotel, not venturing out until late morning when I was sure Guy and his family would be off at Cheddar Gorge. Even after a shower, and the toast and tea that I'd forced down, I could smell the alcohol leaking out of every pore. Just contemplating Barbara's reaction if I turned up at home stinking of booze with bloodshot eyes and a puffy face sent me to reception to book the room for a second night. I tried not to dwell on the guilt of frittering away the money that William and I were saving to move out.

I texted William that I was taking some time to think things through, that I was sure they'd manage without me and to give Theo a huge hug from me and tell him that mummy loved him. I couldn't let him hear my leaden, hungover voice or allow a conversation that required me to be on my toes, to respond to all the criticisms the whole Cottingdale family would have fine-tuned in my absence the previous day. He mustn't find out that the reason I wasn't with our son on Boxing Day was because I'd buried myself in a couple of bottles of wine. Ian's words, so often repeated when I'd laughed too loudly with my friends and woken up Emily or Joey, reverberated in my head: 'What is the matter with you?' The matter with me? Everything was the matter with me.

Christmas Eve, when I'd shouted Merry Christmas to my work colleagues and walked home, the early finish at lunchtime compensating for the freezing rain, seemed a million years ago. I refused to let myself consider what was happening or being said back 'home'. Instead, I ran a hot bath and stayed in there for hours, letting out the cold water and putting more hot in.

I was probably all the bad things they said about me.

No wonder Theo didn't want me as his mother.

The next day, I steeled myself to speak to William. His tone, full of concern initially, turned to irritation once he knew I was all right. 'You've got a son, Vicky. We've got a son. You can't just walk out when things don't go your way.'

I tried, really tried, to explain that I wanted to take responsibility for him, but that it was so difficult when Barbara seemed closer to him than I was. 'I don't think he even really knows I'm his mother. He calls me Vicky, as though I'm just some random woman who lives in the same house. Half of the time, he screams whenever I go near him…'

There was a moment's silence. I could picture William smoothing out his dark eyebrows, his handsome features troubled, tugging at the collar of his favourite blue-striped shirt. His voice was measured. 'Vicky, do you think you need help? I'm worried about you. How you're behaving isn't normal. It's not good for Theo to have all this tension and upset. He just needs a simple, straightforward home life.'

I averted my eyes from the mirror. How was he ever going to get that with a mother like me? One that walked out, got shit-faced with a stranger, who, more by luck than judgement, had accepted my refusal to go to bed with him?

I brought my attention back to what William was saying. The words were different. But it was the same tone all the other people in my life used. Disappointed. Let down.

I was a problem to solve.

VICKY

December 2012

I slept in the car for three nights, unable to justify a hotel room any longer. Every morning, I hauled my aching body into the driver's seat, vowing that today would be the day when I went back, before sitting paralysed for hours, making excuses about the traffic, the fact that the Cottingdales would be getting ready for lunch at the golf club, anything that could stand in the way of Theo not even acknowledging me, with Barbara gloating away, 'Theo, come on, say hello to Vicky.'

But on the thirtieth of December, after five nights away, I drove towards Guildford. At Reading, I pulled off the motorway into a lay-by and sat gathering my courage. What excuse could I possibly give for my disappearance? Stomping off for a couple of nights at Christmas wasn't ideal, but I could probably pass that off as it being a difficult time for me since I'd fallen out with my family. But five? Leaving my two-year-old son?

I rang William. He answered in a voice that was weary, irritable.

I stumbled over my words as though I was pitching for a job I had very little chance of getting. 'I'm sorry I've been away so long. I'm on my way home now.'

'Where are you?'

'Reading.'

'I don't know what to say to you, Vicky. I really don't. You'd better apologise to my parents for ruining Christmas.'

My humble-pie intentions immediately burnt to a cinder on a furnace of injustice. 'I am sorry that I spoilt it. Do you understand even a little bit why I exploded like I did? I know we've got a lot to thank your mum for, but I think she forgets to let us be parents sometimes. She's so used to taking charge of Theo, she acts as though we're just peripheral. She must see that it's hard for us to watch her give Theo everything he wants when we're saving up to rent somewhere.'

'My mother has sacrificed half of her social life to look after Theo so you can go out to work. She does spend more time with him than we do, but that would be the same if he went to a childminder.'

'Honestly, if I'd have known that I'd have to schedule in time to see my own son, I'd never have gone to work.' I fought to sound contrite rather than enraged.

'I don't think that would have been a good idea, do you?'

'What do you mean?'

'Oh nothing.' He said it in a way that people do when they think they've got the killer argument, the winning nugget tucked away, designed to make your brain rush down fifty different avenues trying to identify what they've discovered that gives them power.

'What? Go on, you've obviously got something to say.' I didn't know whether it was my fury or the phone that was making my ear hot. I put it down and switched to speaker.

'It doesn't matter.'

I knew William would have that face on, his whole family had nailed the expression – head up high, shoulders squared, eyes intent in a gaze that always made me look away first. I thought I might implode with frustration, might lean my head on the steering wheel until the horn sent the whole car park rushing over to see if I'd had a heart attack. I waited for him to say something more but the silence squatted on the line like a drawer we were afraid to open. I gave in first. 'Is Theo all right? Has he missed me?' I asked, a longing to see his little hand clutching the blanket to his cheek as he slept coursing through me.

I heard William take a sip of coffee. 'I was going to wait till you got home, but that was what I wanted to talk to you about. He keeps saying, "Vicky hurts me."'

'What?' I could hear the catch in my voice. 'Why would he say that?'

'I don't know, Vicky. Has something happened that you haven't told me about?' I could hear the effort he was making to keep the accusation out of his voice.

'NO! How could you even think that? I mean, he sometimes falls over when we go to the park. He banged his head on the towel rail when I got him out of the bath the other week...' My mind was racing, examining the times when I'd held his arm firmly – too firmly? – when I thought he might run off when we were near a busy road. When the kitchen door had swung shut on his fingers and I'd put an ice pack on them. His words turned my stomach. 'You don't actually think I'm hurting Theo, do you? Actually believe I'm deliberately harming my son?'

He hesitated. 'I don't know what to think. Why would he make that up though?'

'Oh my God. I literally can't believe you would think that.'

'Well, it was odd that he fractured his leg that time.'

'I told you what happened. It was an accident.' I fished around in my mind for occasions when Theo had injured himself with William. 'He fell off the bed and hurt his shoulder when you were tickling him. He's got a scar under his chin from where he ran into a branch when he was in the park with your mum. But, of course, no one ever talks about that. If it happens when I'm in charge, it has to be because I've deliberately set out to torture my two-year-old!'

William back-pedalled. 'I didn't think you were hurting him, I wondered if something had happened, *by accident*, and you hadn't mentioned it and it had grown into a big thing in Theo's mind. That's all.'

'I would never do anything to harm him. You know that.' I wanted to swear, to use words that usually wouldn't ever feature in my vocabulary, but my voice cracked. There was so much more to say, lists of things that I did right – taking Theo to storytelling at the library, helping him learn the letters for his name, braving the cold pool at the leisure centre for Saturday morning swimming lessons. Instead, I ended the call and sat sobbing in the car, 'Vicky hurts me' going round and round in my brain. Had I been rough and impatient and trapped his soft little baby skin in a zip or button somehow? Or had he picked up on my repressed anger and become fearful of me?

My head was heavy with fatigue. Rage was gathering, giving me a crackling energy, the type that was out for revenge, that wanted to 'make them sorry'. The sort of anger that comes from the pain of being accused of something that someone close to you should have dismissed instantly: 'Vicky hurt Theo? Never.'

My phone rang. I debated between proving to William I was a kind and forgiving partner and hurling my mobile out of the window so he could never contact me again. But it was Barbara. 'Mamma'. I braced myself for her talking to me slowly, kindly, as though my brain – my university-educated brain – couldn't keep up with her lightning-sharp thought. I let voicemail kick in. She rang again. And again. Until I was getting a perverse pleasure from picturing her strutting around the kitchen, saying, 'Silly girl! This just isn't on!'

The longer I sat there, the more self-doubt engulfed me. Maybe Theo was frightened of me. I did get irritated with him, often because our time together never seemed to match up to the fun, carefree times he had with Barbara. Half the time, we'd walk to the park, with him whining about where Daddy was or when Barbara was coming and I'd feel like the last person Theo wanted to spend time with. I marvelled at the easy way the other mums seemed completely uninhibited, dashing about with their kids, shrieking with laughter. It was as though I was making an effort to be fun but Theo was just waiting to get back to the people he liked better.

Barbara's number flashed up again. God knows why she was phoning instead of William. If we were to have any chance of surviving, he needed to tell Barbara to butt out. I checked myself. What alternative was there to surviving? Where would I go with a toddler in tow? William would have to take responsibility, instead of passing the buck to his mother. I went to my phone settings to block Barbara's number as a small act of defiance. There was already a number on the list. I didn't remember blocking anyone before. In fact, I'd fished about a bit to work out how to do it. And I certainly didn't remember blocking my own mother.

I stared at it. I fiddled about, but I couldn't see when it had happened. Had I done it when I was drunk? Did I do it when I first went to Corfu in a fit of pique? We hadn't spoken since I'd left university, though she'd tried to ring me for quite a while afterwards. I struggled to remember when she'd last left a message. Ages ago. Which was hardly surprising if all of her calls were going straight to voicemail because the number was blocked. She must have assumed I was refusing to pick up.

I reinstated her number, wracking my brains for how it had happened in the first place. As the phone lit up again with yet another call from Barbara, I turned the car towards the South Coast. I needed a bit longer to clear my head. I'd go back after New Year.

2018

I understood now what it was like to lose a child. When people had talked in hushed tones about a child dying or being abducted or moving to the other side of the world and never coming home again, I'd nodded, briefly reflecting on their pain, before somehow insulating myself, distancing myself from the possibility of it ever happening to me. That sort of bad luck was for other people, with less fortunate lives. But now I got it. That deep yearning to have one last conversation, to find the words that might make a difference, that might switch the tracks that we ran along to an alternative trajectory at the last minute. Whoever said, 'You don't know what you've got till it's gone' knew what they were talking about.

Now, that searing sorrow, like a friend I never wanted to make, was with me every day. Pointing out the stupidity of my actions, the futility of the plans I'd made.

I hoped we'd still be able to salvage something. That some good could come out of this. Maybe now she was older, she might understand the strength of love that made me behave in the way I had.

VICKY

June 2013

Today was Theo's third birthday. Six months since I'd seen him. Six months since I'd been living and working at the pub where I'd stopped in to go to the loo on New Year's Eve. I'd overheard the manager discussing how half his staff were off sick, leaving him in a pickle. I'd brushed my hair in the Ladies', put on some lipstick and asked if he could give me a job and a place to live. And there I'd stayed just outside Exeter, keeping myself to myself, squirrelling away money, telling myself that I'd contact William at the weekend, next week, at the end of the month. I lived in one room and worked seven days a week. I didn't engage with anyone; I was just polite, efficient and exhausted enough to sleep as soon as my head hit the pillow.

In the early days, it had been enough to continue putting one foot in front of the other. I pictured the family clucking away at the breakfast table, Barbara flapping out a napkin and muttering variations on the word 'selfish'. I brooded about whether William would miss me, what Barbara would tell her friends. Whether she'd quietly suggest that me walking out was a good thing, 'because Theo had said some disturbing things about Vicky hurting him'. Barbara would deliver that with just enough finality in her voice that no one would dare ask for any details. Considering that scenario made my breath come in short, angry bursts.

But, so much worse than that, so bad that I rarely even allowed my thoughts to head in its general direction, was how Theo would react. I went numb when I attempted to imagine him asking about me. Or never asking about me. Or being thrilled that he never had to see me again, the person he claimed had hurt him. Was it possible that I'd had some kind of weird breakdown and done something terrible that I couldn't now remember?

I tried to hold onto the fact that not everyone thought I was bad. At the pub, my boss waved me in every day with, 'Vicky will sort it out. She's amazing at changing the barrels.' 'Get Vicky to have a look at the numbers. She's so sharp.' He listened to what I thought about the menu, remembered to tell the customers that the popular halloumi burger had been my idea. And slowly, so slowly that I didn't notice it was happening at first, little shoots of self-belief made their way towards daylight. Life no longer felt like an exercise in fending off the enemy. What I couldn't figure out was whether telling myself I was an outsider had become a self-fulfilling prophecy or whether William and Theo had withdrawn from me and Barbara had seized the opportunity to undermine me further.

There was only one way to find out.

Today, with the hot June sun in a perfect blue sky, I was going to see my son to find a way forward. I had some money of my own now. I could rent somewhere small closer to Theo.

Initially William had rung and texted me. I never picked up, but I'd composed lots of texts both in real life and in my head. I'd never sent any of them. And with that long silence between us, I didn't dare hope that William would ever understand or accept what I did. There was probably no way back for us as a couple, but even if it took me forever, I was going to make it up to Theo. I forced myself to dismiss the idea that Theo wouldn't recognise me or worse, would cry to get away from me.

I sped through the Surrey countryside, counting my way down the junctions of the M25, the places that were once so familiar and now seemed like names I knew long ago, as though in a story I'd once heard as a child. I turned off at Junction 10, turning in the opposite direction from William's house to kill some time. I wanted to arrive about two o'clock when Theo had finished lunch, when hopefully everything was as calm as it could be.

I'd dressed smartly. Bought new trousers and a blouse. I looked responsible. Grown-up. Not like me at all. I'd have to stay measured, prove to them that I took full responsibility for my actions, that I knew I'd behaved badly but quietly, rationally insist on sitting down with William to have a sensible discussion about how we might either give things another go or work out a plan to share Theo's care going forwards.

Without Barbara's drip-feed of criticisms disguised as helpful suggestions until I couldn't even trust myself to judge the right bath temperature, my maternal love had crept back out from its hiding place over the last few months. I was no longer so convinced that every other mother in the whole world was excelling while I failed. I breathed deeply. No. He was my son. I shouldn't have let her erode my belief in my ability to look after him.

I drove round past the park, the place where I hadn't even been able to push Theo on a swing to Barbara's satisfaction: 'Not so high!' 'Push a bit harder!' Where he'd fallen off the steps of the slide and cut his lip open. 'I always stand behind him, ready to catch him.' I slowed as I drove past Bathfield House, the little prep school where Barbara had been so keen to enrol Theo. Anywhere that made a three-year-old wear a cap wasn't going to work for me.

Suddenly, like a punch in the stomach, I caught sight of William with Theo, his chubby little legs poking out of grey shorts, his dark curls squashed under a cap. Barbara had got her way, fed into the school sausage machine before he could even ride a bike. His face was slimmer, more angular. As he laughed, I saw his cheek dimple, just like William's. And without me willing it or searching for it, my whole chest filled with a love so fierce I wanted to abandon the car there and then, rush towards him and pull him into my arms, sucking in all those missed moments and reacquainting myself with every angle, every soft curve of his body.

A cyclist swerved to avoid me, with a Land Rover hooting impatiently as I dawdled along. I indicated and pulled in just past them, hardly able to tear my eyes away from Theo long enough to park.

I wound my window down, craning backwards, noticing for the first time that the blonde-haired woman walking alongside them was holding Theo's hand. His nanny?

They stopped to talk to another woman with a little boy in the same uniform. William was all smiles, his easy charm leading to much nodding and flicking of the hair from his listener. Occasionally Theo looked over to me. I kept waiting for his eyes to widen with recognition. I was ready to spring out of the car, to shout, 'Stop!' if he looked like he might dash out into the road. But his eyes kept flickering past me, his attention caught by passing cars. He shouted out their names. 'BMW! Look, truck! Motorbike!'

After a while, Theo pulled at the blonde woman's hand, impatient to be going. She swept him up into her arms, kissing him all over until he arched away, giggling and squealing with delight. It was ironic that someone employed to take care of him had established a bond that had eluded me. Eventually the other woman moved on and William swung round to his companion. The understanding when it hit me was ferocious; distress pounded through my body, blurring my ability to reason: I recognised that look. He used to give it to me, that slow smile that made me feel I was so special. He leaned towards her and hugged them both. I could hear Theo's chuckle of glee from where I was sitting. And with that sweet note of joy came the bitter realisation that whatever future I'd hoped for with both William and Theo had drifted irrevocably out of my reach.

She spoke with a slight accent, not one I could place, her words filtering over to me as she said, 'So, Theo, birthday ice cream for my gorgeous boy?' Her relaxed manner, the way she was so natural with him made me sink back into my seat in despair. This woman had walked into his life and charmed him, little squeals of laughter carelessly tossed her way. The exact opposite of when I used to trudge home from work, planning how to approach him, what to say to elicit a hug, even a smile. Or at the very least, to stop him from screaming at me.

He clapped his hands. 'Strawberry and choc'late?'

'You can have whatever you want. That's the brilliant thing about birthdays.'

And with that, she leaned over to William and kissed him on the lips.

While I'd been harbouring ideas of the whole family discussing how it might work if I came back, perhaps examine their role and responsibility in my leaving, they'd obviously all breathed a huge sigh of relief that an unfortunate chapter of their life was behind them. The hole I'd left was so minimal, a little dent in the sand, washed over within a couple of waves. Theo didn't look like he'd ever noticed I'd gone. That blonde woman with her swishy hair, slim, in white jeans, reminded me of my friend Liv from university. She had the same air of belonging. The right shape, the right fit, that slotting in that I'd never manage to achieve. With painful clarity, all the thoughts, all the questioning, all the doubts I'd raked over in the last few months distilled down into one resounding truth.

My son was better off without me.

I indicated and pulled out in front of a bus, leading to a flurry of horns and heads turning to marvel at how we'd missed each other. In my rearview mirror, I watched Theo's dark curls recede.

PART TWO

CARO

23 December 2016

To hear Gilbert on the phone, you'd think he'd discovered not only that Father Christmas was real but that he'd decided to stable his reindeers on our farm. 'Brilliant, darling, brilliant! Well, not brilliant about the house, obviously. But marvellous news that you're coming. Stay as long as you like, of course. Shall I pop over and give you a hand?' A little drop in his voice. 'Okay. If you're sure. You know where I am.' He put the phone back in its holder. 'India's house has flooded. The river burst its banks last night.'

I sighed. 'So they're all coming to stay here until it's sorted?'

Gilbert did his big eyes. 'Don't be like that.'

I bristled. 'I'm not like anything.'

'I know, love. But it's still good that she turned to us and not Andy's parents in a crisis.'

'I suppose even India would rather put up with us than cram in the five of them with her in-laws. At least they can all have their own bedrooms here.'

'Oh come on, it'll be great to wake up with a houseful on Christmas morning. Just like old times.'

Gilbert and I existed in different universes. My desire to scrub the rosy tint off his and replace it with the volcanic ash on mine had rarely been stronger. I wasn't sure the 'old times' he remembered so fondly had existed since India left for university nearly two decades ago. And certainly not since my mother's funeral, ten years earlier.

I stood up to stop any memories of that night squeezing in like an unwanted guest demanding a chair at a dinner table. With all of us cooped up for the foreseeable future, there'd be enough fuel in the family dynamics to blow the lid off the secret I'd buried since that day. I was a far worse mother than anything even India could conjure up.

I felt guilty for wishing that the holiday cottages that we rented out on our farm hadn't been fully booked. If only we could have accommodated our daughter and her family without the need to have her come and live with us. I took my frustration out on Gilbert by snubbing his offers of help, instead waving him off into the village to pick up more supplies.

I tried to take pleasure in his pleasure. And it would be lovely to have the three grandchildren here. Apart from the oldest one, Ivy, who was fourteen, they never seemed to notice that India found fault in everything I did. And with that thought, I added the forensic cleaning of their rooms to my list of things to do. It was too late to get Lou up from the village to help. But there was no way India was going to blame Rowan's asthma on my haphazard dusting. My stomach clenched as I considered the days, maybe weeks ahead of avoiding expressing any opinions on school, children or parenting. I'd have to make sure I didn't start a game of Monopoly half an hour before bedtime and get India all in a twitch about the dangers that lack of sleep posed to children's brains. I'd probably be okay if I avoided anything that could be considered fun.

And, worst of all, India would act as though the things I didn't get right were deliberate, planned specifically to annoy her. It pained me to say this about my daughter, but she'd obviously been composting her carrot peelings when the humour gene was handed out.

I realised as I pulled out the bed to hoover up the hairballs from the cat – surely we'd cleaned in here since last March when Soots died? – a dull dread was filling my whole body. It dawned on me that over the years, India's refusal to come for Christmas had shifted from something that had me wringing my hands, resolving to do better, to a reluctant relief, with just a short sharp stab of pain at the initial no. The most India had graced us with in recent years was a quick 'pop in' to drop off our presents and pick up hers. I'd grown used to her gulping down a coffee in such record time she must have blistered her throat. She'd whirl off again, practically snatching the Quality Street out of the kids' hands: 'You'll spoil your lunch.' I'd learnt not to say, 'One won't hurt.' In fact, over the years, I'd learnt not to say much at all.

And this year hadn't been any different. These days I'd absolutely locked down the answer to her declining every Christmas invitation. As soon as she started with 'The thing is, Mum...' I leapt in with the 'Of course, you must make your own traditions, do whatever you want to do' noises when she'd explained that Holly, at three, still needed a routine that was easier to manage if they just stayed at home 'in familiar surroundings'. Frankly, I thought the key to being a successful adult was nailing flexibility early on, but I was a bit of a lone wolf howling in the wind with that one. My own husband needed smelling salts if the paperboy only brought my copy of the *Guardian* to our house in the Devon hills, leaving him to huff and puff into the nearest village two miles away for *The Telegraph*. And my daughter, even at thirty-seven, with three children and a marriage under her belt, still thought mealtimes, bedtimes and, for all I knew, sex times were immovable feasts.

It wouldn't matter how much fun the kids were having on Christmas Day, which lovely film we were watching – assuming we'd even managed to agree on one that ticked India's boxes: not misogynistic, sufficiently feminist, suitably pacifist – Holly would have to go to bed on the dot of 6.30, leading to three hours of her up and down, with India and Andy getting more irate. I'd always been in favour of letting kids fall asleep where they dropped and carrying them up to bed. But that was probably because after about seven o'clock I used to pretend I didn't have children so I could get on with the serious business of drinking wine and they quickly learned to keep a low profile if they didn't want to get shuffled off to bed.

Me, I loved a bit of chaos. Gilbert liked to get in the Christmas turkey order at the butcher's about September. I was more in favour of the frisson of 'Will I, won't I be cooking a joint of beef, a goose or maybe we'll have to make do with sausages?' I loved the bonkers googling of random ingredients from the fridge – butternut squash, crab and okra – and seeing if there was actually a recipe that would corral it into something edible. And Fergus, my thirty-two-year-old son, who lived in the annexe next to our farmhouse, was on my side of the fence with his shrugging and encouraging everyone to 'chill'. I'd have to ask him not to antagonise India by enquiring what colour her aura was today.

Gilbert arrived back with bags of disparate groceries that even a *MasterChef* contestant would have been hard-pushed to create a meal out of. My stomach lurched at the sight of a bumper pack of sugary cereals for the kids. I pointed to it. 'You can take the rap for that one, otherwise she'll immediately have a go at me for undermining her efforts to provide a healthy diet for her kids.' I couldn't resist imitating her: 'I know we grew up on jam sandwiches and chocolate mini rolls, but the world's moved on.' I loved how she plucked out that memory but conveniently forgot all the Sundays I spent preparing a roast for ten, twelve, sometimes fifteen people, including her friends. The baking. The jam I made from the plum trees in the orchard. The chutneys. The soup I stocked up on in the freezer. The fresh eggs I fetched from our chickens to make scrambled eggs before school. Nope. None of that. Just Mighty White and Rowntree's Raspberry in her version of events.

Gilbert tried to jolly me along. 'We'll have a brilliant time. I doubt that they'll stay for long. Just try to keep the peace.'

Those words nearly ignited an explosion in me. I was the one who stood in the bloody toy shop paralysed over the dolls, wondering if choosing one with a party dress would somehow lead to India lecturing me about the sexualisation of children. Gilbert didn't sit with his hand poised over the chequebook wondering how much would constitute the right balance between encouraging India to treat herself to something nice and a sniffy comment about how easy it was to throw money at things. Gilbert didn't even try to keep the peace, but somehow, India waved his transgressions away. She highlighted mine in neon yellow and wrote them in her bulging register of things that MUM DID WRONG. And that was even without the enormous thing I did wrong coming to light. I bloody hoped it never did. Otherwise my dream of ever having a relationship with India – probably with anyone in my family – would be blown sky high, the explosion lighting up the Devon hills so brightly, you'd be able to see it from France.

CARO

Christmas Day 2016

India's middle child, six-year-old Rowan, woke me up at quarter past five. India had told them all they had to stay in bed until at least seven o'clock otherwise Father Christmas would take their presents away. Rowan lifted up my eyelid to see if I was awake.

'Ro, Mummy said you couldn't get up until seven.'

'But my presents are already there. Can I open them?'

'I think Mummy would be quite cross.'

He was bouncing from one foot to the other, his brown eyes pleading with me to give in. I couldn't resist Rowan. He was my favourite by far because he was innately naughty. He hadn't yet mastered the art of throwing a bomb and not being anywhere in the vicinity when it went off. I adored him. Just the night before when India had allowed the two eldest, Rowan and Ivy, to go and explore outside while she bathed Holly, he'd managed to fall into a sloppy manurey mess, appearing at the kitchen door sopping wet and stinking. 'Mum will go mad.' He was spot on there.

I'd scuttled him up the old servant stairs and into my en suite. I washed him and his clothes and we'd sat through supper winking at each other.

And now I could feel my resolve weakening. 'Could you just open one small present, do you think? Bring it in here so you don't wake the others up.'

Gilbert snuffled awake. 'What time is it?'

'About six?' I said, rounding up to the nearest hour.

Gilbert groaned and fumbled for his watch as Rowan came through the door dragging a sack of presents bigger than him, followed by Holly, who was tottering under a pile of parcels.

'Ro said it's presents.'

The words 'I said you could open one' died on my lips as Rowan started a frenzy of ripping. 'Rowan, no, stop! You've got to wait for Mummy and Daddy.'

I nudged Gilbert, who said, 'They probably won't mind the kids opening a few if it means they get a lie-in. It's pretty early.'

Rowan's excitement pulled me in, so I ignored the warning anxiety in my stomach.

'I just want to find the remote-controlled helicopter I asked Father Christmas for,' he said.

'Okay. Let's think about which one it might be. Not that one. It's too heavy. That's too flat…' I was so busy trying to do damage limitation with Rowan that I didn't notice Holly unwrapping all of her presents tucked away on the other side of the bed.

By the time we'd narrowed the helicopter down to two possibles, Holly was sitting in a pile of debris, holding up a Playmobil jet for Gilbert to open.

He frowned. 'Is this yours, Holly? Not Rowan's?'

'Girls can be pilots too, Gil,' I said, shocked to hear India's words coming out of my mouth. And I meant it. I hoped my granddaughters wouldn't even consider hooking up with a bloke who couldn't work a washing machine. It was too late for me, with a husband who disguised an instruction for me to do it as a request for information: 'How long do you think I should cook this salmon for?' I couldn't stomach the thought that my granddaughters would still be the ones remembering to defrost the bread for the packed lunches, know which recycling bins had to go out, have the nous to use eggs in date order. Any food in date order.

Holly looked up at me. 'I want to be a fairy.'

But before I could get any further on gender aspirational train-
ing, India appeared at our door, with Ivy. 'What the hell is going
on here?'

I saw Rowan's eyes widen, then a glimmer of a smirk flicker
across his face and it was all I could do not to laugh.

India immediately turned to me. 'Why did you let them do
that? Why didn't you send them back to bed?'

I wanted to stick my lip out like Holly. 'They've only opened
one or two. I didn't want them to wake you up. I thought you'd
appreciate a bit of a lie-in.'

'We open our presents together when we've all had breakfast.'

'Sorry. I thought I was doing you a favour.'

But India started shouting at the kids to pick everything up, to
put the paper in one pile and the plastic in another and 'to not open
anything else until we're all together downstairs'. She marched along
the landing, saying to Ivy, 'Honestly, thank goodness you came
to get me. Daddy will be really angry about this. He was looking
forward to seeing Rowan open his helicopter.'

Ivy, bless her, did try to stick up for me. 'I think Grandma
thought you'd be pleased not to be woken up. They got her up at
quarter past five.'

'Well, she should have made them go back to sleep.'

India's commitment to gender equality didn't seem to extend to
sharing out the blame for parenting failure. That, apparently, had
always been my domain. Big black mark for grandma. Granddad
still smelling of roses, though.

CARO

New Year's Eve 2016

I encouraged India and Andy to go out for New Year. 'Make the most of it. Babysitters on tap.'

India pulled a face. 'But you've got people coming over tonight. I think it will be far too much for you to get them into bed at the right time.'

'It's up to you, love. We're very happy for you to go out, even if you just pop to the pub for a drink. Dad can take Holly up and read to her while I cook and perhaps Rowan could stay up a bit later and watch a film with Ivy?'

She looked doubtful. I wished I hadn't bloody offered. 'If they don't get to bed at a decent hour, there's always a price to pay the next day.'

I didn't answer. I sometimes couldn't believe she was my daughter, with her endless stream of rules and regulations.

'Who *is* coming tonight?' She managed to say it as though I'd have invited all the local miscreants and some dodgy men with an unhealthy interest in children.

I ran through the list. Our oldest friends from the village, Jan and Keith. Gilbert's drinking partner from down the pub, Bill, and his wife, Jackie. In fact, lots of people we knew from all walks of life, some I'd known for years, some I'd met at my painting class, a few of Gilbert's friends from bowls. And Lou.

'The school caretaker's wife? The one who sometimes helps with cleaning our cottages?'

'Yes.'

'Why are you inviting her?'

'Her husband died this year and I didn't like the thought of her sitting there by herself.'

'You're a right one for inviting all the waifs and strays. What will she have in common with anyone?'

Gilbert had asked the same thing, but it hadn't sounded so judgemental from him.

I laughed. 'Probably nothing other than an intimate knowledge of how slack they are on dusting. She loves the dog, so she'll hang out with Dalí. Can't be worse than sitting in her little house on her own wondering how she'll get through the next year.'

Honestly, India and Andy could tell you about the donations they made so a young girl could have an education in Uganda, how they'd got up a petition at school to ban plastic straws, how they went litter picking on the beach at Exmouth one Sunday a month, but actually being a bit kind to someone who was having a tough time never seemed to feature.

'I'll talk to Andy, see what he says.'

Didn't sound like 'thank you for the lovely offer' was going to be among the words I would hear, though judging by past history, I didn't know why I'd expected anything different.

I chopped the mushrooms for the huge pot of spag bol I was making. India hadn't said anything directly, but she'd raised an eyebrow that made me feel I was letting the side down in some way. 'You're not doing a sit-down meal then?'

As she disappeared upstairs, I wondered, as I always did, at what age we'd stopped being able to connect. When I thought back to her childhood, I did have memories of going to Crealy Park, us sitting together on the roller coaster and her laughing afterwards when I was so dizzy I couldn't walk straight. Not like she did now, a sort of 'Mum's such an idiot' scoff, but that gurgle of joy that comes from shared experience. We'd spent days, weeks, at the beach, bodysurfing. I could see her now, her sturdy legs powering through the water to be the first one out to the waves, always so determined, so driven. So competitive. I'd gone wrong somewhere, but I couldn't pinpoint where.

I remembered feeling really desolate when she went off to university. And I'd loved welcoming her back with all her friends, Andy among them, though I'd never earmarked him as a potential boyfriend for her. I thought she'd choose someone less earnest, more carefree, a counterbalance to her intensity rather than a mirror. Initially I was delighted that she was developing new opinions, different from ours, about politics, the world, who she wanted to be. I hadn't realised that the by-product would be that she'd dismiss us as parochial and ill-educated.

Since she'd had children, she watched me like a hawk in case I made the mistake of commenting on how lovely one of the girls looked. 'Yes, but Ivy's also intelligent, fierce and kind.' 'Yes, but Holly is strong, funny and feisty.' All true. But they were pretty as well and I didn't think it hurt to have confidence about the way you looked.

If I got the chance tonight, I would take the opportunity to show them off to my friends in all their glory. I wanted to have that moment, the one my friends had so often, of family just being there, around, no big deal, instead of the explaining I always had to do, the excuses of why I hadn't seen the grandchildren lately even though they lived fifteen minutes away – 'You know what it's like, with piano lessons and netball matches and there's Rowan taking up tae kwon do… Honestly, I don't know how they fit it all in.' And they'd all nod, and we'd start talking about the freedom we'd had to go out on our bikes at their age and I'd feel that knot of angst loosen. Until the next time, until I had to cover up the truth

I wasn't sure I could ever face, not completely. My daughter didn't like me much and didn't care about – at best – or didn't want – at worst – her kids having a relationship with me.

I imagined Andy and India upstairs, debating the merits of dinner à deux versus the folly of leaving their kids in my care, the potential for transgression from the 'no sweets before supper' rule. I liked to divert my maternal energy to fun things – painting, drawing, baking. I hadn't been all bad. One year, India and I had made such a stunning castle cake, she'd won first prize in a school competition. She never mentioned that, despite always embracing an opportunity to recount anything that portrayed a less than flattering picture of my parenting skills: 'What about that day when Mum went mad spring cleaning?' The mitigating circumstances – that I'd been blitzing the house so we could hold my father's wake there – never featured. In my grief, I'd got it into my head that people would judge me for the grouting and equate its filth with a lack of respect for my dad. So I'd gone from being the mother who never batted an eyelid when the kids trailed in with muddy wellies to the harridan who hovered on the edge of insanity if so much as a biscuit crumb hit the deck. 'Just don't make a mess until after Friday.' And, of course, the kids, but mainly Fergus, who was about eight, had decided to bring in some lambs from the cold and put them in front of the Aga on a bed of straw. They'd crapped everywhere and Fergus, in his oblivious way, had trodden in it and walked the muck all through the house. I'd blown a gasket. The sort of fury that loses sight of the actual issue and races through corridors dragging historic rages out of rooms and gathering a crowd of upset until there's no room for reasoning. I chased both of them up the hallway, shouting like a woman possessed and trying to slap and kick their backsides as they scooted up the stairs away from me. It was over twenty years ago and Fergus still killed himself laughing about it. 'You should have seen yourself, karate-kicking along the hallway with us shooting off up the stairs, trying to tuck our arses in!'

India didn't laugh about it. She used it as evidence that I'd been a volatile and inconsistent mother. I should have challenged her. But I didn't want to get into a discussion about how grief could unhinge a person, make them do things they'd regret forever while caught in that vortex of disbelief and frenzy against the injustice of losing people you loved. I couldn't start any conversation that might lead to her finding out what I had done when my mother died.

In the end, India and Andy decided to go and have a look at their house, see what it looked like now the water had subsided a bit. After much toing and froing, they finally decided to join a 'chin up' party at a cottage a fellow floodee had rented and stay there for the night to avoid the faff of trying to get a cab on New Year's Eve. As soon as they left, I felt the weight in me lift, as though I was coming up from the bottom of a deep swimming pool. I wished I didn't feel like that about my daughter.

Her children didn't seem worried that they'd been left with us. Quite the opposite. Ivy immediately commandeered the remote control. 'Can I watch a film?'

'Of course. Is there something you can all watch?'

'Rowan and I wanted to watch *Jurassic Park*,' Ivy said.

'Isn't that a bit scary for a six-year-old?' I asked.

Rowan looked at me and said, 'They're not real, Nan.'

'Turn it off if you get frightened. Ivy, you fast-forward the gory bits.' I was pretty sure it wouldn't tick India's non-violence boxes. 'Holly, you come and help me cook.' She was soon stabbing olives and mozzarella onto cocktail sticks.

And then everyone started arriving, and once I'd had a few glasses of wine, I forgot about India and danced with some of Fergus's friends. I found it hilarious that I'd known some of them since they were in primary school and they still called me Mrs Campbell. They were good lads, a gaggle of oddballs, who'd never got up the motivation to leave the village. None of them had proper names – Big D, Swanny, Sparks – and half of them still lived at home in their thirties, existing hand to mouth doing decorating here and there, fixing cars, DJing in the local pubs. Despite going to university, Fergus had stayed close to them, picking up where he left off when – much to India's disgust – he came straight back to work in our holiday cottage business. Her favourite refrain was 'It's all right for Fergus. He's never even had an interview. Didn't even try very hard at university because he knew he'd never have to prove anything to anyone. He should try teaching history in a secondary school. I've always got someone sitting in on my lessons, criticising me, telling me how I could do better.'

Fergus just laughed. 'I did all right at university. Still got a 2:2 *and* had loads of fun. Rather have that than revising my backside off any day. Probably just goes to show that I made the smart choices in the end, Inds.'

We all relaxed when India went out. Even Ivy was a different person without her nitpicking. So when she asked if she could have a glass of champagne, I agreed and said, 'Drink it slowly though, otherwise it might go to your head. Just the one, mind.' I'd always let my two have a few sips of wine from an early age and neither of them was a drunkard. In fact, India improved when a glass or two of wine softened her sharp edges.

And then, what with the making sure everyone had a drink and serving food, I didn't manage to get Holly to bed at seven as India had instructed. In fact, when I remembered to look at the clock, it was ten-thirty. I went through to the den where I'd said they could watch a film to see if Ivy could take her up. Holly was fast asleep on the rug wrapped around the dog and Rowan was watching *Live at the Apollo* next to a bonfire of Quality Street wrappers. When I walked in, he screwed his face up and said, 'Nan, what's a wanker?' I was so busy working out how I could answer and simultaneously erase the word from his vocabulary before India got home in the morning that it took me a moment to realise that Ivy had her laptop open watching some scantily clad dancers gyrating to rap music that seemed to have 'Motherfucker' as the dominant lyric.

I had a brief moment when I thought what a perfect painting it would be. My fingers itched to sketch out Rowan's face, his eyes wide with mischief. He might not know what 'wanker' meant, but he had an inkling it was in India's 'bad word' category, requiring a search for a 'more appropriate word'. Holly's chubby little cheeks pressed up against Dalí's snout. Dog and human in perfect harmony. Though it wouldn't fall into India's decrees about hygiene. I'd always subscribed to the 'We must eat a peck of dirt before we die' philosophy, but India was in the antibacterial hand gel camp. And finally, Ivy, that gorgeous slope of teenage indolence arranged on the sofa, shoulders rounded, just begging for a 'sit up straight!' I could title it, 'While the Cat's Away'. I could have left the party right there and then to disappear to my studio.

I was distracted by Rowan, who wasn't going to give up on the answer to his question, but there was something niggling me. 'Ivy, are you allowed to be on your laptop at this time of night?' I knew all screen time was strictly forbidden after nine o'clock. I nurtured a hope that India had agreed a special dispensation for New Year's Eve.

Way too slowly, realisation dawned as she slobbered rather than articulated, 'Not really.'

'Ivy! Have you been drinking?'

She twitched her nose like a hamster sussing out its surroundings. Stripped of that chilly reserve she had, that wary gaze like India's, she looked soft and warm. 'Just a little bit of champagne.'

'You sound rather drunk. Come and have some coffee in the kitchen.' I led her through the guests and tapped Gilbert on the arm. 'Can you get Holly and Rowan up to bed?'

He frowned as though he'd forgotten they were here. Then he nodded and went back to chatting to Fergus's mate.

I was just sitting Ivy down on a kitchen stool and encouraging her to drink a mug of super-strong Nescafé, when a big gust of wind signified that someone had opened the back door. Most of Fergus's friends liked a smoke. I'd decided I'd take it up again when I was eighty, so I could die of something else first, but in the meantime, I banished them outside.

But it wasn't Fergus's friends. From across the kitchen, I saw India and Andy emerge from the boot room.

I hissed to Ivy. 'Don't tell them I let you have a drink!'

She giggled. 'Sure Mum wouldn't mind.' Whereas I was sure she would.

I darted over to Gilbert. 'India's back! Try and get the other two upstairs.'

I turned to see India walking over to Ivy, saying, 'There weren't many people there, so we thought we'd come back.'

As my brain scrambled about for an escape route, Ivy threw up all over the pavlova on the kitchen counter. My simultaneous thoughts were 'What a waste of fresh raspberries at this time of year' and 'What a lot of shit I'm going to get for this.'

The guests all scattered to the side of the room. I gestured to Fergus to herd them through into the sitting room. He couldn't see me because he was doubled over with laughter. Honestly, that boy would be splitting his sides as they pushed the button to slide my coffin away at the crem. 'Fergus! Just take everyone through!'

Not bothering to disguise his hilarity, he spluttered out, 'Come on, everyone, party without puke this way.'

I ran over to Ivy. 'India, sorry, Ivy hasn't been feeling well this evening.'

She ignored me.

I grabbed the kitchen roll and passed it to Ivy, who was crying and saying, 'Sorry, Nan, sorry, Mum.'

'Don't worry, darling, you couldn't help it,' I said.

India put her hands on her hips. 'But you bloody well could. Don't give me that bollocks about it must be something she ate. What were you thinking, allowing her to drink? She's fourteen!'

'You were drinking at that age,' I said.

'I was also shooting air rifles unsupervised, mixing with all your weird painter friends and naked models with their penises hanging out. But that doesn't make it right!'

'I don't have weird painter friends.' She was making my life sound way more interesting than I remembered it.

But we never got to the bottom of that because Ivy splattered all over the floor.

She started crying harder. 'It wasn't Nan's fault, Mum. She just let me have a little glass, but I found a bottle.'

'You should have been supervising her. She could have died of alcohol poisoning. Ivy, you come with me to get cleaned up.'

Rowan came scampering in at that moment with Andy in hot pursuit, shouting, 'Bedtime, it's nearly midnight!' His whole tone smacked of impending world doom rather than something that could be resolved with an afternoon nap or a lie-in.

'I just wanted to ask Mum something,' he said, speeding round the kitchen island like a car around a race track.

India could sniff out a sugar high from a million miles away. She did a dramatic 'Oh my God, the six-year-old is going to die from lack of sleep and sugar overdose' face in my direction. She glared at Andy, I assumed for busting the myth that they were parents who never raised their voices. She then adopted what I thought of as her earnest teacher expression, despite the fact that she was standing there with her boots covered in bits of spaghetti Bolognese. 'Rowan?'

'Mum, what's a wanker?'

CARO

January 2017

Over the next week, the house strained to contain the seething mass of tensions within. No amount of apologising mollified India, whose response was always a version of 'I trusted you with my kids. You let Ivy drink herself to death and Rowan watch entirely inappropriate TV!'

Fergus, in his clumsy way, tried to be the voice of reason. 'Inds, you're not still going on about Ivy throwing up. I seem to remember you not doing so well on Pernod Black at Deano's party at the Scout Hut when you were about her age. And, in the role of wise uncle, I'm happy to explain to Rowan what a wanker is.' He put on a voice that was a pretty good imitation of India: 'It's like this, Rowan, darling, when you're older, you will find wanking an entirely pleasurable and appropriate activity…'

'Fergus, shut up, you're not helping,' I said, though I failed to sound properly annoyed with him as it was so wonderful not to have both my children treating me as though I couldn't be trusted to go shopping for an onion, let alone look after grandchildren.

He walked out, waving his hands in surrender. 'Always available to help keep Rowan on the straight and narrow.'

On the sixth of January, India came in and announced that they were all moving to a Premier Inn until the insurers could find them more permanent accommodation.

I couldn't help crying as I hugged the children. Despite India's role as chief critic for me and joy extinguisher for her kids, I'd loved the energy and life the grandchildren had brought to our home. Rowan waved out of the back window until they were out of sight.

Gilbert gave me a hug. 'Darling, India always has the hump about something. She came out of the womb with a protest placard. She'll soon be back when the kids have got a bug and she's got OFSTED turning up.'

I tried to share his confidence, but after ten days of checking my mobile every five minutes, I couldn't bear it any longer and texted to see how they were, offering them one of the big holiday cottages after the twentieth of January when we didn't have any bookings. Nothing.

A few days later, a letter arrived addressed to Gilbert and me. I recognised India's looping script. I told myself it would be a thank you note from the children for their Christmas presents. It was one of the few things I'd insisted on when my kids were young, and India maintained the tradition with bells on. But I still paused before I opened it to convince myself that the contents would be innocuous, even uplifting, the hard-won letters of 'Holly' that would have taken her ages or a scrawled 'Rowan' probably written as 'Roman'.

Dear Mum and Dad,

I wish I didn't have to write this letter, but after a lot of reflection I think it would be better if we have a complete break from each other for the foreseeable future. You clearly don't respect my views and opinions, especially regarding what's right for the children. I've always been a figure of fun in the family despite working hard, getting a first-class degree and taking responsibility for carving out a career for myself. I'm fed up with everyone acting as though I am the fun monitor when all Andy and I have ever wanted to do is keep our children safe and bring them up as decent human beings who know right from wrong.

You've never really made Andy welcome, always giving the impression that I could have done better. I'm not sure what you base that on as he has two degrees, teaches politics and supports me in everything I do. Perhaps you hoped that I would marry some rich businessman and live a life of Riley, maybe you wanted me to be more than just a head of department at the local grammar. Perhaps I just wanted parents who were happy for me.

I feel that Mum in particular has a toxic influence on my state of mind, so, for the sake of my own sanity, I think it's better that we keep contact to an absolute minimum. If you wish, you can send birthday/Christmas cards with money for the children, but no presents please.

Despite everything, I wish you both well.
India

I sank into the armchair in the den, remembering Ivy, lolling in the corner, Holly cuddled up to Dalí. Less than three weeks ago. India had said awful things to me before. Even her Mother's Day cards hurt me in their baldness, the perfunctory daffodil picture, with the sparse 'Happy Mother's Day' inside, the reluctant sense of duty trapped within. But the written word had a much sharper edge. Someone else's horrible version of you on paper, to replay at will with no right of immediate reply, had a power to wound that the spoken word lacked.

I turned the letter over on my lap, but still her phrases repeated themselves on a continuous loop in my brain. A toxic influence. No mother in the world set out to earn that as an epitaph. Being a good mother to India had been like the rough sketch of one of my paintings, temporarily put to one side because I couldn't get it right but always intending to pull it out and have another go at it later. And now it seemed later might not be available to me.

I sat, watching the winter sun fail to gain height in the sky, the tones of brown across the fields rippling towards tawny and beige as the light moved and the minutes, then the hours, ticked past.

I tried to pin down when my aloof little girl had become this angry woman. There'd always been a restlessness about her, as though whatever we embarked on didn't quite hit the spot. Halfway through a trip to the cinema, she'd wriggle in her seat and say, 'Is it nearly finished?' In the middle of making a cake, she'd push the bowl to me, 'You do it, Mummy.' And when she was older, we'd plan a day out to buy summer clothes and she'd refuse to come at the last minute – 'You choose for me.' As she'd grown up, I'd been overwhelmed by her blacks and her whites, her rights and her wrongs, when everything I thought huddled in a chaotic mass of grey hues, some smokier, some paler, but never extreme.

Except that one secret I wished I'd never had to hold. I was black and white about that.

In the months following India's decree that I was too poisonous to be included in any of their lives any more, a similar pattern to the dark days that followed the death of my father, then my mother, resonated through the household. Except this time, I was mourning someone who wasn't yet dead. I slept, for hours at a time, but never woke refreshed. I forgot more than I remembered. Even things I loved – painting, cooking, walking the dog – became another chore to overcome. Gilbert oscillated between irritated and concerned when we got a newspaper bill for over two hundred pounds and an apologetic note from Betty, the newsagent, asking if I could arrange to pay it as soon as possible. 'For God's sake, Caro. I'm still here and so is Fergus. Life goes on. You can't just give up.'

And now summer had arrived and with it, a long-standing commitment to give a talk about my art at a fundraising lunch. It was organised by a stalwart of our village, Penny Worrall. I'd known her since our kids were at primary school together, but I suspected I was a bit floaty and free-range for her taste. She'd never shown the slightest interest in my painting until the editor of our local *Devon Chronicle* had done a two-page spread on me. Out of the blue, she'd invited me to speak: 'You know, something light-hearted, bring us a few of your paintings to look at and a few tips on how someone might do something similar themselves.' She managed to say it as though any old bod could knock out a painting worth looking at when they'd finished pairing up the socks and folding their tea towels.

I wanted to cancel, but Gilbert wouldn't hear of it. 'You can't let them down at such short notice. Change of scenery, do you good, have a natter with your friends.'

I didn't have the heart to tell him that I didn't even like any of them. That when we'd moved to the village over three decades ago, I'd planned to sieve out the wheat from the chaff later on when I'd got the measure of everyone. Except I never had, I'd just got sucked into saying yes to invitations and then never finding the right moment to say no. So when I arrived at the village hall, where Penny had assembled thirty or so of her friends, I felt like a worm trapped with a whole flock of starlings.

Every conversation took me down avenues I didn't want to follow.

'How are the children? Well, they're not children any more are they? How old's your India now? Thirty-eight!'

'Is it two grandchildren you've got now? Three! You must have your hands full. India's lucky to have you round the corner as an on-tap babysitter.'

'Fergus not married yet? That might be a blessing. In my experience, sons only tend to stay in touch if their wife likes you. Thank goodness you've got a daughter.'

I batted them all away with stories of how busy India was teaching, how she'd set up a library system that had increased reading at the school by forty per cent, how the grandchildren were dashing from piano lessons to tae kwon do so I didn't see them as often as

I would like but when I did, 'we have a fabulous time, such great company'. By the time my talk came around and I'd heard about the villa that Gail had booked with her sons and grandchildren in the South of France that summer – 'Cost us a fortune for ten of us' – and the surprise sixtieth birthday party Penny's daughters had arranged for her – 'So much work went into it! I don't know how one of them didn't let something slip!' – I had that shaky feeling, as though I was so low on fuel, I needed to put myself in neutral and coast out of the door before I collapsed.

Penny rapped a knife on a glass. 'So, it gives me great pleasure to introduce Caro Campbell, whom I've known since our children were at school together...'

If I hadn't been swallowing, trying to get enough saliva in my mouth, I might have been tempted to point out that she'd only spoken to me at pick-up time if her little posse of friends weren't there.

Penny carried on. 'She's been hiding her light under a bushel for years – we had no idea about her amazing painting until the spread in the *Devon Chronicle* last year – and I know you'll all be desperate to learn about where she gets her inspiration from. I'm sure she'll be delighted to share her tips and techniques with anyone who wants to have a go at painting themselves.'

I stood up, my gaze flicking over all the eager faces. All those mothers who must have made mistakes. Who, like me, must have shouted, forgotten to sew on name tapes, run out of milk for the morning cereal, blown a gasket about make-up spilt on the carpet in teenage bedrooms. Those mothers I now saw chatting to their grown-up daughters over tea and scones in the little village tea shop. Who held their grandchildren on the seesaw on the green. Who wore motherhood as a joy, a source of pride, with a sense of a job well done.

The faces grew more expectant.

For a second, I teetered on the edge. A moment when I wanted to admit defeat, to hold my hands up and say, 'Sorry, I'm just too sad to face you all, too confused about how you with your alcoholic husband, you who never held one bloody birthday party for your daughter, you so strict your daughter had to lie about where she was, have managed to have a good relationship with them.'

But Penny smiled encouragingly and said, 'When you're ready...' and I had a sudden image of my own mum saying, 'Go on, love. Don't worry about what other people think. Most likely they won't even notice half of what you say, they'll be too busy thinking about themselves.'

I turned and held up my first canvas. One tiny pair of wellies next to a bigger pair by our back door, Fergus's and India's, circa 1987, when India was about eight and Fergus was three. And there, tucked away quietly in the corner of the picture, a calendar, with a day ringed.

I found my voice. 'This was the first painting I did where I'd understood that objects can represent an emotion. When I looked at those wellies, I wasn't thinking, rubber objects to stop feet getting muddy.' I pointed back to the painting. 'To me, those boots signified my family, protection, freedom to roam, to come back again, to burst into our house with cheeks rosy from the cold and to find warmth against the Aga and a hot dinner waiting.' I heard my voice quiver and cleared my throat. My words came back, stronger and lighter, as though I was telling a story to entertain rather than exposing nerves that had lost their outer coating. 'I suppose that picture represented being a mum. Keeping my kids safe without squashing their spirit.'

I nearly said it, nearly told them what I'd hardly told anyone. The thing that had made me take myself outside to look at the hills, the horizon, to remind myself that life had carried on and that, despite the pain, I had a lot to be grateful for. That had made me weep when I was trying to get the right size perspective for the boots, one large, one small. There should have been a medium-sized pair in-between. I would have called her Tuesday.

I ringed her on the calendar instead. My message that despite miscarrying her at sixteen weeks, I hadn't forgotten. Maybe that had made me soft on Fergus and harder on India. Who knew where I'd messed up?

I scanned the room. Most faces were turned towards me, some with expressions of surprise that this woman they'd dismissed as a bit of a flake with her knackered old Peugeot and relaxed attitude to school uniform actually had some skills that maybe they didn't. One woman wasn't even pretending to listen, jabbing away at her phone and smiling to herself.

I pushed on, talking them through a few more paintings, becoming quite animated as I discussed the ideas behind them, the technical challenges, how the final product differed from what I set out to do.

The last one was of the rhododendrons in our garden. I'd intended to give it to Gilbert on my fiftieth birthday as a thank you for putting up with me for all those years. The garden was very much my department, but he did love the rhodies, especially the bright pink one in the far corner of the lawn. I didn't complete it in time because my mother died. And when I tried to finish it, everything had changed. Mum was the only person I might have told, who just possibly would have understood. But instead I had to tuck my shame away inside me, far from judgement and justice, where I hoped it would wither and die. The opposite happened. It grew and thrived. Back then, I didn't know how bad it would get, though I'd obviously hedged my bets with a scattering of crows, gathered on a telegraph wire, waiting for unsuspecting prey to cross their path. And, in the corner, a single magpie.

I peddled the story I'd told myself, that the birds represented the sadness I felt about losing my mother, and that the brightness of the rhododendrons promised hope, the natural cycle of life. But, unlike the majority of the people in this room, nothing about my life was natural. My daughter was lost to me. I was abnormal. I felt my energy drain away and did a shy, 'That's it, really. The stories behind my pictures.'

There was a round of applause, the woman on her phone had the grace to put down her mobile to tap two fingers on the back of her hand and Penny leapt to her feet. 'Fascinating, Caro. I'm sure there'll be lots of questions.'

I explained my routine, how exhibitions worked, the best way to learn how to paint, the extra challenges of depicting humans rather than objects.

Then a woman put her hand up. I recognised her as Linda, who'd had a daughter in India's class at senior school, years ago, a cocky little madam who came for a sleepover and had a problem with everything I served up – 'I only really like white toast.' 'Is there any apple juice instead of orange?' 'Is there any *strawberry* jam?' In the end, I'd said, 'In my house you eat what's in front of you or you go hungry.' India had been furious with me for 'behaving like a bitch'. I ignored the woman as long as I could but, eventually, I'd answered everyone else. 'Yes?'

'Will you paint me and my two daughters?'

'As a paid commission, do you mean?'

'I thought you could practise on us. We'd give you permission to use the painting in one of your exhibitions.'

I felt my face go tight. 'I'm not really at the stage of my career where I "practise" for free any more.'

The woman looked affronted. 'I was only asking.'

It was that entitlement that did it. India would look as though she'd slipped in a pile of vomit if I asked her to sit for a portrait. But Linda could take for granted that her children would be happy to oblige and that it was such an honour for me to do it for free. I couldn't think of a more perfect torture than painting a woman I didn't respect, who'd somehow managed to produce two daughters who loved her. The thought of sitting opposite them, witnessing their ease and warmth, made me feel sick.

Whatever hurdles I jumped through, ease would never be part of my relationship with India. I couldn't even be sure I'd ever see my grandchildren again. And yet this woman, who had probably never done one single generous thing in her life, never offered anyone a helping hand, was cruising around with two healthy daughters who hadn't sent her a letter rejecting her as a parent. That searing pain ripped through me, lighting the fuse to the words that should never have left my mouth. 'Do you ask your plumber to work for free? What about your cleaner? Your gardener maybe? Am I supposed to be grateful for the pleasure of sitting opposite your ugly mugs for hours on end for the price of some Earl bloody Grey and a chocolate digestive?'

What I *would* have loved to paint was the Mexican wave of mouths opening all the way round the room. There was a rattle of coffee cups and a synchronised turn of heads towards Linda to see how she was going to react.

I burst into tears, waving an apologetic hand, 'Sorry, sorry, I'm not myself at the moment. I'd better go. Thank you for having me.' I gathered up my paintings, while everyone sat in stunned silence.

Lou, who Penny had paid to clean up, ran to help me. 'Let me carry some of these out for you, love.' When we reached the car, she loaded them into the boot and said, 'I wanted to cheer when you said that. When I was selling raffle tickets for the hospice where my Les died, she wouldn't buy one. Said she donated to *so many* charities already.'

I wish I'd been brave enough to explain that Linda had poked a screwdriver into a gangrenous wound. But Lou was the sort of person who never required you to say more than you wanted. The world needed more people like that.

CARO

Jan 2018

Our whole festive season had stumbled along under the guise of fake cheer. I spent more time in the kitchen than usual, mainly dabbing my eyes with a tea towel before plastering on a smile and insisting that we pulled our crackers and put on our paper hats. I wasn't sure I'd fooled anyone, but if Fergus and Gilbert noticed, they were happy to go along with the charade. In the first week of January, when I was gearing up to face another twelve months without India and her children, Fergus summoned us to a meeting.

'Is there a problem?' I asked, aiming for light-hearted but hearing my words tremble with the irrational fear that he was going to divorce us too, just as India had this time last year.

'Nothing that can't be resolved, I don't think. But, Dad, you and me need to have a proper sit-down.'

He sounded matter-of-fact, calm rather than a man on the verge of listing his mother's faults. My treacherous heart did an optimistic leap at the possibility that India was using him as a go-between to make peace with us.

We'd had crumbs of hope during the last year. Gilbert had hit the nail on the head when he'd said India would get in contact when she needed emergency childcare. The first time she'd rung Gilbert at seven in the morning after about three months of silence saying she needed him to come 'now' because Holly had an upset stomach and India had a special assembly she couldn't miss. Only

Gilbert was allowed to go. I'd been curdled with envy yet relieved that she'd poked out an olive branch and we could start to put this behind us. He'd taken tons of photos of a pale-looking Holly, and Rowan when he got home from school. None of Ivy, who was out at judo – a new development. I spent hours poring over them, my chest heavy with longing.

'How was she? Was she friendly?' I'd asked, without turning round. I didn't want to see him protecting me.

'She was a bit harassed, late for school, so we didn't have much time to chat.'

'Did she look well?'

'Thin.'

My frustration was rising. 'Thin ill, thin she's been on a diet, thin she looks good on it?'

Gilbert had frowned as though reporting beyond immediate observations was not part of his remit. 'Just thin because she's always on the go, I think. She said she'd been really busy, but she'd give you a ring in the next week or two.'

I waited. I ran through my opening lines, trying to find ones that wouldn't have her slamming the phone down. I faltered after 'It's so lovely to hear from you.' Anything else – 'I've missed speaking to you.' 'I've missed you.' 'Could I pick the children up from school one evening when you are working late?' – felt as though it had the potential to pull the pin on one of the hand grenades India had permanently tucked in her pocket. I'd have to practise keeping silent and letting her fill the space.

For the next fortnight, I couldn't concentrate on my painting even though I had an exhibition coming up. I didn't want to go out in case something banal like buying loo paper was the *Sliding Doors* moment that stopped me making peace with my daughter. I came to hate the way she'd turned me into a passive recipient of her bounty. So at the beginning of April I texted her, three lines that took me forever to compose, sifting and sieving for anything that could come over as critical or needy.

Hello India, Dad showed me the photos of Rowan and Holly. They look so gorgeous and grown-up. Please give my love to all of them. Look forward to hearing from you when you have time. Lots of love Mum.

I lost another week to straining my ears for the ping of an incoming text. After a month, it dawned on me that 'the next week or two' might mean the next year or two. Or never.

And for the rest of 2017 the pattern had been the same. A flurry of activity when India summoned Gilbert – never me – to help out. He'd come back, hopeful and positive, mention they'd talked about perhaps a dinner out for one of the children's birthdays or us going to see Ivy play the clarinet. And we'd both say, 'Let's see what happens. It's a step in the right direction anyway.' And Gilbert would suddenly know where his mobile was at all times, and I'd start baking flapjacks and putting them in the freezer just in case, neither of us settling to anything despite not acknowledging it to each other. Then gradually we'd realise that we weren't going to get that call to see Holly in her nursery nativity play or Ivy in her concert.

Gilbert would walk miles with Dalí, arriving home with red eyes – 'so windy out there'.

I'd nod and say, 'The exercise is good for you though.' Then sit in my studio, the disappointment and hurt smashing any creative instinct like a wave against a breakwater.

'How's the painting going?' Gilbert would ask, searching for a lifebelt of good news to stop us going under.

'I had some really great ideas today, just need to corral them into something a bit more tangible.'

And we'd smile and another sadness would go unremarked and unchallenged, left to sink a deep tap root into our souls.

So it was with a mixture of anticipation and trepidation that we waited for Fergus in our dining room, hoping that if he wasn't the bearer of good news, he might at least avoid plunging us into further family disasters. I would have preferred the informality of the kitchen but Gilbert always defaulted to our shiny mahogany dining table for anything that could be deemed 'a serious meeting'. I couldn't come into this room without thinking back to the day of Mum's funeral and that stupid moment I should have avoided. After twelve years, I still recalled looking at the stars and wondering, childishly, if Mum was somewhere up in the sky. The noise of everyone inside, moving to that stage of a wake where you're done with being sad and just want to laugh and live and find another bottle of red and figure out why you haven't seen the cousin you really like in so long.

I glanced at the bench outside the window. I remembered sitting there, the chill of the March wind drying my tears to a tight sting. That voice behind me, gentle and compassionate, telling me to come inside. My head lolling, heavy, as though all my grief was trapped inside my brain, weighing me down. My heart aching – physically aching – from the peculiar loneliness that comes with being an orphan, the irrevocable acceptance of becoming a proper adult because I was no longer anyone's child. I wondered whether I was indulging myself, being overdramatic in my grief, as though wanting my mother was something I should have grown out of at fifty. Along with all the other things I should have known better by then.

Fergus bowled in, interrupting the train of thought I tried so hard never to climb aboard by putting his hands up. He seemed nervous, skittish. 'Right. I'll keep this brief. With all the Brexit uncertainty, we've not had as many foreign bookings as usual and business was down generally over the winter. The roofs at Elm Cottage and Hawthorns need a complete overhaul – the winds in the last few weeks have done some serious damage. And there's a brand new complex opened up over the other side of the valley, with a pool and a games room, which is bound to take some of our regular families.'

Gilbert frowned. 'So what are you saying?' If he was disappointed that Fergus wasn't here to explain how India wanted to reconcile, he hid it well. With a great effort, I forced myself to focus.

Fergus looked down, then stared Gilbert straight in the eye with a mixture of belligerence and defensiveness. 'We need to get a loan to sort out the roofs at least. I've spoken to the bank about borrowing around eighty thousand, to allow for some refurbishment as well. We'd have to put up one of the cottages as a guarantee.'

'And what would the terms be? How long would you expect it to take us to pay that back?' Gilbert was in full business mode. I was still struggling to banish the little images flitting through my mind of Rowan's cheeky giggle, Ivy's face when a teenage sulk morphed into a smile, Holly's little legs running towards me.

Fergus shuffled in his seat. 'I still need to go through the detail, but I just wanted to put you in the picture.'

'I'd like to know the facts before we go ahead. I wish you'd told us about this earlier.' Gilbert sounded accusatory, as he often did when he was worried.

'If I'd done that without going to the bank first to find out what was possible, you'd have said, "Don't come to me with a problem without offering a solution."'

I could see a grain of truth in that, but I wasn't sure Gilbert would view it that way. My stomach did a little flip. We'd already fallen out with one of our children.

I stepped in. 'How about we do a radical rethink? We haven't really marketed the properties for ages. Why don't we get a slightly bigger loan and employ someone to do some advertising and manage the bookings, while Fergus concentrates on the property maintenance, upgrade side of things? We've not really invested in the cottages since we had a bit of a spruce-up with the money that Mum left me.'

Gilbert and Fergus gazed at me, if not with admiration, at least in silence. I burbled on, desperate to distract Gilbert from entrenching himself in a battle with Fergus, who looked excited, as though I'd thrown him a lifeline, playing to his skills.

Gilbert said, 'When I ran the business, we never borrowed any money. Just ploughed the profits back in and built it up slowly.'

Fergus shook his head as though Gilbert had stepped straight out of a seventies sitcom. 'But there wasn't so much competition then. Now you've got glamping, Airbnb, yurts, spas… A few cottages on a farm, lovely though they are, isn't really a unique selling point.'

I saw Fergus's fingers flutter up, then resist the urge to turn his phone over. I'd noticed that all young people did it when conversations got awkward. Though, in fairness, Gilbert and I never addressed the fact that India only contacted us when she wanted something.

Fergus swallowed. 'Why don't we do what Mum suggests for six months? Give it a go? A strong marketing push could make a real difference to the summer season.' He looked to me for support.

'What do you think, Gil?' I asked. 'We could save a bit of money by offering live-in accommodation, with a responsibility to organise the bookings and promote Applewood Farm as a family destination?'

Gilbert acquiesced so graciously I had one of those little reminders why vintage love should never be abandoned for anything glittery or new. 'We'd better draft an advert then.'

By the end of February, Fergus, Gilbert and I were interviewing a hotch-potch of candidates.

One woman was an immediate no by waving Dalí away. 'Off, off my shoes. Presumably the dog isn't allowed to roam freely when the guests are here?'

We all looked at each other until, with great restraint, Gilbert said, 'We use the dog on the website to *encourage* families to come. Four out of the eight cottages are dog-friendly.'

I almost did a cheer when Dalí cocked his leg up the wheel of her car.

Another woman took one look at the farm and the lack of lighting up the lane and said, 'Too isolated for me, I'm afraid. I'd be worried about axe murderers behind the hedges.' In my experience, used condoms and loos left in a disgusting state were far more likely than a weapon-wielding maniac but I didn't try to persuade her.

Then a young woman who introduced herself as Vicky Hall pitched up in a battered Mini with an Irish wolfhound mongrel sitting on the front seat.

As soon as she got out, she said, 'Wow. Look at these views. Would you mind if I bring Lionel in with me?' indicating the dog. 'He tends to howl if I leave him in the car, but he'll just go to sleep if he's with me.'

There was an inaudible cheer as we all watched her talking to Lionel as though he was a human being. 'Come on. Sorry to disturb your sleep, but there are things to do, people to see.'

Once we'd all said hello and Lionel and Dalí had done the obligatory bottom sniffing, we got down to the nitty-gritty, with Gilbert grilling her on the job-related stuff – 'Are you a self-starter?' 'Are you good at proofreading?' 'Could you sort out our website – are you good with technology?'

Vicky gave a short explanation about how she'd revamped the website of the library where she used to work in Surrey.

'Long way from there now. What brought you down here?' I asked.

Her expression was similar to the one I adopted when people enquired how India was. The facial equivalent of a stop sign, blank but firm. 'I wanted to be nearer to the sea.'

The one that interested me though was 'Could you deal with difficult customers?' because I was getting too bloody old to put up with idiots in brand new walking boots complaining about the patchy Wi-Fi.

'I have first-hand experience of dealing with extremely difficult people, so the occasional tricky holidaymaker won't be an issue.'

'Can you give me an example?' I asked.

Fergus raised his eyebrows as I pretended to be some hotshot employer, when in fact I was just being nosey. We all knew she'd got the job from the minute Lionel had put his paw up to Gilbert for a second biscuit.

'I will compromise and try to find solutions up to a certain point, but then I am not afraid to cut loose. And with some customers, you'll give way on one thing to make them happy, but then they'll find another problem they hadn't mentioned initially and there'll be no pleasing them.'

We discovered that she had a degree in English and over five years' experience working in various live-in pub and restaurant scenarios.

'What about the isolation? Do you have family and friends locally?' I asked.

She laughed. 'Lionel will love it here and if he's happy, I am.'

We all turned to see Lionel snuggled up with Dalí in his bed. I registered that she'd only answered one of my questions, but Gilbert stood up, shook her hand and said, 'If you'd like to take Lionel for a stroll round the garden, while we have a quick powwow...?'

She'd barely gone out of the door before I said, 'I think she'd be brilliant.'

Gilbert said, 'Is thirty a bit young though? I wonder if someone in their mid-forties might be better, someone with a bit of gravitas?'

I shook my head. 'No, I think she'd be great, if she doesn't find it too boring living out in the sticks. She'll know how to do all the technology and website stuff and she'll have new ideas about social media. We're too old for that, and Fergus isn't really interested in that side of things.' I said it lightly, because one of the reasons Gilbert had agreed to let Fergus run the business was that he felt too old to learn how to manage everything online. He'd still insisted on telephone bookings until about five years ago. Fergus had made a fair stab at building a website with a friend from the village, but it had fallen short of moving us into hi-tech, high-discoverability territory.

'I think we would really complement each other,' Fergus said.

Gilbert narrowed his eyes while he was thinking. I was desperate to make sure we had as little scope as possible for falling out with Fergus.

To bring Gilbert on board, I said, 'Maybe you need to schedule some meetings with her, Fergus, so you're both clear on who's doing what.'

'Thanks for that lesson in business management, Mum,' Fergus said. 'I love how the fact that the bookings are poor is uniquely down to me. It's not actually my fault that the UK has had a political meltdown and there have been high winds and storms all winter. I bet if you asked any of the holiday places around here, they'd all say the same.'

I put my hand up to stop him. 'I didn't say it was your fault. I don't think it is. We need to move with the times and now's a good moment to do it.'

He turned sulky. 'It just feels as though no one ever looks at the things I do right. Maybe I should start throwing my weight around like India and then you'd be hopping through hoops to make me happy.'

I could have put my head on the table and cried. I'd held my babies close when they were born, my mind full of the fun we'd have, the places we'd see, the idea that we'd be this solid unit, each one of us standing firm, providing fortification against the outside world. It never occurred to me that we'd all turn on each other.

Gilbert acted as though Fergus hadn't spoken, the master avoider of conflict. 'Right, shall we call her back in then? Are we all agreed that she's the right person for the job?'

Fergus nodded. And the moment to tell him how much I loved him passed. Motherhood often felt like trying to catch a butterfly threatened with extinction and resolving to be quicker, quieter next time. Followed by the realisation that I'd had my chances and there wouldn't – couldn't – be a next time. But in true Campbell fashion, we lifted up the corner of the carpet, got an industrial-sized brush, swept the multitude of familial grudges under it and called in Vicky to tell her we'd love to have her join us.

2018

I wonder if she'd come back if she knew what had happened. Whether she'd want to come. Whether she'd been waiting all these years for us to stretch out an olive branch. Or maybe all the things she was angry about have flourished and self-seeded over the years, the plant of parental errors sturdy and strong.

I never thought she'd have the confidence to cut off contact like that. She was stronger than I gave her credit for, more determined. I thought she'd go for a couple of weeks, maybe a few months, but I was sure she'd be back by the end of the summer. And now here we are, all this time later, a family that has had to involve the help of a complete stranger to right the wrongs. If it hadn't become so urgent, and my heart wasn't so utterly and completely broken, I might have felt a grudging admiration that she'd survived on her own and never felt the need to creep back to us with her tail between her legs.

Good strong genes. There's an irony in that, which might save us all.

VICKY

June 2018

As the weeks passed, I began to see results from my hard work. Bookings were creeping up. With some cute photos of Dalí and Lionel and a promise that the dogs loved to be stroked, I'd hit upon the idea of increasing the appeal of the farm to families with children desperate for pets. I'd also identified an area behind the cottages where the kids could camp out at night, and Fergus had built a chicken coop where an army of ginger hens now resided and guests could help themselves to fresh eggs for breakfast.

Fergus had an easy-going way about him that had the parents, particularly the mothers, falling for his sunny charm, especially when they got the added bonus of free childcare in the form of the dens he built with visiting kids, the impromptu obstacle courses, the collecting of wood to make a campfire for toasting marshmallows. My forte lay in making sure everything worked, that any practical problems were resolved immediately.

I told myself it was the perfect set-up. I had my own cottage with Lionel. Caro had tried to get to know me, dropping in little questions as we sorted the linen or inspected the crockery. 'So, where is your family from originally?' and more intrusively, 'Are your parents still alive?' I muttered something about not seeing much of my family and diverted her by asking about retiling some of the kitchens. Eventually, we'd settled into the sort of relationship that I'd become an expert at forging – a friendship that existed in the here and now, without any need to fill in the preceding years.

The other two weren't interested in anything personal. Fergus seemed delighted to have someone to take the heat off him and Gilbert just wanted the job done without any hassle. They were so pleased with me, I didn't want to watch the horror on their faces as they realised that I'd walked out on my two-year-old son six years ago. At worst, they probably thought I was a bit of an oddball, perhaps that I'd had my heart broken and was trying to forget. I had and I was. But not in the way they assumed.

By the middle of June, I was as settled as I'd been for a long time when a family arrived with an eight-year-old boy. I couldn't look at him, couldn't be in the same space as him. I'd trained myself to be welcoming and friendly, but I couldn't wait to leave their cottage. I didn't want to wonder whether Theo would be tall and confident like this lad or reserved, the quiet boy in the class whose – whisper – mother walked out. Unfortunately for me, the boy took such a shine to Lionel, he ended up hanging around me constantly, chatting away whether or not I responded. I found myself being dragged in, despite the futility of learning about the things Theo might be interested in now – 'What's your favourite subject at school?' 'Do you play any sport?' 'What music do you listen to?'

I told myself that I was offering great customer service, not clinging onto something that was lost to me. But for the first time in years, I acknowledged Theo's birthday, admitting to myself I was remembering it, rather than suppressing the melancholy that hung heavy in my chest every 25 June. I sat on the bench overlooking the valley at seven o'clock, the time he was born, with Lionel at my feet. I wondered what my little boy would look like now, what he'd play with, whether there'd be something of me in him, if not a resemblance, a fleeting mannerism or expression. I hadn't afforded myself this indulgence in ages. Occasionally, I'd get an unexpected rush of longing when mums and dads looked so – I was never sure what it was that sparked the envy in me – so unified, unruffled maybe? So confident with their children. I'd never felt that. How did parents know what to do? Maybe I'd just been too young. Too immature. William had had a strong bond with him. He'd be looking after him. Barbara too. She'd definitely loved him.

Even the eight-year-old guest had eventually said, 'You don't know anything about children, do you?' when I'd asked if he liked school.

I marched off, telling him he needed to go back to his mum and dad because I had things to do. I went inside, drawn to the one thing I tried to avoid, that both soothed and scorched. With a click of the mouse, I brought up the single photo I'd found of Theo on the internet. His school team had won the touch rugby tournament and their photo was in the *Surrey Mirror*. A black and white picture that blurred when I tried to enlarge it to study every detail of his face. He was smiling. That had to be enough.

CARO

July 2018

I'd just come in from my painting studio when I saw a big shiny Audi pull into our drive.

A man in his thirties got out, very London-looking. Expensive jeans, the sort of faux-vintage jacket that cost a fortune, similar to the ones Gilbert had had hanging in his wardrobe for thirty years and refused to get rid of – 'That cost me nearly a week's wages' – even though he'd never wear one again. Not as long as he was married to me, anyway. He walked towards the front door, his head swivelling about with a curiosity more intense than that of someone who was just checking out the location for a walking holiday.

I opened the door before he got there.

'Excuse me, good morning, I'm looking for Vicky Hall.'

I put my hands on my hips and studied him. He looked a bit debonair for Vicky with her penchant for tie-dye, dreamcatchers and Doc Martens. An ex-husband finally tracking her down? Wide boy just out of prison? Might explain why she changed the subject every time I asked her about her life.

'Who are you?' I didn't care about living up to the suspicious village crone stereotype.

'I've come to give her a message from her family.'

'But who are you? Are you a relative? How do we know you're not some dodgy ex-husband with a cache of machine guns in the boot plotting for revenge?'

The man laughed. 'Whoa. That's some imagination. I'm Liam Smallfield. I'm a private investigator.' He handed me his card.

'Is she in trouble?' I asked, just as Vicky started walking across the drive towards the laundry room with a bundle of bedding.

He shook his head. 'No, she's not in trouble.'

I invited him in so I could at least warn Vicky before he spotted her himself. 'Here. Take a seat in the kitchen. I'll see if she's around.' I paused. 'Aren't private investigators supposed to sit in their cars using cameras with long lenses rather than announcing their arrival? You're not very Hollywood, are you?'

Liam grinned. 'Sometimes we do just that. But if the client wants us to, we also make initial contact to pass on messages.'

I called Fergus down from the study and filled him in. 'Make Liam a cup of tea.'

I scooted over to the laundry.

'Vicky! There's a private investigator looking for you. Says your family have sent him.'

I watched her carefully. She screwed her eyes tightly shut and held the bridge of her nose.

'Do you know what it's about?' I asked.

'Not exactly.' She folded her lips together, but it didn't stop her cheeks trembling.

'He's in the house with Fergus. Shall I come with you?'

She nodded. I took her arm and this prickly, self-contained girl leaned into me. I could feel her shaking.

'It might be good news. He said you weren't in trouble. It could be a long-lost aunt leaving you a fortune.'

We walked into the kitchen, where Liam and Fergus were discussing the weekend's rugby. 'Fergus, let's give Liam and Vicky a bit of privacy.' I indicated the dining room. 'You can go and sit in there if you like.'

But Vicky seemed to lose control. 'Is it Mum? Is she dead?'

Liam motioned towards us. 'Shall we talk privately?'

'Just tell me if it's Mum?' Then with a strangled howl of anguish, 'Please tell me nothing's happened to Theo?'

There were two people who mattered to her then. Which was a revelation in itself as I was beginning to think she did only have Lionel.

'Let's just pop next door,' Liam said.

Vicky looked as though she was about to resist, but even though the word to describe my interest in what revelation might come our way was 'agog', I ushered them into the dining room.

Behind the closed door, I heard Vicky cry out, 'No!' Then with real venom, 'There's no way I'm going back to Guildford. I don't care what they want. Just ask them what they need and I'll give it to them.'

More muffled speech. I was ashamed that I was moving about so lightly, putting my finger to my lips when Fergus looked like he was about to speak. Our little village didn't see many private investigators arriving with life-changing news.

'It's like being in an episode of *Midsomer Murders*,' Fergus whispered.

After about twenty minutes, Liam came out and Fergus and I did some random opening of cupboards and drawers to disguise the fact that we'd been whipping up a hurricane with the flapping of our ears.

'I'm going to head off now. Thank you.'

Fergus saw him out.

I left it about thirty seconds. I gestured to Fergus to stay in the kitchen.

'Vicky?'

She was sitting on a straight-backed chair, gazing out the window, huge tears gathering silently along her lashes, then burning a trail down her cheeks.

'What's happened?'

'My son's father wants to emigrate to Denmark and I need to give consent so he can move abroad with him.'

Vicky had a son? I stood in the doorway trying to compute the fact that she'd been with us for over four months and hadn't mentioned a word about him, or left Applewood Farm in that time. I hesitated. Vicky wasn't someone I could pull into a hug – not even in these extreme circumstances. Even when she had coffee with me, there was an underlying sense that she wouldn't allow the time to drift into a second cup or another biscuit, that she always had her eye on the exit. I couldn't make her out. Personally, I craved the human touch when I was upset. I loved to fold myself into someone and abdicate from being an adult for a moment. I put my hand over hers. She sat motionless for a few seconds, then her hand relaxed under mine.

She started crying. 'They want to have a meeting to discuss Theo's future. They're pushing for William's wife to have parental responsibility.' Vicky wailed, the sort of sound that has to be released before your heart implodes with sadness.

I needed a list of characters like you get at the beginning of Shakespeare plays.

I let her cry. 'Who is "they"? And where are they?'

'My ex-boyfriend's family. They're in Surrey. I can't go back.'

Vicky folded forward as though someone had punched her in the stomach.

I went through to the kitchen and brought back tissues and a pint of ice-cold water.

She gulped down a huge mouthful. 'Sorry. You don't need my drama. It's just such a shock to have any contact with them after all this time.'

'Do you want to tell me?'

Everything about her sagged. 'You'll judge me. Everyone judges me.'

'Try me. It's a brave person who believes they've never cocked up.'

I sat open-mouthed as she told me that she'd walked out on her son when he was two and a half and never spoken to him since.

'But why?'

She cried, but through it all, she kept repeating, 'He was better off without me.'

I shook my head as I listened to the sorry tale. I struggled to hide my astonishment that a mother of a two-year-old, a toddler still depending on her for everything, would just disappear like that, whatever her mother-in-law was like.

The story was disjointed, bursting out of her in fragments that I endeavoured to cobble together. 'I couldn't be a good mother.' 'Theo broke his leg because of me.' 'I frightened him.' 'He called Barbara, William's mother, "Mamma".' 'I could never get it right.' She paused. 'I wanted him to be happy. That was *all* I wanted.'

I trotted out some platitudes about how parents don't get it right all the time, that we do our best. I worked hard to stop the words in India's letter echoing round my head as I spoke, fighting back my growing frustration that Vicky wasn't snatching the opportunity to see Theo again. He hadn't forced her out of his life in the way India had rejected me. From what I could make out, she'd chosen to leave. What two-year-old boy was better off without his mother?

'So what happens now?' I tried to soften my words.

She turned away from me and gazed out across the valley. 'William got married to a Danish woman called Clara a couple of years ago. Liam said her father is ill, so they've decided to move out to Denmark for the foreseeable future, but apparently, because I have parental responsibility, William can't take Theo abroad without my consent. Otherwise it's like child abduction.'

'You're not just going to let him go, are you? You can't give another woman parental responsibility without even meeting her, surely?'

'Theo probably won't even remember me. I haven't seen him since 2012, so what do I know about what's right for him? William sounds very settled with Clara and that's got to be good for Theo.'

I couldn't allow her to let her boy move to another country, make a life somewhere else entirely with a woman she didn't even know, without examining all the options.

'Women who give away their babies for adoption spend years looking for them. You've got a chance to get back in touch with Theo. Even if you do allow William to take him to Denmark, at least let the boy understand where he came from, who his real mother is.'

The shutters came down. 'He'll think of Clara as his mother now.'

I couldn't help myself. 'And you've got no interest in having one meeting, even if it's a bit uncomfortable, to double-check you're making the right decision? This is your son we're talking about, after all.'

Vicky stood up. 'This is the reason I never discuss it. No one will ever understand.'

I watched her walk out, marvelling at how little we know about people we see every day.

VICKY

July 2018

Liam had left me Barbara's number. I kept telling myself that I could post anything they needed, that I shouldn't give it any more thought, just carry on with life as it was, routine, settled and easy.

But I couldn't. I'd assumed I'd drawn a line under motherhood, that I'd accepted that I'd failed, that someone else would do a better job. But despite what I'd said to Caro, that kernel of curiosity was there, sprouting away, making me wonder if I should just see him one last time, an elected, elegant closure, rather than the chaotic disappearance of six years ago.

Every time I walked past the card with Barbara's number on the back, I frowned. Surely William should be handling this? I suppose he was a hugely important person in the City by now and had delegated it to his mother. The mere thought of phoning made me come over all hot. That pause before Barbara had to make herself polite to get what she wanted. I could never justify what I'd done, not to her anyway.

I lay on the bed with Lionel. I hadn't anticipated that I'd have to accept definitively that I'd never have a relationship with Theo. Secretly I must have been clinging to the nebulous idea it might somehow work out in a distant future. Now separation was being imposed upon me, I felt bereft all over again. Knowing I didn't deserve any consideration didn't change the leaden longing for a thread of connection, that tenuous link that still existed in my heart, despite my mind insisting otherwise.

The next morning, Caro knocked on my door bright and early. 'I've spoken to Fergus. Take the week off and go and see William and Theo and come to some arrangement.'

I stood, thick-headed from the red wine the night before. 'I can't just turn up.' I imagined pulling into the drive. All the roses would be out by now. Theo's face turning to see who'd arrived, then away again, disinterested, without a glimmer of recognition.

Caro frowned. 'Think about your son. Even if you saw him twice a year, it would give you some basis for a relationship to build on when he's older.'

'No. It's not fair. I gave up my rights to Theo when I left. He won't *want* to see me. Why would he? I just didn't realise the day would come when it would all seem so final.'

When Caro spoke, her voice had an odd strained note to it. 'As mothers, we don't always make the right decisions. We make mistakes. But it's not often we get a second chance. Have a think about it.' Then she jumped up, as though I'd annoyed her in some way.

I buried myself in work. Ironically, my job that afternoon was buying some stock photos of happy families to use on the website. Little memories of Theo crept out as I scrolled through the chubby babies held aloft like trophies by their fathers, cradled by their mothers. My favourite time was nursing him on the rocking chair just as the dawn was breaking but everyone was still asleep, the boiler downstairs revving up for morning duty, making the pipes hum. Theo always seemed contented then, his eyelids drooping with satisfaction as he drained his bottle. There had been good times.

Two days later, Barbara contacted me. I should have known she wouldn't sit idly by now Liam had found me. I had to stand up to answer the call, to open up a channel to get breath in my body. Even before I spoke, I could feel the tremble in my throat.

She ignored my enquiry about how she was. 'When are you coming to sort out the legalities?'

I hadn't expected her to be so blunt.

'Barbara, I'd prefer it if you tell me what you need from me and I'll send it to you. I don't think any good will come from me turning up.'

I hated myself for the wobble in my voice. And Barbara was like a vulture descending on carrion.

'Personally, I think the least you can do is have one civilised face-to-face conversation about your son's future, if only to assure us that you won't ever be part of it. Some things need to be talked through properly... You won't have to see Theo if that's what's worrying you.'

There was something about her dismissive manner that sparked a defiance in me. Contrarily, her assumption that I wouldn't want to see my own son made me want to prove her wrong. 'I'd like to discuss this with William. He's the one I should be making arrangements with.'

'William's not here at the moment. We haven't got any time to waste, Vicky. Clara has everything packed up ready to ship to Denmark. We've already lost weeks to tracking you down. You get here by Saturday or we'll all come to you. I know where you are now.' The line went dead.

I slumped into the armchair until Lionel barked at me to move to the sofa so he could cuddle up with me. I rubbed his ears while my mind whirled. Barbara was perfectly capable of bringing her caravan of drama to me. I couldn't have her flouncing around with Caro and Gilbert as onlookers. They saw me as confident and capable. I'd hate them to witness my kowtowing to Barbara. And I certainly didn't want an audience if they brought Theo. The thought of seeing him emerge from the car squeezed the air out of my body. Just contemplating that little boy fast-forwarded to eight years old pressed on something sore inside me that I couldn't acknowledge.

Caro banged on the door.

'How's it going?'

I explained about Barbara and her Saturday deadline.

'They're very welcome to come here. I'm happy to sit in on any meeting with them if that helps?'

I tried to smile. 'I can't. What if they bring Theo? They've probably been feeding him all sorts of lies about me. At best, I'm no one to him – a distant aunt or cousin he's heard very little about. At worst, every variation on a cold-hearted wicked witch. How would I even begin to explain?'

Caro sighed. 'I don't think they would bring him, would they? Not without much more preparation. But a tiny part of you must want to see him? You are his mother.'

'Well, only in the sense I gave birth to him. I can't see the point of trying to rekindle a relationship now when he's going to move abroad.'

Then out of the blue – I was pretty sure it was out of the blue – she shouted at me. 'Just listen to yourself! All about what you can't do, what would be difficult for you, what wouldn't fit in with your life now. Have you stopped to think for a second what might be right for that poor boy? Maybe he's been dying to see you. Maybe he's the motivation behind this meeting. Why don't you ask yourself what he might need instead of letting everyone else tell you what's going to happen to a boy you gave birth to? Are you really going to let them just whisk him away to a new life without even attempting to understand if you could be part of it? Do you know how many women in your position would love to have an opportunity to put things right?'

Lionel jumped off the sofa and ran between us. I pulled him to me. 'Lionel. Here darling.' I buried my face in his fur. I had no right to be angry. But I was. 'What do you know about how complicated it can be? It's all right for you with your perfect little family. One easy-going son with the same husband you've been married to for years. You've no idea what it's like to feel that every person you've ever loved is just a little bit happier without you. That it wouldn't matter how you behaved, you'd always be a crap mother. It's because I love him that I can't ever be part of his life.' I stood up. 'I can't stay here. This isn't going to work.'

Caro folded her arms, a sneer on her face. 'So you're going to run away again, are you?'

I put my hand up. 'You can think what you like. You can call it running away. I see it as stopping him harbouring any hopes of a relationship with a mother who'll never be able to deliver what he needs. I'm going to set him free to go and live his life with Clara and William without wondering about what he might have missed out on.'

My whole body felt as though all the emotions of the last few years had been rumbling away in a hidden seam and ignited on contact with the air.

I strode past her into my bedroom and grabbed my suitcase from the top of the wardrobe. A little part of my brain was going, 'Congratulations on your mature handling of conflict. You've lost your home and your job in one temper tantrum,' but I flung open my wardrobe and started throwing things into the case, far more noisily than necessary. I wanted to shout, 'Judge away. Go on. Fill your bloody boots.'

Lionel crept in and slunk onto the bed. Out of the corner of my eye, I could see Caro sitting in the armchair. My heart was thumping. Where the hell would I go now? I'd be lucky to find somewhere that took dogs in a hurry. I slammed the wardrobe doors shut.

She was glancing over at me. I just wanted her to leave. No one would ever understand how frightened I was of seeing Theo. Frightened of an eight-year-old. The thought that he'd shrink away from me, that he might – I found this hard to admit to myself – be scared of me, threatened to finish me off. I'd never been enough for anyone. I hadn't been dazzling or interesting enough to claim a solid place in Mum's affection. And my own son, the person with whom I should have shared an unbreakable bond, gravitated towards another woman. Had called someone else Mamma even though I saw him every day. However generous-spirited William and Clara were, it was impossible to see how they'd welcome me springing back into their lives when they were on the cusp of a clean slate in a new city, free from the last vestiges of any lingering memories of me.

Caro came and leaned in the doorway. Her voice was gentle. 'Don't leave without knowing where you are going.'

'I can't stay here. I'm so sick of being judged. The worst mother in the world. The woman who did something so unnatural. Men do it all the bloody time and no one even passes comment.' My temper had subsided to that level where it could peter out but an ill-judged word could also act like a blast from a pair of bellows.

'I do understand.'

I'm not sure that I actually said, 'Bullshit' out loud, but the word certainly buzzed on my lips. 'Don't patronise me. No mother I've ever met has understood. Which is why, unsurprisingly, I never admit to it.'

'I understand more than you think.'

I looked up. 'I can't work for you knowing that there'll always be this taint of disappointment hanging in the air, that you'll always think less of me because I abandoned my son. As you see it.'

She shuffled on the spot. Her mouth opened, then closed again.

I couldn't bear it any longer. 'Could you leave me now, please? I'll drop the keys in when I've finished.'

She shook her head. 'Why are you being so stubborn? Just listen to me for a second.'

And there it was, that little breeze that set the embers of my anger glowing again.

'Do you know what? I'm not listening to you or anyone. Why does everyone else always assume they know what would be right for me? Or my son for that matter? So let me finish packing up, and you can pretend you never knew me.'

The energy drained from her. Just briefly with her face in the repose of disappointment, she looked old and drawn. 'You're making a mistake, Vicky.'

Another one.

VICKY

July 2018

It was surprising how little I had to pack in the end. It was ironic that my fake 'wherever I lay my hat' persona had actually become who I was – a woman whose life consisted of two suitcases, a rucksack, a couple of carrier bags, a duvet and a dog bed. The thing that took the time was the cleaning. I wanted to flounce out and leave it, but for some reason, I couldn't bear Lou thinking badly of me along with everyone else. And it didn't seem fair that at sixty-five she had to bleach the toilet of someone half her age.

I was just piling my belongings in the hallway, resisting the childish desire to stand in my bedroom and say goodbye to the four walls, when there was a banging at the door.

Fergus. He was all out of breath.

'Vicky! You can't leave me!'

I'd hoped to sneak off without seeing him.

'I've got to. I can't stay when Caro is so angry about something that's nothing to do with work. She has a fundamental problem with my life choices and that's never going to go away.'

He wrinkled his nose. 'Can I bribe you to stay? You're brilliant with customers. I love how you tell them to bugger off so politely they enjoy the journey.'

I felt something in me soften. 'I'm sorry to leave you in the lurch. I've loved working with you.'

Fergus sensed the weakening in me. 'You'll never find a better colleague! Or a more handsome one. Or a funnier one.' He threw his arms out expansively. 'Come on, Vick. You don't really want to leave us. Don't get sucked into what Mum says. She's not exactly mother of the year – only got a one-in-two hit rate herself.'

'What do you mean?'

He shrugged. 'She didn't tell you? I've got a sister she doesn't have any contact with. I don't see her either for that matter.'

'Really? Since when?'

Fergus said, 'About a year and a half. Don't know what happened really. India was always difficult, you know the sort that gets offended by a passing flea that's accidentally showed its arse? I think Mum let India's teenage daughter have a glass of champagne at New Year or some shock-horror thing and it all went downhill. They've never spoken again. No big loss, to be honest, though I miss my nieces and nephew.'

'Does she live locally?' I asked, as I adjusted what I knew about the three Campbells I'd met to fit a picture of a family of four.

'Yeah, she's a teacher in a secondary school over Honiton way. I bumped into her once in Exeter. She was more interested in explaining how she came to be carrying a Primark bag, which goes against her ethical principles, than in hearing how we all were.'

'Do you miss her?'

'Nah. There was a big age gap anyway so we never had the same social group and she married a bit of a pompous knob. They both think I sponge off Mum and Dad and couldn't get work anywhere else.' Fergus's nonchalance slipped for a moment. 'Of course, they might be right.'

'Don't be silly, the business is really picking up. You've done a great job fixing up Sunnywell cottage. And the kids love the chickens.'

'I'm not finished yet. I've got a plan to put in one of those above-ground pools for next summer. And on the grass field at the bottom, I think we could set up a mini pitch and putt.'

'That would be brilliant!' I forgot for a second that I wouldn't be there to see it.

'I'll really miss you, Vicky.' The tone of his voice stopped me responding. Fergus, who never sounded serious about anything. He looked away. 'Mum's only having a go at you because she knows she messed up with India. From what I understand, you've just got to sort out some legal stuff. Wouldn't it be worth one more conversation, even if it's really awkward? I mean, who you are now at thirty is probably pretty different from who you were at twenty-four?' He tried to joke. 'All that newfound maturity.'

'Don't you start, Fergus. I can't stroll in and have a view about a child I don't even know any more. I can't face them all.' But more than that, I couldn't risk wanting Theo, couldn't allow myself to jeopardise the stability of his life now.

'You know best. But there's no reason for you to up sticks and leave.' He smiled. 'You must have dealt with far trickier situations than my mother having a go at you.'

I sat down in the armchair, suddenly exhausted. 'I've packed everything now. And it's not about Caro. It's about not living up to other people's expectations. I'd just rather cut loose than have this dark cloud of disillusionment following me around.'

'Okay. Here's my suggestion. I do a fantastic barbecue outside on the terrace and bring some beer and instruct Mum to stay well away, while you make up your bed again and agree to stay for one more night while you sleep on it. See, Lionel doesn't want to leave.'

And Lionel, traitor that he was, was sitting with his head on Fergus's lap, looking at him as though he was a god.

That night, by the time I went to bed, I'd somehow agreed to go to Surrey with Fergus on Friday and do what I had to do.

CARO

July 2018

On Wednesday morning, still reeling from my argument with Vicky the day before, I put a cheque for fifty pounds into a birthday card for India. I'd bumped into her in the village once in the last six months and she hadn't quite ignored me, but it was fair to say she also hadn't employed much vocabulary beyond 'fine'. I couldn't form the words to unpick that, so I wrote what I always did: 'Have a lovely day, darling. Treat yourself to something nice. Love you.' I took Dalí with me to the Post Office in the village, wondering why I was bothering. But I couldn't bring myself to ignore her birthday. Although I didn't understand her, she was still my daughter and the mother of my grandchildren. And I still hoped her bolshie, rule-driven, critical self would come back to me one day.

The following day, I tried not to think about the expression on India's face as she opened my card. Gilbert was out again. I didn't know where he went. Always popping off into Exeter or giving another farmer a hand with a fence. We had enough to do here, especially now the cottages were at full capacity. He hadn't even bothered to drag in the bins from the bottom of the drive. Bloody man. And now he'd disappeared off on India's birthday. Tears of frustration prickled my eyes. He'd asked me if I was going to send a card earlier in the week. He knew it was today.

After forty-one years of marriage, I should have stopped hoping Gilbert would become a mind reader and stay at home in case

I wanted to explore why we never saw our daughter any more. I decided to take my mind off it by washing the kitchen floor. I might as well be miserable in a clean house.

I'd just sprinkled some Flash on the tiles when Vicky knocked on the door. At Fergus's instruction, I hadn't been near her or her cottage since Tuesday.

This morning was not an ideal time to have a discussion about estranged children, with my daughter blowing out her birthday candles without me.

'Vicky.'

'Caro, I'm sorry. I'm sorry for losing my temper. I think you did understand more than I realised.'

Contrarily, I didn't want to touch on my own failings right now.

'Fergus filled you in, I take it?'

She nodded. In typical Vicky fashion, she didn't expand, which immediately made me blurt out, 'It's her birthday today. She's thirty-nine. She's got three kids and I'm only allowed to send them a birthday card. Not see them. Heaven forfend that they are allowed to talk to me.'

Vicky didn't react. Just stood there in that neutral way of hers that meant you didn't know whether she was listening or planning how to escape. But it didn't seem to matter. I was like the drunk at the party who'd drifted onto their favourite rant and couldn't be steered away again.

'I've missed out on everything. All their plays, their sports days. I've missed out on being a part of their lives. Not just me, but Gilbert and Fergus as well. She cut off ties with all of us. And I couldn't even tell you why we've fallen out. It was something and nothing, letting the oldest one have a drink, the youngest one fall asleep in the den instead of putting her to bed.'

Vicky had that look people adopted when confronted with emotions that are so raw, they can't get away with the catch-all platitude of 'It'll be fine, you'll see.'

With difficulty, I reined in my diatribe. 'Anyway, Fergus tells me you're staying, at least for a bit.'

Her voice was small. 'Is that all right?'

'Of course. What about Theo?'

She put her head up and looked me straight in the eye. 'I'm going to go and sort out the legal side of things, but only on the condition that I don't see Theo.'

Despite the rage coursing through me, I restricted myself to, 'Fergus said he'd drive you.'

'He did. It was very kind of him.'

I still had no idea whether she'd accepted. I was surprised Fergus had offered to be honest. For all his apparent openness, he wasn't one to plunge himself into the middle of tricky situations. Whenever I tried to bring up what was happening with India, he usually huffed out a bored breath and said, 'It's not like she adds much value, is it?' Personally I wasn't sure most people had kids so they could 'add value'. Child-rearing was supposed to be a bit more selfless than that, for mothers at least.

I wanted to end this pulling of teeth with Vicky, so I gestured to the Flash on the floor and said, 'I'd better get on.'

Just as she turned to leave, Lou came in, beaming.

'Didn't know it was your India's birthday today? Penny said she just saw Gilbert having lunch with them in Exmouth. Apparently the whole restaurant joined in with the singing. I was pleased to hear that.'

That was the closest she'd ever got to commenting on any gossip she'd heard about the rift between us all. I stared at her, my brain refusing to digest the magnitude of that piece of information. Her smile faltered. I couldn't admit even to Lou that I didn't know Gilbert was seeing India. I took a breath. 'Yes, I would have gone too, but I felt a bit off this morning and I didn't want to risk passing a bug around.'

I managed a weak smile, the force of betrayal sinking me down onto a stool. How long had Gilbert been meeting her behind my back? All the while listening to my heart breaking, the endless churning over of history, the what ifs, the should haves? I thought he was on my side. That we were a team of two, wronged and wounded but leaning on each other in the crossfire.

Lou nodded, warily, not looking convinced. 'Shall I start upstairs today?' she said, ferreting under the sink for bleach. That discretion was the reason she was the most popular cleaner in the village.

Vicky caught my eye. There was no judgement there. Just compassion.

Like her, I'd just discovered I was in this on my own.

VICKY

July 2018

The house looked smaller, more dilapidated than I remembered. The paint was flaking on the automatic gates and some of the bushes lining the drive needed a serious pruning. As the gates swung shut behind us, I wanted to run, slip between their closing jaws and fly down the road. But it was too late. Barbara was at the door, with another woman, young with blonde hair. There was no sign of Theo or William. I pretended to myself I was having a difficult meeting with a couple of unhappy customers who were expecting a much more luxurious holiday home at Applewood.

Fergus said, 'Shall I come with you?'

'Would you?' I couldn't get away from the feeling that I'd regress to that twenty-three-year-old again, explaining to a doctor how Theo had broken his leg and doubting myself as Barbara barrelled in with her own version of events.

As I walked up to the door, I had to stifle my natural response to hurry, to appease her, to alleviate the impatience I could read in every angle of her body. I wasn't late.

'Hello, Barbara.'

I'd been braced for a hug, but she ignored my greeting. 'Who's that?'

I only got as far as, 'This is my boss, Fergus, he was kind enough to drive me' when he stepped forward to introduce himself, all smiles and 'Pleased to meet you. Would you mind if I come in,

just to take a few notes about what's being discussed so we don't
miss anything?'

The woman next to Barbara nodded. 'Of course, come in,' she
said in slightly accented English. 'I'm Clara, William's wife.'

I waited for William to appear as we followed her into the
sitting room, which looked exactly the same with its floral curtains
and peach-coloured walls. A memory of Theo furniture surfing,
staggering on unsteady legs from armchair to sofa and back rose
up, unbidden.

We took a seat, with Fergus making heroic efforts to recall the
names of places he'd visited in Surrey. I felt as though I was looking at
one of those old-fashioned slide projectors clicking through moments
of my life – Theo picking dandelions, Theo on Derek's knee, eating
a boiled egg sitting on the stool in the kitchen – which brought the
bittersweet recognition that I could remember but had chosen not to.

I sat rigid in my chair, wondering where William was, where
Theo was, a little fillip of fear every time I heard a noise in case it was
my son making his way down the stairs to pass vicious judgement
on his feckless mother.

Vases of lilies adorned every surface, but instead of bringing
cheer, the effect was stifling. I scanned the table, then the armchairs
to see if there were papers at the ready, speeding my escape.

Without waiting for us to have a cup of tea to be fascinated
by if the conversation grew uncomfortable, Barbara launched in.
'William was killed on a motorbike a month ago.'

I gasped. The image of him in his shorts, his curly hair swinging
as he turned and looked over his shoulder that night in Corfu,
surged into my mind. 'Call me.' Followed by a slideshow of William
cradling Theo as a newborn, talking to him about whether he'd be
a prop or a fly half on the rugby field and me shaking my head and
warning him about cauliflower ears. William rushing out of our
bedroom with wet hair to catch his train. That amazing energy he
carried with him, turning heads in the doctor's surgery, the dentist,

the Co-op, attracting attention without seeking it. And all those memories against the backdrop of shame at our angry exchanges of texts in the months after I'd left. The final childish one sent after I'd seen William kiss Clara outside Theo's school, a rant about his own hypocrisy. I'd deleted his response without reading it.

I sat, my hand over my mouth as I understood why it had been Barbara who got in touch. 'I'm so sorry. I don't know what to say. What a terrible thing to happen to you.' I turned. 'You too, Clara.' I brushed at the tears that were coursing down my face. 'Sorry. Sorry. I don't know why I'm crying when it's your husband.'

Clara said, 'Don't apologise. We've had a bit of time to get used to it.' She pressed her lips together. 'Not that I ever will.' She got to her feet. 'I'll make some tea.'

'Thank you.'

I watched her go into the kitchen, elegant and dignified, even when faced with comforting the woman with whom the only thing she had in common was that they'd both slept with the same man who was now dead.

I glanced at Fergus, who looked stunned, as though this far exceeded the drama he'd geared himself up for today. I dragged my attention back to Barbara. She was ramrod straight as though relaxing any muscle might lead to total collapse. So many questions were crowding into my mind, I couldn't seem to pick one to get started. Barbara put her hands on the arms of her chair as though to steady herself. 'Anyway, in light of William's death, we need to discuss the next steps for Theo.'

I interrupted. 'I understood he was moving to Denmark. I assume Clara's Danish? And you needed me to give permission allowing that to happen?'

Barbara gazed down at her hands and twisted her wedding ring. 'Clara and William had been trying for a family over the last year. Just before he died, William discovered he was completely infertile.' She paused. 'Since birth.'

'But he couldn't be,' I said.

I didn't think I'd ever seen such disdain on anyone's face, as though I was the most stupid person Barbara had ever had the misfortune to encounter.

'Theo isn't William's. We did a paternity test to make sure,' she said.

Heat flooded my face. Freddie. I'd dismissed the idea that he could be Theo's dad so easily. I didn't know then that it was possible to bleed in early pregnancy. Looking back, I didn't know much at all. I'd have to untangle the guilt about robbing Freddie of an opportunity to be a dad to Theo when Barbara's eyes weren't boring into my skull. He'd have loved being a father. He had a natural ease with children, an affinity that made all the kids who came to the bar compete for his attention, beg him to show them one of his coin tricks that they'd then spend all evening practising.

Barbara tapped her fingers on the arm of the chair. 'William wanted to keep Theo anyway. He loved him. Clara did too.' She sniffed. 'Against my wishes.'

Fergus did a sharp intake of breath. I took comfort that, in a family not short of an emotion or two, this still registered on the absolute outrage scale.

Five and a half years had not dulled my anger, just stored it for a later date. I swallowed. Again and again as though I couldn't get enough moisture into my mouth. Fergus was nodding gently, encouraging me to take my time. I flailed around for something that wouldn't rehash Barbara all but excluding me from mothering my own child. If that was what had happened. I'd never been able to decide what was me making excuses for myself and what she had done to estrange me from Theo on purpose. In the end, I was weak. I'd let her push me out of the family. In my darkest moments, I'd even asked myself if it was what I'd wanted, someone to take over and someone to blame.

'So is he staying here with you then? Or still going to Denmark with Clara?' I asked.

'I'm not committing the rest of my life to a boy who's not blood. We've spent thousands of pounds on that school, you know, Bathfield House. It's cost us a fortune.'

'I didn't want him to go there in the first place. I would have been happy with the little school in the village.'

'Your horizons always were rather narrow.'

Fergus shifted in his chair. I gestured as if to say 'I've got this', whereas I wasn't at all sure I had. In fact, I had to sit on my hands to stop them trembling. It was a mystery to me how I'd spent the last few years living in pubs, dealing with rowdy men twice my size, refusing to let anyone intimidate the staff working for me, but one old lady could turn me back into that naïve twenty-two-year-old so desperate for her approval that I'd let her separate me from my own son.

Fergus's presence gave me courage. 'So what do you want from me, Barbara?'

'You'll have to take the boy.'

I shook my head. 'No. No. I can't do that. I've been gone too long. You were the one who encouraged Theo to call you Mamma, who undermined me at every possible opportunity. And now, when it suits you, you want to click your fingers and have me playing happy families. You practically forced me out!'

Barbara leaned forward, her hands spread on her knees. 'I did nothing of the sort. You were far too immature to be responsible for Theo. You let him fall off his changing table and break his leg.'

I stood up, pointing my finger at her. 'Take that back. Take that back now. You know that was an accident. It happened in a split second, which was not because I was negligent or stupid. It was just *one of those things*.'

She waved her hand as if to say, Have it your way. 'Nonetheless there must have been something wrong with you to walk out like that.'

Fergus tugged at my sleeve. I sat back down, my mouth slack, with air where retaliation needed to be. My cheeks burned with the humiliation of my shortcomings being discussed in all their glory in front of Fergus.

'It was complicated and you know that.' The words wheezed out of me like the last breath of a bagpipe. I'd thought about this over and over again, wondered if I'd been depressed or mentally ill or if I did just have a terrible character flaw that no other mothers shared, a lack of compassion or love that made it possible for me to leave.

Fergus cleared his throat. His voice was so reasonable, so measured. 'What did you want to achieve at this meeting, Barbara? Obviously Vicky can't just pick up a boy she's had no contact with for years and say, "Never mind about that, you're coming with me".'

'It's not what I want from this meeting. It's what's right. Vicky killed my son and now she needs to take responsibility for the outcome.'

I stared at her. 'What do you mean?'

My voice sounded as though it might fragment like a fine glass dropped on a flagstone at any moment.

'You killed him. If it wasn't for you, he'd still be alive.'

I dithered between storming out after giving her both barrels of every swear word I'd ever known and taking her seriously, the ramblings of a grieving mind that I might be able to soothe. I leaned towards Fergus, who had all the wide-eyed horror of a kid at an aquarium where a shark has turned on a tank mate.

Clara came in with a tea tray, clicking her tongue. 'Barbara, you can't blame Vicky for William's death. You had a row with him about wanting to bring up Theo even though he wasn't his biological son and he drove off in a temper on his motorbike. That was not Vicky's fault.'

'If she hadn't *tricked* him, if she hadn't made him believe he was Theo's father in the first place, we would never have been in this situation. Why should William have wasted his life on a boy who wasn't his son?'

The boy who Barbara had spent hours building blocks with, sorting shapes, pushing on the swing. The boy she was now talking about as the human equivalent of Lionel at his dog rescue centre, with prospective owners weighing up whether he could walk nicely on a lead and be relied on not to shit on the carpet. And whether his lineage was enough to find a forever home.

Clara closed her eyes. In her crisp Danish accent, her gentle words carried a power that no amount of shouting could ever hope to do. 'He didn't know eight years ago that Theo wasn't his son. As I understand it, nor did Vicky.'

Barbara let out a snort.

Clara carried on. 'William loved Theo. As far as he was concerned, he was his father.'

Pain etched into her face. She'd obviously adored William. She was a much better match for him than me. Posh, kind and able to handle Barbara. And brave. Despite not being able to have a child of her own, she hadn't jumped ship at the first hurdle. Unlike me. Now the memories were crowding in – Barbara darting a look at William every time I used a word she considered to be common or forgot to use the bloody jam spoon, pulling a face when Theo threw a tantrum as though no other two-year-old ever did that – it was incredible that I'd even had the courage – or the cowardice – to leave.

My breathing steadied. 'How long had you been married to William?'

'Just a year and a half. But we were in a hurry for children because I am thirty-five.' She rubbed impatiently at her eyes. 'We thought the problem was me because he already had a son, but the tests showed...' She tailed off. 'You know what the tests showed.'

I wanted to jump up, to explain about Freddie, anything that would make me seem less of a terrible person. Compared to abandoning my son though, I supposed the odd night of sex overlapping with a previous boyfriend would have been neither here nor there if it hadn't had such far-reaching consequences.

'You'd be a great mum for Theo. You've probably already bonded with him.' I wanted her to have Theo. She had all the patience and kindness to bring up a boy who'd lost the only dad he'd ever known.

Clara shook her head, waves of pain working across her face. 'I would be very happy to have Theo. He's a gorgeous boy and William and I loved him very much. But it didn't seem right to me to keep him when, perhaps, well, you, his own mother, might see things differently now and, possibly—' Her eyes welled up, but she drove herself on. 'He should be with you. We had planned to move back to Denmark to my family, that was true. But I don't think it would be good for his development, now, as things are, when he's still in shock for William, to take him to a new country.' A few tears spilt over her lashes. 'I didn't realise you didn't know he wasn't coming with me.' She glared at Barbara, who displayed a nonchalant innocence as though it was news to her as well.

I moved my head so I wouldn't be able to see Barbara out of the corner of my eye, then leaned forward, searching for the right words to make Clara understand my position. She was so much more competent than me. Everything about her made me feel sparse and insubstantial, as though I was being asked to make decisions when right there in front of me there was a vastly more capable woman available. 'Thank you but—'

She put her hand up. 'Theo needs to be with his own family.'

I floundered about, feeling myself herded down a route I couldn't go. 'What does Derek think about it all?'

Clara's eyes darted towards Barbara. 'He's in a home. He suffers from dementia.'

'I'm sorry.' I had that odd sensation of finding out huge things about people I once knew so well long after the event.

Barbara waved fingers at me, her teacup rattling in the saucer in her other hand. 'I should never have discouraged you from finding your own mother. She could be picking up the pieces. Or that silly friend of yours. She came looking for you. Got the address from one of William's friends out in Corfu.'

The conversation was moving along at such a pace that I had more questions than answers.

'Liv? Tall with blonde hair?'

'I can't remember what she looked like. She didn't think much of you having a baby and not telling her.'

It must have been Liv. I was touched she'd bothered to look for me. I doubted we'd have anything in common now. The girls we were skinny-dipping in the sea in Corfu, testing each other until the early hours of the morning at university, fortified by coffee and crisps, seemed like something out of a sepia photo. I'd never mustered up the nerve to tell her I was pregnant so soon after leaving university, especially when she'd landed such a good job. I knew how she'd react: 'Who saddles themselves with a baby at twenty-two?'

With a reluctant clarity, I realised I rarely made the decision to cut off contact with people, I just faded away whenever things became emotionally uncomfortable, thinking that 'one day' I'd somehow pick up where I left off.

Clara said, 'She was very worried about you. Said that your mobile number had gone out of use.'

I wanted to explain that for two years after I'd walked out, I obsessed about my phone. Took it to the loo with me. Kept it by my pillow at night. Waiting, longing, for someone to call, to help me find a way back when I was so lost. So desperately, unbearably lost that it was all I could do to work a shift at the pub where I lived before crawling back into bed, my head full of my own worthlessness, the muffled shouts floating up from the bar below, the laughter, the casual belonging that I could never imagine being part of again.

I'd lain, night after night, staring at the ceiling, wondering how all those mothers who breezed through not one baby, but several, managed. How they didn't fall into a pit of self-doubt and self-loathing, how they ended up with children who adored them. I hadn't even met the low bar of producing a son who didn't yell every time I went near him. In the end, the phone had dropped out of my back pocket when I was changing a barrel and smashed. It seemed like a good time to get a new number rather than live in the push-pull limbo of wanting/dreading that Mum or William would call.

'I changed phones.' It had been a relief of sorts. They couldn't ring and, finally, I could stop waiting, stop being disappointed that no one was looking for me. Stop hoping. I turned to Barbara. 'But what I can't understand is why you've turned against Theo now. You loved him, I know you did. Does it make such a difference that he isn't William's?'

A sneer crossed her face. 'It's not the fact that he isn't William's. It's that he is yours. Now William's not here to care what happens, there's no point in my being involved any further. All that work for nothing.'

'What work?' I could tell by the way she said it, she didn't mean childcare.

Clara slammed down her cup. 'Barbara! That's enough. It's water under the bridge.'

I leapt to my feet. 'Tell me what you're talking about.' My voice didn't sound like my own.

She laughed. 'You don't frighten me.'

I stared down at her, repressing the urge to slap the satisfaction off her face.

She gazed back at me. 'I taught Theo to scream every time you came near. It was our game. I told him I was his Mummy and to pretend you were a monster trying to take him away.'

Behind me, Fergus was muttering, 'What the hell...?'

'Why? Why would you do that?' My words were like a football kicked without enough power, dribbling to a halt just short of the net. I should have been shouting, roaring at her but disbelief had stripped me of anger. There was too much to process to funnel any of it into a reasonable response. There was nothing rational here, just the madness of a woman who couldn't give up control.

Barbara threw herself on the bonfire as though she had nothing left to lose. 'You were too stupid for our family. William was getting all those left-wing notions from you. Forest school? Not starting formal education until he was seven? I couldn't have that. William's grandfather went to Oxford. I certainly couldn't risk your parents popping up out of the woodwork and taking my grandson away from me. Sorry, your mother. I don't think there was a father on the scene, was there? History repeating itself! Did you even realise I'd blocked her number so she couldn't phone you?' She clapped her hands together, more animated than she'd been for the whole visit. 'No. I bet you just thought she'd given up on you.'

I remembered sitting in the car, baffled that I'd managed to block Mum. It had never occurred to me that Barbara would be capable of such cruelty. I was amazed she'd even had the technological know-how. Testament to the power of her determination. Or duplicity. While I was living with them, she'd probably played up the 'Just show me how to find the torch on my phone again' so if I confronted her, she could duck behind her 'old lady barely got the hang of a video recorder yet' façade to make me think I was losing the plot.

The heat of having trusted her, on a few rare occasions, with the intimate vulnerability of my relationship with my mother raged through me. In the early days, I'd longed to bond with Barbara, hoped she'd compensate for the lack of support I'd felt my whole life. I remembered watching her smiling right into Theo's eyes as she cuddled him. I'd said, 'Maybe one day I'll sort things out with my mum. It would be weird for him not to know my side of the family at all.'

Barbara had waved dismissively. 'When the time is right. In the meantime, we're your family.' At the time, I'd felt flattered, but actually I'd just dropped right into her trap. I cursed myself for being so gullible, for letting her take my confidences and use them to isolate me from anyone who might stand up to her.

Now she looked almost bored, as though telling the truth was just something she had to get over and done with in order for me to agree with what she wanted. I couldn't find any words to relieve the pressure building inside my chest, where my own stupidity swelled like a lump of proving dough, nurtured with shame and leavened with regret.

Fergus was on his feet at my side. 'Vicky, let's just grab some fresh air.'

I couldn't make out the look on Clara's face. She seemed as though she had something she wanted to say, but I didn't want to hear it, didn't want to have anything else to torture myself with.

Fergus led me out of the front door. An image of Theo refusing to put on his wellies and Barbara behind him with her arms folded, satisfaction all over her face, popped into my head.

Fergus put his hands in his pockets. 'You all right? That's some crazy shit in there.'

I bent over, my elbows on my knees. I didn't want to see the pity or puzzlement on his face that I'd let another woman drive a wedge so successfully between me and my son. I wasn't the only woman in the world to live with her in-laws and to find them difficult. But I couldn't bring a single mother to mind who'd rolled over and said, 'This is too difficult. I'm off. You have him.' Not in fiction. Not in film. Not in life.

Fergus put his hand on my back.

I stood up. 'Sorry, this has turned out to be a bit of shocker. Bet you wish you'd made me get the train.'

'What I actually wish is that my mother was here. She'd give the old witch a good run for her money.' He pulled a face. 'It would take the heat off Dad as well.'

'What shall I do?'

'I think there's only one thing you can do.'

'I can't take Theo, if that's what you mean. He'd probably scream the house down if I said he has to come with me. Can you imagine the trauma of being bundled into a car with a stranger, who is actually the mother who walked out on you years ago? I think Clara should have him. She seems kind.'

Fergus sat on the wall, his toes flicking the osteospermum. I had to stop myself saying that Barbara would be furious if she saw him kicking the flower heads. The woman had just told me she'd deliberately turned my son against me and I was worried about a few petals. If I wasn't careful, some journalist would track me down as a case study for a feature on how some women should never be allowed to have children.

Fergus stared right at me, more serious than I'd ever seen him. 'Vicky, I'm sorry to say this, but my mum did have a point. You'd rather let your son who's had a really horrendous time – with the dad who's not his dad and now dead anyway, the grandmother who's some kind of psychopath – go and live in another country with a woman you've known for five minutes than actually take a good long look at yourself and step up to the plate.'

His words winded me. Even Fergus was disappointed in me. The man who wouldn't send back a cup of cold coffee in a café, who lived at home, still relied on Caro to cook and fill the fridge. But right there, in the injustice of his words, was a grain of truth that stopped me detonating the 'What the hell do you know about being responsible?' button.

'I can't give him what he needs. It's not that I don't want to put myself out— '

'I'm not going to let you do this. If you walk away now, you'll never forgive yourself. You'll be stuck with the "what if?" forever.'

Clara came out. 'Are you okay? I'm sorry. I know this is all a bit of a shock.'

I nodded. 'I don't know how you've put up with her. I'm not going back in to speak to her. Could you bring out the papers I need to sign? Then we'll head off.'

Clara frowned. 'Papers? There never were any papers.'

'Weren't there some documents about parental responsibility so that Theo can stay with you?' As the words left my mouth, I realised Barbara had played me completely. Just as she always had. But on this occasion, I couldn't go along with it, couldn't pretend it didn't matter. 'She didn't tell Liam what she was really planning, did she?' I asked. 'She knew I wouldn't have come,' I said, answering my own question.

Clara's face softened. 'I thought you knew why she'd called you here. I can't take him, Vicky. And Barbara won't keep him.'

I looked at Fergus, panicked. 'He can't come with us. I've no idea how to look after an eight-year-old boy. Or girl. Or child of any age.'

Clara took a step back. Her pale eyes swept over me. 'My father is dying and I have to go back to Copenhagen next week. Barbara says she will call social services if you don't have him.' She grasped my forearm. 'There is no alternative unless you want him to go into care? Barbara has been preparing him. He knows his mummy is coming to get him. She's been showing him the photos of you.' She swallowed. 'You and William, with him as a baby.' Her eyes filled. 'You've no idea how lucky you are, if only you could see it.'

I didn't feel lucky. I felt as though everything anyone had watched me do, then grimaced and said, 'Vicky, not like that!' was distilled into this moment, boiled into a concentrated collection of every time I'd failed, every occasion when I hadn't lived up to someone else's expectations.

Clara's fingers were digging into the tops of my arms. 'He's your son. You have to look after him.'

Fear was coursing through my body so strongly that my arms were shaking under her grasp. I squinted into the sitting room through the window and felt my heart stop. Barbara was on her feet, hugging a boy in a red T-shirt and jeans. I could only see the back of his head, his dark hair. Barbara pulled away. She raised her hand to him in a gesture of farewell. The expression on her face was lost behind the reflections on the windows. Clara released me from her grip and I swung round to look at Fergus, who wasn't looking quite as together as he had been a moment ago.

I peered back into the sitting room. It was empty. The front door opened. And he was there. My son. Standing on his own, a thin boy with huge dark eyes, his face a mixture of hope and fear, struggling for control as he tried not to cry.

'Are you my mum?' His voice was uncertain and vulnerable as though he'd squeezed his last remaining courage into those four words.

I was going to have to try to be.

July 2018

She's tougher, much tougher, than I remembered. Tough is good. She's going to need that to get through. I had to make her hate me to get her to agree. In the absence of a more positive emotion, her contempt for me and a desire to prove me wrong should carry her a long way. I deserve it. I nearly wavered when Theo hugged me. That little face full of confusion. It's incredible I had any heart left to break. Maybe one day he'll understand that making him leave was the only solution. I mustn't allow myself to think I might see him again, even though in that last moment of weakness, I promised I'd talk to him soon.

I guess that little lie in the face of everything else doesn't make much difference now.

CARO

July 2018

When Fergus rang from the car, I could barely take in the fact that they were bringing Theo back with them because his dad was dead. A big knot of emotion cluttered my chest, tears springing to my eyes as the implications for Vicky – and the boy himself – sank in.

For once, Fergus was practical – 'Honeysuckle Cottage is clean and empty for the next few weeks. I suggest they stay there until we work out a more permanent solution.'

There was so much I wanted to ask, but instead I confined myself to, 'Is everyone okay?' Fergus's non-committal grunt told me what I needed to know.

I changed the subject. 'Have you spoken to Dad?'

He sounded exasperated. 'No, Mum. We've been driving for most of the day. Have you?'

I didn't answer. Just as I had a hundred times before, I wished I could turn back time, erase that moment when a decision that I'd played no part in started off as a ripple that I'd hoped would fade away over time but ended up becoming a wave that might sweep us all away.

After we finished the call, I started making some chocolate brownies. When India was Theo's age, they were the magic button for solving problems. If only life were still that simple.

Gilbert came through. 'What are you baking?' he asked in that neutral tone, carefully honed in our marriage to signify a willingness to talk, but not so apologetic I could consider him a walkover.

'Brownies.' I filled him in on the situation with Vicky as far as I knew it.

Gilbert raised his eyebrows. 'So is the boy going to be staying here permanently? Will he go to school in the village?'

I measured out the flour. 'I don't know. I suppose he could be at school with Rowan? He's about the same age.'

Gilbert nodded. He sank down onto one of the kitchen arm-chairs. Dalí immediately hopped up onto his knee, leaving Gilbert perched at an awkward angle. 'Caro, I'm sorry I didn't tell you about meeting up with India. In the beginning, I thought it might not lead to anything and I didn't want you to be disappointed again. Then I thought if I built a bridge, she'd eventually come round to seeing us both.'

'But I'm guessing that hasn't happened?'

'Not yet.'

I stirred in the chocolate. 'How often do you see her?'

A betrayal scale formed in my mind. Once every six months. Once every two months. Once a month.

'It depends.'

'Roughly?'

Gilbert wandered around the kitchen, picking up things I needed for cooking and putting them away in places where they didn't belong.

'Gilbert. How often do you see India?'

'About once a fortnight. I've seen her a bit more lately because Holly's been off school with a bug.'

I didn't think I'd ever gasped in my life. I'd always associated that with women who expected men to hold an umbrella over them when it was raining. But I heard the air shoot into the back of my throat. I squished some flour against the side of the bowl. 'So that's where you've been. Not helping Sid with the fences or popping into Exeter for a special drill bit?'

Gilbert looked abashed. 'No. I would have told you but—'

'But what? You might have had to communicate with me? You would have had to face a difficult discussion? God forbid, you might have had to examine your feelings rather than saying, "There's no point in talking about this again." Maybe if we'd been a bit braver, put it all out on the table, I wouldn't be sitting like the bad guy in jail while you get to be part of their lives.'

'It's not like that.'

'It feels like that to me because I'm the one who is left out!'

I made myself stop shouting because I knew Gilbert would walk away.

'When did you start having contact with her again?' I banged the sieve against the mixing bowl.

'At first, just what you saw. When the kids were ill and she needed childcare. A bit more in the last six to eight months.'

'And there wasn't any point where you thought, "I should probably mention this to Caro?"'

'I wanted to make sure that I'd established a firm footing before we tried to push it any further.' Gilbert put the kettle on, irritating me even more by filling it right to the top.

'By "push it any further" you mean asking my own daughter to see me? I bet you've had a bloody wonderful time discussing my shortcomings. Honestly, motherhood is so fulfilling – look at me – doing the nappies, the nits and all the other crap that goes with young children, listening to recorder practice, making sure they knew their times tables. And you, what did you do? You were away for work a lot of the time and when you were here, you were off on the farm, more interested in creosoting fences than helping out with homework or having a kick around with Fergus. But who gets the grief when it doesn't go to plan? Not you. Me.'

I stopped, not because I'd run out of examples of how unfair all of this was, but because tears were clogging my throat.

Gilbert sighed. 'I can't help how India feels. Maybe she finds me easier to deal with because we're very different. You both have a tendency to get entrenched in positions.'

I put down the whisk, toying fleetingly with tipping the whole lot over his head. 'Oh, to see ourselves as other people see us, Mr Flexibility of Thought! You go into a decline if I tell you that dinner is going to be half an hour late.'

I poured the mixture into a baking tray. I wanted to know if he saw the grandchildren, how they were, whether they remembered me, even queried why Gilbert went to see them but not me.

I wondered if what had happened at my mother's wake had already come to light. Whether that was at the root of it all. I couldn't figure out how to investigate without chucking more petrol on the bonfire and watching the inferno rise.

Gilbert crossed the room to stand near me. The sort of standing near that would bring me comfort on another occasion but made me want to lash out today. 'Don't.'

I snatched up the baking tray and put it into the Aga.

'I didn't mean to hurt you.'

And in that moment, I should have accepted that people who love each other can screw up on an Olympic level and only a forgiving heart can bring everyone back from the brink. A vengeful one can push everyone over it. Soundlessly, like a kiss in the night.

I turned. 'But you did hurt me. I think you've probably broken my bloody heart.' And as the words left my mouth, 'hypocrite' echoed in my head.

The door banged. Minutes later, the sound of the lawnmower filled the summer air.

After a couple of hours, I heard the crunch of tyres on gravel. I ran to the window and saw Fergus helping a young lad out of the back of the car. He had the same air as one of the little deer that sometimes darted out in the lane, as though he couldn't judge which way to run for safety. Vicky didn't look much better. I put Dalí on a lead.

'Hello, hello, come on in, welcome. You must be Theo. I'm Caro and I was so excited about you coming to stay here.' I added, 'For a bit.'

He nodded but didn't speak.

'You've had a long journey. Do you fancy a chocolate brownie? I've just made some.'

'Would you like that, Theo?' Vicky asked.

He shook his head.

'Come on, everyone loves a chocolate brownie. Shall we go in with Caro?' Her words sounded strained, desperate.

He didn't respond. Just stood looking at us as though he might burst into tears at any minute.

I knelt down. 'I tell you what, Theo, I've got to go and collect the eggs from the hens, and Dalí here doesn't like to be left on his own. Could you hold him while I gather the eggs? The hens are just round the corner. Then, perhaps after that, your mum—' I stumbled on the word in case he was calling her Vicky, 'can show you where you'll be sleeping.'

I smiled up at Vicky as he put out his hand for Dalí's lead. She appeared on the verge of tears herself. 'That's a great idea, Caro. I'll take Theo's case inside and come and find you in a minute.'

I walked around to the back of the house, saying to Theo, 'Dalí really likes you. He doesn't walk nicely on the lead with many people. You must be really good with dogs.'

In a little voice, Theo said, 'I love dogs.'

'Your mum's got a lovely old dog. Do you know what an Irish Wolfhound is?'

He nodded and started talking about what made a good dog, and how his dad had promised him a puppy. 'We were thinking of getting a rescue dog, but then Clara wanted to go back to Denmark, so Dad said we had to wait.'

And then as though he'd only just remembered that his dad was dead, his little face crumpled and he started crying. I stood there with my arms around him until the shaking stopped.

I was working out what to say to comfort him when Lionel came tearing round the corner, paused to sniff Dalí's backside, then stuffed his nose in between us, nuzzling at Theo for a stroke. Vicky came haring round whistling for him.

Her face softened when she saw the three of us. I mouthed, 'He's a bit upset, but he'll be okay' over Theo's head.

She whispered, 'Thank you'. This woman who stood up to some of our trickiest customers, who got workmen running an extra mile, sometimes with charm and sometimes with a hint of steel, looked terrified at the thought of caring for her own son. Whereas to me, it felt like the most natural thing in the world. And for the first time in a long time, I felt the distant flutter of hope.

VICKY

July 2018

I tried to learn from Caro. She had the knack of speaking to Theo when he wanted to talk and being quiet when he didn't. I, on the other hand, burbled on whenever there was a silence until he would say something really formal like 'Could I go to my room now, please?'

Yet again, I'd reply, 'This is your home, you don't have to ask.'

I took him into Exeter to buy some things so he could put his stamp on his room, but I'd relied on him telling me what he would need. 'Posters? Cushions? A new duvet cover?' He shrugged. It was optimistic on my part to think a picture of Harry Kane could make a difference to a young boy who'd just lost the dad-who-wasn't-his-dad, plucked away from everything he knew. We went into John Lewis and wandered aimlessly around the homeware department. 'Shall we buy a photo frame so you can put up some pictures of your dad?'

'Granny said Dad wasn't really my dad. That's why I had to come to you.'

He said it as a bald statement of fact. I attempted not to hear it as a reproach. Or to imagine how those words must have ripped through everything Theo took for granted, a hurtful hurricane of truth bulldozing life as he knew it.

'That's not really accurate. Your dad – William – absolutely adored you. He might not have been your biological father, the one who… well, anyway, he *was* your dad. He loved you.' I paused, wondering how much an eight-year-old knew about the facts of life. My own sex education had involved the teacher putting a test tube inside a gas jar to show us what intercourse looked like. I hoped things had moved on a bit since then, but I didn't know what words to use to explain that there was a bit of an overlap and even I hadn't realised William wasn't his dad. So instead I fluffed the opportunity to have that difficult conversation in favour of going to get an ice cream.

Caro never seemed like she was thrashing about to find things to say or worrying about what Theo thought of her. I, on the other hand, now existed in a state of self-consciousness, even feeling obliged to clean out the whole fridge in case the cheese crumbs and yoghurt smears were the deal-breaker for competent motherhood.

It was a relief to get home and ask Theo if he wanted to watch telly while I caught up on some work. When I saw him lying on the floor with Lionel, murmuring into his ear, I wondered whether I'd ever be anything more than a reluctant carer with a polite but distant charge. He glanced up and I was embarrassed at being caught watching him.

'Will Granny Barbara come and visit me?'

I shuddered inside. There was no way she was coming into my space, sprinkling her venom in my safe haven. 'I'll take you up to see her one weekend if you like?'

Theo ignored my question. 'Will I be able to go and stay with her for a bit?'

'Once you've got really settled here, I'll see if you could go for a little holiday.' I was too much of a coward to confront him with the truth.

He turned his face away.

'Are you okay, Theo?'

He nodded without making eye contact.

'It's hard getting used to being somewhere new, where everything is different, especially the people, isn't it?' My voice sounded sickly-sweet even to my ears. I longed to cuddle him and tell him everything would be okay. But I wasn't sure it would be. And I didn't know what I'd do if he screamed.

He didn't respond, just snuggled into Lionel, who stretched and flopped onto his back as though his world was complete. A human giving him full attention and a cuddle. Thank God for Lionel because I had no idea how to reach my son.

CARO

Summer 2018

As the weeks passed, Theo gradually became more confident around all of us and Applewood Farm seemed to absorb his presence as though there'd always been an eight-year-old boy in and out of my biscuit tin and running around on the lawn with Dalí and Lionel. Fergus carried him off to play football with his group of mates who adopted him as their mascot.

Gilbert, who initially had been sceptical about how Vicky would continue to work as hard as she needed to over the summer with a young son to look after, was the most enchanted of all of us. I nearly keeled over in fright when I saw Theo on the ride-on mower, chugging past the kitchen window, until I realised Gilbert was puffing along behind him, shouting instructions.

My heart ached for how we were missing out on India's children growing up. So many family memories weren't about birthdays or Christmas or big days. They were about silly little things that once you'd been shown, you never forgot. I thought about my mother every time I made her Yorkshire puddings: 'Get the fat really hot, Caro.' My dad was there in my memories every time I filled up my windscreen washer bottle: 'Have you checked your water?'

I wanted the grandchildren to be telling their children in thirty years' time, 'My Granny Caro showed me how to make brownies.' Instead, they'd say, 'I didn't really know her. Granddad Gilbert used to come and see us though, but we never went to their house.' And they wouldn't know that my heart broke over that. Maybe they'd just think I didn't care.

Vicky was grateful for everything we'd done to accommodate Theo – moving her to one of the older cottages that needed a bit of renovation but had a bit more room, talking to my friend at the council so that Theo could get a place at school to start in September – but she still had the air of someone asked to find a holiday cottage for twenty at a day's notice. If I made a discreet enquiry about how Theo was settling in, she'd say something like, 'It's early days' or 'It's hard to tell.' I never saw her hug him, though I found him to be quite the little cuddler, sidling into the sitting room when I was reading the paper and slowly shuffling up the sofa until he was leaning on me. When I turned over the page, I casually put my arm round him and felt him melt into me, that glorious sensation of offering up a shelter to someone who was desperate to take it.

There was something about him that reminded me of Rowan. And just thinking about that little boy with his mischievous eyes, the boy I would have read to and baked with and showed how to paint properly when he was older, tapped into something raw and bitter inside me. India's three children would never have a relation-ship with me, even though she seemed to call Gilbert round for emergency childcare more and more.

When I pressed Gilbert for any clues that India might consider a ceasefire, he sighed. 'I don't know. You are a force to be reckoned with and she's very headstrong.'

I worked to keep my voice neutral. 'What does Andy think? I mean, they're quick enough to run to you when they need help. Is it India who's really adamant?' I tried to sound casual. 'Or is Andy stirring the pot?'

Gilbert frowned. 'Good question. He keeps out of it really. I used to think he was a good influence on her, a bit more outgoing and fun, but he seems to be quite prickly these days. Maybe it's the responsibility of having his own kids. Though India is probably quite difficult to live with. I think he thought he'd be a bigwig at Westminster by now, not stuck in a small-town school juggling the A level politics expectations of middle-class parents.'

But we didn't get any further into the conversation because Theo waved outside the French windows. Despite Gilbert telling me not to get too involved, the sight of him always cheered me. I opened the door.

'Can I take Dalí for a walk with Lionel?'

'You can, but I was about to go into the village to buy a new dog bed. I wondered if you wanted to come with me?'

His face lit up. There was something so flattering about a child wanting to spend time with you because it was real. Theo hadn't yet learnt to put his mask on for the outside world.

'There might be ice cream in it for you…'

'I'll go and ask.'

I hadn't yet heard him call Vicky 'Mum'. She hadn't insisted on it: 'I feel such a fraud. I can't waltz back in and have opinions about what title he gives me.'

'But maybe it stops him feeling confident that you're a permanent fixture because you haven't told him that's what he should say.'

'Let's just add it to all the other things I'm not getting right.' And then she'd walked out, leaving me wondering whether to go after her and apologise. It was amazing how clearly I could see the flaws in other people's mothering but would need surgical intervention to patch up the gaping wounds in my own.

Theo came into town with me. We laughed in the pet shop as he adopted Dalí's various poses on the dog beds. 'He likes to lie with one foot stretched out like this, so this one is too short. Maybe this one, because when he's curled up, it's still big enough for all of him to fit on.'

We were just choosing some food for the bird feeders when the bell jingled above the shop door. Over the years, I'd stopped expecting to bump into India as she disdained the village – 'They're all so bloody parochial' – and always went into Exeter. Yet there she was.

Sam, the shopkeeper, was obviously abreast of the gossip and hurried off into the back, muttering about 'checking on the stock of dog chews'.

'Hello India.' She was thinner than I remembered, and wearing glasses, which was new.

'Hello.'

Theo stopped chattering about the different bird feeders and how he'd seen the squirrels hanging off them and how Gilbert needed to coat the poles with oil. I'd never mentioned India to Theo, but he seemed to pick up the awkward vibe immediately and shrank behind me.

I winked at him to reassure him. 'Theo, this is my daughter, India. India, this is Theo. His mother, Vicky, works with Fergus at the cottages.'

Theo whispered a hello. India gave a nod in his direction.

I took a step towards her. 'How are you, love? How are the children?'

'They're fine.'

Her breathing was coming in short, sharp bursts as though she was engaged in a battle she was terrified of losing.

I smiled, pretending to take her comment at face value rather than the implied 'What do you care anyway?' 'That's good to hear. Give them all my love.' I moved back again. 'It would be great to see you anytime you want to pop in.' I bent down to pick up the dog bed so I could avoid the look on her face. I hoped she'd be finding the cat litter interesting by the time I straightened up again. But she was standing with her hand on her hip, looking over her glasses.

'Ivy's as tall as me now.'

The unexpected nugget of information, containing as it did, the passing of time and, with it, everything I'd missed, made tears threaten.

I struggled for a response, unable to find the words I needed.

I had to get away. I leaned over the counter, shouting through to the back, 'Sam! Can I pay?'

He came scuttling out, fumbling at the till in his efforts to hurry things along. He didn't look at either of us, instead directing his attention towards Theo while he processed my card. 'How are you enjoying living in Okeridge then, young man?'

I don't know whether it was a reaction to the uncomfortable dynamic in the shop or whether he'd become the master at putting a brave face on things, but Theo rushed out with, 'It's really cool.'

Sam laughed. 'That should make headline news that Okeridge is cool. What's the best bit?'

'I like having a dog. I want to be a farmer one day like Gilbert. He's teaching me to drive the tractor.'

'Is he now? Aren't you lucky?'

India slammed a tin down on the shelf. I snatched up my credit card and, in a whirl of goodbyes, hustled Theo out of the shop, my heart thudding, my body a confused whirl of emotions it didn't know whether to embrace or suppress. It took all my grown-up rationale not to steam back in and blowtorch India with my guilt about knowing a hundred times more about the life of this boy when I knew nothing about my grandchildren.

Theo turned to look up at me. 'Was that really your daughter?'

'Yes, darling.'

'Does she like you?'

And there it was, a simple, astute question with a painfully simple answer.

'No, Theo. I don't think she does.'

CARO

August 2018

A fortnight after I'd bumped into India, Gilbert told me that she and Andy were coming to visit. He carried the message like a wise man cupping a gift of myrrh, reverential, with a sense of ceremony, big man coming through with big news. His delivery that they were going to 'pop up for a cup of tea, nothing dramatic, just a quick visit' implied that I should be bowing to his peace envoy skills, falling on the floor with gratitude. I tried to smother my resentment with the awareness that if it weren't for Gilbert, I'd probably never see India again.

'How did you make that happen?'

'I just said that we'd all made mistakes and it would be nice to draw a line under it before we got much older. She said she didn't get to speak to you properly the other day.'

I allowed myself a quiet snort at that.

I didn't voice it out loud, but I was pretty sure India wanted to place her bets on timing a reconciliation before I kicked the bucket. The only ace I held in my hand would be to disinherit her. Which I actually had no intention of doing, but if it focused her mind on building bridges, I would take it.

Now that India was actually coming to visit, I was frightened to look forward to it. Gilbert kept saying, 'Just stay calm and don't look for problems. Keep it light.' Which infused a certain level of fury into me.

I'd baked India's favourites – Bakewell tart and peanut butter biscuits. I didn't know whether she was bringing the children. I told Gilbert to ask, but he said the more we texted her with questions, the more opportunity she had to change her mind.

I tried to look like the mother she wanted. I searched in my wardrobe for something that didn't suggest 'old hippy', which meant discounting most of my wardrobe. Nothing long, nothing flowing, no scarves. I settled for a pair of linen trousers and a fitted blouse, chasing away the thoughts of India in her mid-teens when she wouldn't let me go and watch her play hockey anymore, grudgingly relenting when I queried it. 'Only if you don't turn up looking like some mad artist.' If her friends ever asked me about my paintings, she'd shuffle me away as though I had some contagious disease. Ivy was a natural though. I tried not to think of the times we could have spent together in my studio.

I was just pencilling in my eyebrows and doing my lipstick, twenty minutes before the allotted arrival time when the doorbell went. I hoped Lou had finished hoovering. I'd asked her to do it at the last minute because Dalí moulted so badly; I was aiming to get through today without India tutting at a stray black hair that had managed to float onto her plate. I hurried to the stairs, pausing on the landing to take a deep breath and to allow my heart to settle back into a normal rhythm.

Tears sprang into my eyes when I saw her. Without anger to cloud my judgement, she looked like the teenager hovering on the edge of the party, not knowing whether to join in with the drinking games or call me for a lift home before it all got out of hand. I raced downstairs. 'Hello! It's so lovely to see you, come, come on in.'

'Sorry we're a bit early.'

I went to embrace her, but we ended up in a clumsy clash of arms and faces as she held back, offering me her cheek.

Andy gave me a brief hug, mumbling 'Nice to see you'.

We went through to the sitting room, which, thanks to Lou, sparkled, without a dog hair in sight.

'How are you? How are the children? Well, not really children anymore, Ivy's sixteen, isn't she?' My words were running away from me, eager, desperate. 'Dad said she did really well in her GCSEs. She'll be starting in the sixth form in September then?' I remembered too late that Gilbert had mentioned the great furore because she'd decided to enrol at college in Exeter rather than stay on at school.

India sagged as though I'd deliberately chosen to poke at something they were irritated about. 'Didn't Dad tell you?'

'Oh yes, I forgot, she's going to college. Anyway, she's a very capable girl, I'm sure she'll make the right decision.' My words fell into a silence. I jumped up. 'I'll just make some tea.'

'Have you got any peppermint?'

'Yes, I think so. I'll bring it through. Help yourself to cake or biscuits.'

I ran into the kitchen and ferreted about in the pantry, rejoicing in the dusty box of peppermint tea probably tucked there since the last Christmas India had been with us. I sniffed the teabag to check it wasn't stale.

Just as I put the kettle on the Aga to boil, Lou came through. 'Shall I make the tea and coffee before I head off?'

'That would be brilliant, thank you.'

Lou smiled, the discreet smile of someone who wouldn't dream of commenting on other people's business.

I walked back in. Gilbert and Andy were discussing a detective series they liked on TV. India was perched on the edge of the sofa. Very gently, I said, 'It's lovely to see you, darling. I've missed you.'

She turned towards me. 'Have you?'

I couldn't work out the tone. Disbelieving? Straightforward question?

'I really have. I miss the children too. How are they? Growing up lovely, I bet.'

Her face pinched. She ignored my question. 'I gather you spend a lot of time with that boy I met, the son of one of your employees.'

'Theo? Well, he's had a very difficult life, he—'

India cut me off. 'Dad told me.' She gestured towards Andy. 'It's really hard for Rowan to hear what you've been up to with him. Off to the beach, out fishing for the day with Dad. I heard you even went on the roller coaster at Crealy Park. You always said it made you sick.'

'It does make me sick, it was just that Dad had a bad back and Theo really wanted a go and he's not had an easy time because his dad died a few months ago...' My words petered out. The knot of tension in my stomach that had been there since the door opened was tightening, minute by minute. I understood how the pigs felt when they were herded onto the trucks for slaughter. I turned to face India. 'I'd absolutely love to take Rowan to Crealy. Any of them. All of them.'

'What would your new grandson think of that?'

A sigh escaped me. I raised my hands in surrender. 'India, if I was able to spend time with your children, I would love that more than anything.' I fumbled around for some words that wouldn't apportion blame and came up empty-handed. 'As I understand it, you're not keen for me to spend time with them at the moment, although I hope that will change in the future, so I'm just getting on with life. Taking pleasure where I find it. In my painting. I've got a new exhibition coming up as part of a Devon artist initiative. I go out for the day with my friends, with Dad, and sometimes with Theo.'

It was like being on *The Chase* losing against the clock with someone much smarter than you.

'Vicky's part of the family then, now? Is she good at her job?'

'We work closely together, yes, and she's come up with some great ideas for expanding our appeal to families. She has her own life with Theo, I mean, they're not in and out every five minutes. But obviously we can't avoid seeing them because we live in such close proximity.'

I clenched my jaw to stop it clanging open in total disbelief that India didn't like the idea that I might get close to someone else when she hadn't texted me in a year and a half.

I tried to catch Gilbert's eye in hope of rescue, but he was too busy telling Andy about our plans to refurbish the last three cottages on the farm and build an indoor swimming pool so we could become more of a year-round destination.

'How are you getting on teaching? Have you enjoyed the holidays?' I realised I had no idea about her life. Gilbert dropped a little trail of crumbs so I could just about keep her in my distant sights, but every conversation felt like such a two-way struggle of loyalty for him, I ended up frustrated and, more often than not, pissed off with the messenger.

India shook her head. 'Holidays? I've been into school just about every day to get things ready for next term. I'm teaching the A level sets for English this coming year and you wouldn't believe the amount of pressure we're under to make sure we get the top grades.'

'Do you enjoy it though?'

'Mum, it's not a question of enjoying. Andy and I have to work. We don't have anything to fall back on. Fergus gets a free house and a guaranteed job, but Andy and I have to keep producing A* students or we'll all be round with our begging bowl. It's hard enough to make ends meet as it is.'

Though I knew from the chap at the newsagent that the five of them had spent three weeks touring Thailand and Vietnam. When he'd casually asked me whether India was spending any time in Bangkok, I'd tried hard to disguise the fact that I didn't even know they were on holiday. I was too proud to let on that the daughter who lived eight miles away on the other side of the valley didn't tell me anything, which left me dissecting everything Gilbert passed on.

I always tried to fathom why she'd allowed us a particular nugget of knowledge. To hurt us? To get money out of us? To prove how well she was doing without us? Gilbert thought I was too suspicious. I hadn't yet said it out loud, but it was only a matter of time before the words 'Gullible Gilbert' left my mouth.

For the moment, I decided not to compete with what I knew and clung onto my attitude of appeasement, though I could feel the fabric fraying under my grasp. 'Fergus also never really gets a break though. In the end, the buck stops with him. He doesn't have the collective wisdom of colleagues to help him. Even when he's on holiday, Dad and I still ring him if there's a problem. That's really why we got Vicky in to manage the bookings.'

'He never has to worry about getting the sack though, does he?'

'No, but it still has to work as an ongoing concern. And, actually, family businesses are really hard because you never have the luxury of getting up and saying, "Sod this, I'm off." You just have to keep turning up for work, however bad it gets.' I stopped short of saying, 'It's all right for you. You could walk into another teaching job tomorrow.'

India leaned back into the sofa, positioning a couple of cushions behind her back.

I really wanted to say, 'Would it make you feel better if he was facing the sack every Friday night?' Followed by 'What would make you feel better in general? Would you be happy if we were all as endlessly disgruntled about life as you are? Is a condition of us having a relationship that you snipe at me and I swallow down everything I'd like to say in return?' Instead I said, 'I've baked your favourite cookies. I've never met anyone who loved peanut butter as much as you.'

India refused to take one: 'We've just had lunch.' I had to stop myself rushing off to pack them in Tupperware for her kids. I marvelled at how many mothers managed a relationship with their daughters without much thought or effort. I couldn't utter a sentence without inspecting my words for anything that could sound accusatory before I dared to let my thoughts make contact with the air.

Finally, Gilbert caught my frantic semaphoring. 'Where's that tea got to?'

'Lou said she'd do it. I'll go and check.'

I leaned on the kitchen worktop, revelling in a moment of not being judged.

Lou was wringing out a cloth at the sink. 'I'm so sorry. Dalí jumped up to get a biscuit off the tray when my back was turned and sent it all flying.'

Andy wandered in. 'Everything all right?'

'Yes, just coming.'

Lou finished filling the teapot and smoothed her hands on her trousers. 'Right. I'll be off then.'

I waved my hand in goodbye and rustled about in the pantry for some sugar. The back door banged. The words I'd wanted to say for so long sat in my chest. I stirred the teabags in the pot and without looking at Andy, said, 'Is there any way back for India and me?'

'You'd have to change your attitude to her, for sure.'

I spun round. 'What do you mean?'

Andy did that pseudo-intellectual frown, which stopped short of him adopting Rodin's 'The Thinker' chin-on-hand pose. 'I think it's fair to say that you're really hard on her and let Fergus get away with anything.'

I felt injustice crackle like the popping candy Fergus and India used to buy down at the newsagents on the way home from school. I remembered to breathe. Not to 'shoot from the hip', as Gilbert always said I did. I heard my voice grind out, rasping with hurt: 'I'm not sure that is fair actually.'

Andy did that thing of pulling himself up to his full height, amusement dappling his face. 'Oh, come on, Caro. Fergus is always getting a new car, while India runs around in that battered old

Polo. She's working her backside off while he skips out midweek to go surfing with his friends. I bet he gets more than twenty-five days holiday a year.'

I smiled with a warmth I didn't feel. 'Didn't you both have six or seven weeks off over the summer, plus several weeks at Easter and Christmas?'

'Yes, but we really need it. I don't think you have any idea how hard we work. It's not just the hours at school, it's everything we do outside that time, all the preparation. And I coach rugby every Saturday. I often don't get home until the evening.'

'I know how hard teachers work, but India had the opportunity to come into the family business and she chose not to.' I stopped. Right there. Before we descended into a slanging match. But Andy carried on.

'We've worked for every penny we've got, whereas Fergus just lives rent-free. And presumably he'll inherit the business?'

I tried to laugh it off. 'I'm not planning on dying yet. But anyway, we don't just hand over money to Fergus, he runs the business and gets paid for doing it. Which doesn't seem unreasonable to me. It's kind of how business works, isn't it?' I paused. 'Surely this whole thing with India isn't about money?'

Andy shrugged. 'Not specifically about money, though India does find it hard to see your employee's son milking the pot now too.'

'Milking the pot? Theo's not milking the pot. Far from it. He never asks for anything. Occasionally we take him out for the day and because Vicky does a great job for us, we don't make him pay.' I stopped short of yelling, 'As he is *only eight years old*, we don't insist he brings his own wallet. I'd be very happy to take your kids out. And I wouldn't expect them to pay either.' I tried for a wink, which proved beyond my reach as my eyeballs were bulging out of my head with rage. I picked up the tea tray. 'I'd love to have a conversation about money with India. Or anything. It breaks my heart that she doesn't want to speak to me. I don't know what I did wrong.'

Andy snorted. 'You don't know what you did wrong? How about never taking her seriously? Always making her feel that you liked Fergus more? Can't you see what you're like when Fergus is around? India could be telling the most exciting story in the world, but if he came in with a broken fingernail, you'd jump up and rush over to him. I've seen it myself. It's why we're so fixated on treating our three equally.'

'Well, aren't you the perfect ones? I have tried to treat them both the same, but they're very different personalities so one size doesn't fit all. And I don't know what you mean about not taking India seriously. We paid for a tutor to help her do the Oxbridge exams. Okay, it didn't go her way, but we encouraged her to try.' My voice was shaking. I couldn't believe I was digging back two decades listing what I had done to prove to my daughter's husband – not even my daughter – that I'd done a reasonable job.

'But you never really believed she could get in.'

'I didn't know whether she could. I hadn't even been to university. I had no idea about any of it. I just thought she should have a go, but it wasn't the end of the world if she didn't succeed.'

'It was to her.'

I stared at him. 'But it wasn't our fault they rejected her. She still went to Nottingham. That's a really good university.' I pressed my fingers into my eyes. 'Why are we even talking about this? It's twenty years ago.'

He rocked back on his heels. 'Someone needs to fight her corner.'

I shouldn't have let him goad me. I'd made a pact that I'd bury it, forget it ever happened, the result of a convergence of circumstances, unique in that particular moment. But that cold chill of injustice had morphed into a torrent of white-hot rage that knowing I should walk away wasn't going to divert.

'Fight her corner? We're not the enemy. And I'm sorry to bring this up, but I think you've had moments when you haven't covered yourself in glory.'

He tilted his head on one side. 'What do you mean?'

If ever four words had been invented to make the speaker ponder the wisdom and accuracy of what they were about to say, those were they. I walked over to the French windows, seeking to block out Andy's presence behind me, to ascertain once and for all that my memory of what happened was actually a memory and not a wish list of events I'd imposed on history to present me as a shinier, better person than I was in reality.

I stared at the bench outside. In my mind's eye, I could see me sitting there on the night of my mother's wake. It was so starry. I'd just had words with Gilbert because he'd decided to go to bed, said he was worn out. I'd wanted him to stay up, indulge me, let me cry, laugh, reminisce, go over my regret – again – at leaving the hospice instead of staying the night when she died.

I recalled him saying, 'It is what it is, Caro. She probably waited until you left. You'd been there every day for weeks. It doesn't matter that you weren't there when she actually died.'

'It does to me.' He'd got fed up with me repeating something that couldn't be helped, couldn't be changed, as though my regrets were logical, something I could take a step back from, nod and say, 'You're right. I shouldn't feel bad,' and tidy my messy grief into something that he could cope with. Something that didn't frighten him, unlike this fragile wife, a far cry from the one who usually dealt, sorted and got on with stuff.

I'd been shivering in the chilly air, almost to make myself more miserable, a kind of homage to how much she'd meant to me. Andy had come out to see if I was okay. He'd told me to come inside out of the cold, but I'd refused and said I wanted to be alone with my thoughts for a bit, that he shouldn't worry about me. That he should go and find India who'd been chasing around after four-year-old Ivy all day. He went away and I sat, wondering if Mum had been frightened on her own, weirdly obsessed with whether she'd known the second before she died that the next breath really would be her last.

Andy came back with brandy. 'Here. If you won't come in, this should warm you up a bit.' He took off his coat and draped it round my shoulders. I was grateful. And angry at Gilbert for leaving looking after me to someone else's husband.

We sat listening to the owls hooting. The security lights flashed on and off as rabbits ran across the lawn. The brandy scorched through me, as though it was gathering all the loose threads of emotion as it went. Every now and then, I'd come out with a random thought that seemed important to articulate but probably sounded like the ramblings of a miserable mind. 'While Mum was alive, I felt someone really understood me. And I don't think I've managed to do that for India. Fergus maybe. But not India. I did try. I wanted that connection that I had with my mum, but, I don't know, maybe she was too clever for me. I hoped we'd find some common ground when Ivy was born, but I think she finds me interfering.'

My eyes were aching as I'd turned to look at Andy, from the tears, from the brandy, from the red wine I'd had earlier.

He'd nodded. 'She's quite complicated, as you know. She doesn't like admitting she doesn't know how to do something. But she does love you. She might need more help when we have another baby. If she ever manages to get pregnant again.'

With a jolt, I'd realised that my assumption that she was too focused on her career to have a second child was wide of the mark. 'I didn't realise there was a problem.'

Andy took a long swig of his brandy. 'Not really a problem. Just not happening to India's timetable.'

'She's always been so capable. She never depended on me like Fergus. He needed so much more help through life. I tried to treat them both the same. It was probably easier for my own mum because there was just me. She made me feel as though I was amazing, even though I was ordinary.'

Andy had patted my hand. 'You are amazing. Don't do yourself down. I've always found you so interesting and creative.'

The lights in the kitchen went off behind us. India had called from the door, 'Andy? I'm going up now.'

He'd turned. 'I'm just finishing this drink with your mum. I'll be up in a few minutes.'

I jumped up and went to give her a hug. 'You don't mind me borrowing your husband for a minute? He's listening to me ramble on about grandma. Five minutes and we'll all be going to bed. Thank you for supporting me today.'

India, as always, couldn't accept a compliment the way it was intended. 'Well, what else would I have done? She was my grandma, as well as your mother.'

'Night, love.'

I'd sat back down and pulled Andy's coat around me. 'Aren't you cold? Don't let me keep you out here if you want to go up.'

'I'm made of strong stuff. I was born in the North.'

I'd laughed. 'That won't stop you catching pneumonia, will it?'

And then he'd said something like, 'I'd better sit close to you to keep the cold out' and shuffled up next to me.

I'd tried to pin down the exact sequence of events in my mind so many times, but it was like a piece of paper, blowing along the street, lifting and whirling just as you got within grabbing distance. I did recall a moment of his arm going round me and me relaxing, as though someone else was propping me up, absorbing a fragment of my sadness, sharing for an instant the burden of something I was going to carry forever. I'd felt comforted that he was taking time to let me voice the feelings everyone else backed away from. Grateful my prickly daughter had a kind husband who would look after her when she was upset.

I knew for definite that after we'd drained the last dregs of brandy, I'd said, 'I think it's time to call it a day' and handed him back his coat. I thought he was leaning in to put it on, but instead he pulled me towards him, planting his lips on mine and muttering something about always having a soft spot for me.

I'd leapt to my feet, shock piercing the alcoholic haze. 'No. No. Sorry. No. Sorry, oh God, Andy, no.' I couldn't gather my thoughts. I'd laughed in the sort of way you do when you're trying to pretend something is a joke before your brain wraps itself around the fact that what just happened has changed a relationship forever. 'Andy, it's bedtime. Thank you for listening to me burble on. Come on, you go in. I'll lock up.'

He'd picked up the brandy glasses. 'You're right, it's been a long day.'

I hoped we could just ignore it. Because if we couldn't, would I have to tell my daughter that her husband had tried to kiss me? She'd never believe that I hadn't led him on.

The next morning, it was my first thought. The fear of India finding out, the stomach-churning terror that she would blame me for what happened, overshadowed the rawness of losing my mother.

I'd spent breakfast fussing around India, chopping up melon, bringing out every possible variation of herbal tea until she got irritated. 'Peppermint is fine.' Every time that image of Andy lunging forward to kiss me wormed into my head, I feared I might shout it out, just to have done with the panic that was making my heart thump and lurch.

When Andy had carried their cases out to the car, I'd slipped out, 'I'm sorry about what happened last night. I blame the brandy.' As I said the words, I knew I shouldn't be the one apologising, but it just seemed more elegant to shoulder some of the responsibility, easier for Andy to save face.

He'd looked straight at me. 'Don't worry, Caro. I think it's better that we just forget about it. You'd had a bit of a day of it. I don't think it would be in anyone's interests for India to find out what you did. Or Gilbert, for that matter.'

I'd frowned. 'What I did?'

He'd pulled a face, laughed, disbelievingly. 'Trying it on with me?'

And before I could knit together a coherent response, India came out towards the car with Gilbert. 'Take care, Mum. We'll see you soon.'

And I'd stood waving, Gilbert behind me, fear rolling through me.

In the ensuing years, that lack of respect I'd given to the days following Mum's death swamped me with guilt, that the need to save my own skin took precedence over grieving for her. I tried to assuage the sickening self-loathing by clinging onto Mum's mantra that life was for the living.

Today, I'd reached a tipping point. I turned to face Andy, hands on my hips. Over the last twelve years, I'd allowed him to control not only my interaction with him, but also with India, always appeasing, accepting their abuse of our generosity, allowing them to take, take, take, without requiring any consideration in return. I'd surrendered my right to address problems in exchange for his silence about something that wasn't my fault. And where had it got me? India was perched stiffly on an armchair, the daughter I'd loved, who might as well live in Timbuktu rather than on the other side of the valley, barely able to say a civil word to me, primed to assume that everything I did was to belittle, hurt or undermine.

'Did you tell her? Did you tell her about that night?' I wasn't sure whether I would act on the threat that my questions contained.

'You throwing yourself at me, you mean?' He looked almost amused, as though he was humouring the confused recollections of an ageing relative.

My breath was coming in gasps. 'Could you repeat that?'

'You threw yourself at me. You know you did. The night of your mother's funeral. On the bench, out there.'

'You know that's not true. You kissed me when I was vulnerable and upset.'

While the words were coming out of my mouth, I knew I was wading to a far shore from which there'd be no return journey. 'Did you tell India what happened?' I was hissing, my voice unlike anything I'd ever heard before.

'Tell me what?'

We both swivelled round. My mind was racing, thinking of a get-out, some way of fudging the truth, distracting her.

But before I could, Andy dropped his arms to his sides, all theatrical and floppy. 'You shouldn't have to hear this, India. Really. It was all so long ago.'

Something in me surrendered. Just seeing her standing like a snake coiled ready to strike made me realise there was no exit for me. Somehow, our family dynamics had become so skewed that I was the cause of all that was amiss in India's life. It was incredible how love, poured freely and without question, could turn on itself, a lethal rip tide, churning truths and facts until they solidified into a bank of irrevocable perceptions, rising higher as the years passed, forming a barrier that could never be breached or broken down. Even with love from both sides, my relationship with India never seemed to fuse into a stable, straightforward base. After years of Andy drip-feeding her my shortcomings, pouring petrol onto the grievances she already had – my perceived favouritism for Fergus, my lack of generosity, my disinterest in her achievements – she wasn't going to believe me now.

'What? What shouldn't I have to hear?' There was accusation in her tone before she even knew what we had to say.

It was like perching on the window ledge of a burning building, twenty storeys up. Everything to lose, whichever option I chose.

Andy opened his mouth to speak, but I burst in.

'This is going to be very hard for you to hear, India, and you'll never understand it, but on the night of Gran's funeral, I had way too much brandy and kissed Andy. He didn't tell you at the time because you were already upset about not being able to get pregnant again and he wanted to protect you.'

Something splintered inside me as her lip curled. A flash of surprise passed over Andy's face.

India turned to him. 'My mother made a pass at you? My own mother tried to get off with you?'

He stood, frozen to the spot, his whole face wrinkled in disbelief.

Gilbert shouted through from the sitting room. 'My God, what's happening with this tea? Are you sending for it from China? Or is the party in the kitchen and no one's bothered to tell me?'

We ignored him while India flung her arms about, screwing up her face, saying, 'I can't believe what I'm hearing. I just can't take it in. This was, what, twelve years ago, and you're only just telling me now. How did this even happen?'

I tried to put myself somewhere else in my mind, to defend myself from the blows that were heading my way. I hadn't found the right way to love her, or to make her feel loved, but I could stop her marriage crashing down on the back of my failure. No good would come from putting the blame onto Andy. It might even make her hate me more.

Gilbert came through and took in the unhappy panorama. His shoulders slumped and inevitably, he looked accusingly at me. 'What's going on here?'

India – who knew the least about any of it – filled him in.

Gilbert shut his eyes as though his brain needed the darkness to process the magnitude of this fiasco. For a brief moment, I was tempted to argue my case, to tell him the truth – though I was coming to understand that, in families, there is never one single version.

He looked so devastated. I put out my hand to him, but he shook me off.

'Can we talk about this later?' he asked.

The sadness in his voice nearly undid me. I swallowed. I reminded myself that my relationship with India was done and dusted a long time ago. What mattered now was keeping her together with Andy, so my grandchildren could have a stable home life. And convincing my sweet husband that it wasn't what it looked like.

India was crying, screaming insults at me. Andy was trying to calm her down, his face bewildered as though he couldn't believe he'd got off scot-free. Just as India stormed through to the sitting room to fetch her coat, there was a timid knock at the kitchen door. *Please God, don't let this be Theo.*

But it was Lou. 'I'm so sorry to interrupt, I left my handbag on the chair.' She cast her eyes down, obviously party to far more of the conversation than any of us would have liked.

'I'll get it for you, Lou, just a second.'

She wouldn't look at me. Another person in my world who would never view me in the same way again. I marvelled at the fact that my voice sounded so normal when inside everything felt not just broken, but shattered.

I handed her the bag. 'Thank you.'

She bit her lip and turned to go, but before she did, India came hurling back through, in such a state that I didn't think she'd even registered Lou's presence. 'Let's go. Mum, I hope you're proud of yourself. I hope you got the ego boost you wanted from kissing someone twenty years younger who was married to your own daughter. On the night of your mother's funeral!' As though an ordinary Sunday night, Monday morning or Wednesday afternoon would have been better.

I didn't respond. Just stood there with conflicting emotions thundering through me – relief that we could all stop pretending that we could ever get on, devastation that I'd hurt Gilbert and the agonising recognition that I'd lost my daughter for good. That was it. On this sunny day in August, our square-shaped family with one of us at all four corners had become a triangle. It remained to be seen who would remain forever outside the shape.

I stepped towards Lou. 'Sorry, Lou. You've picked a bit of bad time. I'll see you next week.'

She nodded and made to walk out, then stopped. I wanted to push her out of the door. This was not the moment to remind me to get some bloody limescale remover or flaming woodworm treatment. She turned very deliberately towards India.

'India, you should know, it was not your mother who tried to kiss Andy but rather the other way round. She pushed him off.'

Complete bemusement that Lou knew anything about it balanced the rush of joy that someone in the room was fighting my corner. But it was much easier if we all just believed it was my fault. I needed to let Andy and India salvage themselves.

I shook my head. 'I don't think you're right there, Lou.'

In that quiet stubborn way of hers, she said, 'I was tidying up the glasses in the kitchen, remember? Right by the door I was, picking up a sausage roll before Dalí got to it. I heard you talking to him, one minute all normal and then the next you were jumping up, shouting and telling him no, that it was all wrong and that he should go to bed.'

It wasn't going to change anything, India was already shaking her head and saying, 'Did she pay you to say that?'

She heard what she wanted to hear. I couldn't change that.

I wondered if I could stop waiting for her to listen.

VICKY

September 2018

I didn't want to take Theo to school on his first day. I was dreading speaking to all those other mothers, proper mothers, who knew instinctively what books they'd be reading in class, whether 'white trainers' really meant no blue stripe allowed, what would be an acceptable packed lunch because I had no doubt that there'd be some flipping sandwich/cake/biscuit combo that would mark you out as a weirdo among the kids and a failure as a parent among the mothers.

I tried to tell Caro my worries. She waved me away. 'You're his mother. That's enough. All kids think their parents are a variation of normal – because that's all they know – and embarrassing, because we just are.'

I wasn't all Theo knew. He'd had years with William and some with Clara, whom I was sure had correctly-sized carrot sticks and answers that were friendly but not overfamiliar to teachers in her DNA.

Theo continued to maintain polite non-committal responses to me. It was like living with a lodger who didn't really want to be there but had nowhere else to go. I couldn't work out how to reach him. I was thirty and couldn't relax around him, so goodness knows how daunting it was for him. I wondered if he lay in bed crying for his dad/not dad. Missing Barbara even. Perhaps looking longingly at Denmark on the map and working out how to escape there. Even the most simple things seemed beyond me. He'd shrugged when I'd asked him what he liked for breakfast. I'd bought about seven different cereals and three types of bread, but I still felt he was making the best of an incompetent job.

The only thing he showed any enthusiasm for in my presence was starting school, which made me think he couldn't wait to get away from me. On the day, I didn't know what to wear. I definitely couldn't look like all those mothers in the smart work suits or the white trousers/navy fine-knit jumper combos I'd seen that day I'd sat outside Theo's school. This was far more rural. Would jeans be too casual for a first-day impression? I only really had one dress, which my mother would have called 'a bit Greenham Common'. Just remembering that made me miss her. I'd noticed that I didn't automatically follow every nice memory of her with a criticism now I'd started to understand that motherhood was such an imprecise science.

I asked Caro about the dress code for school drop-off.

She waved her hand. 'Oh, anything goes. I used to turn up in an old painting smock if I was running late.'

So that first morning, with Theo being pulled along by Lionel and me trailing behind with his book bag, I was a smart version of my scruffy self. I almost baulked when we got within a hundred metres of the school. All those mums hugging each other and catching up on who went glamping where while their kids ran in and out of the little cliques.

I steeled myself and patted Theo's shoulder. 'This all looks very exciting.'

Theo was quiet. I stood on the edge of the playground with him. I wished I had the courage to walk up to those other mums and say, 'This boy, my son, he's new and he's had so much trauma, can you make your really kind offspring come and be his best friend?' Instead, I was frozen, ashamed that I couldn't overcome my own feelings to help Theo with his.

I couldn't think of anything to say, something to give him confidence. How did those other mothers do it? I felt as though my ineptitude was announcing itself via a loudspeaker, that everyone was subtly moving away, exchanging the *look* that denotes an outsider blundering into their territory.

Eventually a teacher came over. 'Mrs Cottingdale?' She didn't wait for me to correct her. 'This must be Theo. We're all just about to go in, so if you want to give Mummy a hug and come with me?'

At the exact time I stepped forward, Theo stepped backwards, leaving my hand floundering in thin air and eventually finding an ear to brush. 'I'll see you at pick-up time then, Theo,' I said, blushing as though my fraudulence was obvious to all.

I watched him walk away, his teacher smiling down as he spoke. He looked so small and vulnerable and I had no idea how to protect him, no idea who to be so that I could be part of that group of mothers, laughing and talking about their holidays, their husbands, their lives, smoothing a path into his own friendship group.

I wandered home, Lionel walking at my side as though he sensed the huge vacuum inside me. I was just turning up the hill when Fergus came past in his car. He gave a blast on the horn, making us both jump. He never seemed to care what any of the villagers thought. Or anyone really, which was beginning to look like a life skill I might never master.

'Hop in, I'll give you a lift. How did drop-off go? Did you cry?'

I knew Fergus was teasing, but the fact that I hadn't cried was another tick in the unnatural-mother box.

'No. I'm not that big on crying.'

He turned sideways in his seat, making me want to tell him to keep his eyes on the road. 'I don't think you're as hard as you make out.'

I wasn't in the mood for someone who came from a fruitcake family himself psychoanalysing me. 'I never said I was hard.'

'You are a bit "lived on t'motorway and licked it clean" though. You get chippy around people who've had a lot of privilege.' He grinned. 'People like me who inherit businesses, for example. Or whose parents still help them out even though they're adults.' He winked. 'Love it when Mum does my ironing.'

I knew he was trying to cheer me up, but I wished I'd walked. He had no idea what a luxury it was to sidle up to Caro and say, 'Be a love, just iron this for me.' He took advantage of her and she knew he was doing it and let him because she loved him. If I tried to explain that to him, he would have missed the point, frowned and said something like, 'But I'm not very good at ironing.'

I didn't answer him.

I stared ahead, ignoring Fergus throwing provocative statements out into the world like a teenage boy insulting a girl he fancies to see if he can get a reaction.

We got held up in the lane by a flock of sheep. He switched the car off. 'Sorry. Have I done a bit of a "Fergus foot in it" again?'

'It's okay.'

He pushed back against the door. 'You are quite hard to help, Vicky. You're very loved by the Campbell family. Even dad sings your praises and, believe me, that's as rare as an egg from Hilda.'

I couldn't help smiling at that. It had become Theo's job to collect the eggs and he'd made a chart to keep a tally of which ones produced the most. Hilda was in danger of not earning her keep and Fergus was always kidding Theo that one day he'd turn up to the dinner table and Hilda would be on his plate. I'd been all protective initially, but Fergus had waved me away. 'Boys' stuff. This is how blokes communicate, Vick. We don't do all that hair-plaiting, we tease each other. Theo gets that, don't you? Being a boy and all that?'

I had to hand it to Fergus, Theo did seem to covet his company. Occasionally, I sat with Caro on her terrace overlooking the bottom field and watched them throw a rugby ball around. If I strained my ears, carefree, uncensored laughter floated up, injecting tiny amounts of hope into my heart. I'd usually spoil the moment that they came panting back together, pushing each other and wrestling as they walked, by asking a question – 'Did you play rugby at your old school, Theo?'

He'd look down. 'No, not really, just with—' and he'd stop speaking, but I didn't know whether it was because he didn't know what to call William anymore or because it was too painful to mention him.

Fergus and I had just about reached a truce when we drew up to the cottages and saw a couple parked by their suitcases, arms folded.

'What are they doing here already?' I asked. 'I bet it's the guests for Yew Tree Cottage.'

'Is it ready?'

'Lou was coming back to clean the kitchen this morning. She ran out of time yesterday.' I sighed and got out of the car. 'Morning! Mr and Mrs Cosby? Welcome to Applewood Farm.'

The woman pursed her lips so tightly, I wanted to tell her that in twenty years' time, her lipstick wouldn't bleed, it would haemorrhage. 'Yes, well, we've been all round trying to find someone to let us in.'

Her husband was rubbing at a smudge on the bonnet of the car, looking as though he wished he'd hired a lighthouse on a Hebridean island for one.

'You are rather early. Check-in is two-thirty. It does say that on the paperwork we sent you.' I tried to sound polite but firm.

'I haven't had any paperwork.'

I was aware of Fergus walking up to us. 'You must have done, otherwise you wouldn't have had our bank details to make the payment for the holiday.' I sounded less conciliatory than normal but I was pissed off that this woman was making me look as though I hadn't done my job properly.

The woman fluttered her fingers at me as though the mere mention of money was offensive to her ears. 'I haven't seen anything that said we couldn't get into the cottage until the afternoon. So can you get us our keys please?'

I adopted a pleasant but professional manner. 'I'm afraid the cottage isn't ready just yet. If you'd like to leave your luggage in my office and go and have a little walk round town…'

The woman slumped as though I'd asked her to sleep in a ditch for a night or two while we got our shit together. She raised her voice. 'We've paid seven hundred pounds for this week. Do you know how much money that is?'

I could feel my temper rising. She'd obviously looked at me and decided that she was far superior. Infuriatingly, I found myself wishing I'd had my hair cut and coloured, that I was dressed in the work suit that gave me a bit of authority in confrontational situations.

Fergus said, 'Is there a problem?'

'Who are you?' the woman asked, as though Fergus was a casual passerby spotting a bit of aggro and deciding not to miss out.

'I'm Fergus Campbell, the owner of the holiday cottages.'

She did a whole shoulder ruffle of satisfaction that she was now talking to the organ grinder rather than the monkey. 'First of all, we couldn't find anyone to let us in and, now, the cottage isn't ready and we're expected to amuse ourselves until two-thirty.'

Fergus explained how we needed the mornings to make sure the cleanliness was up to scratch, but we'd call them as soon as the cleaner had finished.

'Oh, for goodness' sake. We've been on the road since six o'clock this morning. We just want to unpack and start our holiday.' She turned to her husband. 'I told you this looked like a one-man band. I knew it would lead to them cutting corners. If you're going to stay afloat, you need to work on your customer service.'

Fergus stepped forward. He opened the boot of their car and put the suitcases inside.

'What are you doing?' the woman asked.

'I've decided to work on the calibre of my customers instead. Now get lost. Vicky will transfer your money back to you today.'

For the first time, the husband lifted his head. 'You can't talk to my wife like that.'

'I can. I'm not having self-important idiots come here, shouting about what we've done wrong when actually we're offering exactly what we said we would – accommodation from two-thirty. I know your type. You'll get in there and you'll moan that the water isn't hot enough, you don't like the shape of the plates, there are only ten teaspoons. Whatever it's like, you'll whine your arses off and I'm just not in the mood for it.'

The woman stood open-mouthed. So did I. Until TripAdvisor fear clapped my lips together and kicked my brain into gear.

'Fergus. I don't think that will be necessary. How about I drive you down into town and sort you out a brunch and we'll be as quick as we can?'

Before they could reply, Fergus shook his head. 'Nope. No. Sorry. Off you trot. I'm not having anyone talk to my staff like that.'

I stared as their jaws gaped open like ventriloquist dummies.

Fergus waved his hand at them, just like she'd fluttered her fingers at me. 'Go. Goodbye.' He grabbed hold of my arm. 'Come on, let's go and get a coffee. Bloody people.'

We sat in Caro's kitchen while he recounted the story to her. She was torn between laughing and telling him off. 'Fergus!' She frowned. 'What if she goes and slags us off on TripAdvisor? We could lose loads of business.'

'I can't stand bullies. Vicky works really hard to keep everyone happy. Old bag got right up my pipes. Anyway, even if she does go and vent her spleen, most of the other reviews are five-star, so hopefully people will just dismiss her as a sad old troll.'

It was the first time in forever that someone had stood up for me. That I hadn't had to accept someone else's bad behaviour because I was too poor, too vulnerable, too desperate for a roof over my head. And I couldn't deny it, it felt brilliant to know someone had my back.

VICKY

Autumn 2018

Fergus defending me like that brought a lightness to my spirit, giving me more confidence to bounce ideas about for the business. Despite my peering nervously at TripAdvisor for several weeks, nothing came of his unceremonious dispatching of the Cosbys. Theo had adjusted well to the routine of school and we'd started a tentative, fragile bonding over reading. I nearly burst into tears when his teacher said he was one of the best readers in the year: 'A pleasure to have in my class.'

One of the mums nearby smiled as though I'd won first prize for parenting. I managed not to say, 'I walked out when he was two. It's down to the man we both thought was his dad but turned out not to be.' I did feel a puff of pride though, quickly followed by a wave of guilt that Freddie – gentle, kind Freddie – had a gold-star son he knew nothing about. God knows when I'd be brave enough to address that.

As the autumn term wore on, and the nights drew in, we developed our own pattern of walking home with Lionel, eating crumpets together and working on the model of the Globe Theatre he was building for his history project. He was far more diligent than me, meticulously gluing lolly sticks and tiny pieces of paper. Good old Freddie and his patient genes. But as I struggled not to glue my fingertips together, I still loved hearing about fragments of Theo's day, eager for any information that might fill in some of the blanks.

Over the last few weeks, however, Theo had withdrawn from me, refusing to involve me at all. 'I can do my homework on my own, thank you.'

Was that a normal part of growing up? A step towards independence? Or was there a problem, obvious to everyone except me?

'I'd like to have a little look at what you're doing before I sign your homework journal,' I said.

He picked up his books and went to his bedroom.

I hovered outside his door, exasperated as always by my ineffectiveness.

'Could you just show me very quickly what you're working on so that I'll have some idea if I have to speak to your teacher?'

I hated the pleading in my voice, the leaving myself open to refusal.

'No thank you' came the reply.

I knocked on the door and went in.

'Theo?' I made my voice gentle. 'Are you all right? You seem very quiet. Is anything worrying you?'

He shook his head, his face blank.

'You know you can talk to me about anything, don't you? We haven't had the traditional mother/son relationship, but I am here for you.' I wanted to say, 'I love you, give me a chance to protect you,' but I was frightened he'd pull away from me, throw it back in my face. I needed to be braver, but I just couldn't make myself say the words.

He burst into tears.

'Theo! What's the matter?'

Which was probably up there as far as stupid questions went.

I sat on the end of his bed, my whole body aching to reach out to him. 'Would you like a hug?' Caro did this sort of thing so naturally as though no one had ever shrugged her off. Fergus had inherited her warm nature; I envied how he lifted Theo up and clowned around with him, always looking as though he knew what was an acceptable amount of tactility without having to ask.

Theo shrank back into his pillow, thrusting the outline of a shield with the title 'Family Coat of Arms' at me.

In that moment, I longed, *longed*, for my mother. The way she could soothe all those jagged and prickly feelings, bring fear and upset down to a level that suddenly seemed within my capability to overcome. I remembered how she'd get up to me when I had a nightmare. She'd read to me until I was engaged in the story and not afraid to shut my eyes in case I fell back into my bad dream. She did it with a mixture of firmness and kindness, swapping pillows with me so I could smell her Anne French face cream and pretend she was there right next to me as I dropped off again.

'Is it not being sure of what – or who – to put on this that's made you so unhappy today?'

He didn't show any sign that he'd heard me.

Shame that I couldn't reach him, couldn't fix him was making me impatient. My voice was snappier than I'd intended. 'Theo, if you don't tell me what the problem is, I can't help you.'

With that he leapt off the bed, hurling his exercise books at the wall. 'I hate being here. I hate school. I want Dad and Clara and Barbara. I hate you!'

In the days that followed that outburst, everything in me shuttled between two opposing forces – protecting Theo, which required me to make myself vulnerable, and protecting myself in case I failed so resoundingly, I eventually had to admit defeat and let him go to another family.

Before we'd even made a millimetre of progress towards unravelling any of the complex circumstances surrounding us, I arrived at pick-up to find Theo waiting with Mrs Devlin, his teacher.

'Mrs Cottingdale? Could I have a word?' These days I just went with the whole 'not my surname and not even really his surname' thing.

I followed her in, trying to catch Theo's eye for a clue of what I might be in for. But Theo stared at the ground, not even acknowledging me. I didn't care what had happened, I just wanted to be in this together, not shut out.

'I'm sorry, but Theo has had a fallout today with another boy. We've had quite a few instances of inappropriate behaviour recently.' Her tone was already getting on my nerves. Didn't eight-year-olds sometimes fall out without it turning into a world drama?

I looked at her, immediately feeling that even though I had no idea what had happened, she'd got out her judgement stick, waved it in the general direction of my single parenthood and decided I had somehow *not done a good job*, which is why we were now having this conversation.

I didn't say any of this. I smoothed my eyebrows into something I hoped was neutral. 'What happened?'

'Theo. Do you want to tell Mummy?'

Theo looked as though he wanted to cry.

I bent down, longing to pull him into my arms but not wanting to add his screeching at me to get off to the teacher's growing tick-boxing of messed-up family shit. I went for a hug in my voice and hoped it was enough. 'I'm not angry. Just tell me what happened.'

The response came out in a rush of choked sobs. 'It was Rowan. He said I didn't have any family, so I'd taken his. That I'd stolen his Nan and Gramps.'

I should have come up with something that showed I was a reasonable, right-on mother, encouraging my son to see the best in everyone. Instead, I burst out with, 'That's his mother talking. She's made him feel jealous of you.'

The teacher had her 'Really, Mrs Cottingdale' face on. But I wasn't inclined to be 'Really'd' today. I hadn't rushed down to the school to fill them in on every last detail about Theo's tricky childhood – I wasn't sure a little Devon village was ready for the gossip onslaught that a few months before Theo started at Okeridge Primary the dad who wasn't his dad had died and the mum who'd abandoned him as a toddler had had to step in because the woman he thought was his grandmother had shut off not just the cash flow but apparently also the love supply for a boy who wasn't her grand-son. However, I'd talked about how much change he'd experienced and how he was adjusting to 'unusual family circumstances' and I'd hoped that they'd cut him a bit of slack.

'What happened when he said that to you?' I asked.

'I shoved him and he fell against the desk and banged his head really hard.'

I sighed.

Mrs Devlin said, 'It's not the first time Theo's temper has got the better of him. We don't want to take sanctions, but Rowan did have to go to the drop-in centre to be checked for concussion.'

Theo seemed to shrink in front of us. Given that I was pretty sure Theo's behaviour came from a place of roaring pain, I decided we'd talk about it without Mrs Devlin having a view.

I put my hand on his shoulder and he didn't shake me off. 'I'll ring the school to make an appointment to discuss it at an appropriate time.' I gave myself a little clap for boomeranging 'appropriate' back to her.

When we got home, I made cheese on toast for Theo and said, 'Is there anything I should know before I go in to see your teacher? I promise you I'm not cross. Are you being bullied by Rowan?' That probably broke all the parenting manuals of not putting words into his mouth, but I could see by his face that I'd guessed correctly. 'Could you tell me what happened?'

'He told everyone to stay away from me in case I stole their families because no one wanted me.' He sounded more resigned than sad and the guilt that his expectations of the world were so low required me to breathe deeply before I could carry on.

'Has it been happening for a while?'

Theo nodded. 'He won't let me join in the football at lunchtime.'

'Is there someone else you could play with?' I asked.

'No. All the boys play football.'

'So what do you do?

His answer – 'I just sit under the oak tree at the end of the field until the bell goes' – contained such a mixture of loneliness and stoicism that I fussed about with the washing-up until I could gather myself enough to continue.

I told him I'd sort it out with Mrs Devlin and tried not to take the mumbled 'You'll just make it worse' personally. He didn't argue when I suggested a bath and an early night.

It was a welcome distraction after I'd got him into bed when Fergus floated by with a couple of locally brewed beers he was thinking of offering on the honesty bar. I filled him in. 'Sorry, I know it's your nephew. And your sister.'

He sighed. 'Poor Theo. And poor bloody Rowan. He was such a lovely, open kid. All that sounds like the dead hand of India behind the scenes. Rowan never sees Mum anyway, so I don't understand why he'd suddenly think he was missing out unless India has been poking the wasp's nest.'

There was an impatient knock at the door. I raised my eyebrows at Fergus.

'I bet it's that couple with the Rottweiler. They started moaning that there wasn't enough room on the terrace for the dog as soon as they arrived.'

I opened the door. 'Hello?' I said to a woman who had something familiar about her but I knew wasn't a guest.

'I'm India, Rowan's mum.'

'Hello. Would you like to come in? Fergus is here.' I hoped I hadn't accidentally said out loud, 'THANK GOD Fergus is here.'

'No thank you. I'll make this brief. I've been in A&E with my son this afternoon.' Her voice was rising. I was conscious of the conversation reaching all the guests around the courtyard, where no doubt some of them would be sitting under the heaters enjoying the star-studded skies.

'Are you sure you don't want to come in?'

Fergus moved behind me. 'India, get inside. You don't want the whole of Applewood Farm knowing your business.'

Reluctantly, she stepped in. Her gaze swept round my little sitting room. Her eyes lingered on the huge turquoise vase Caro had lent me and flicked to a painting she'd done of Lionel and Dalí together.

I clasped my hands. 'I'm really sorry about what happened today. Is Rowan all right?'

'He's shaken and a bit bruised, but there's no lasting damage. Luckily. Can I speak to Theo about what he did?'

She was such a force of nature, I almost turned on my heel there and then to go and fetch him. But her harsh tone pulled me up short.

'What do you want to say?'

'I'd like to understand why he pushed Rowan over.'

I didn't have any experience of dealing with other parents or the altercations between their children. But I'd had plenty of experience of one-sided blame in a two-sided story. I tried to remember how I talked to difficult customers without inflaming them. Nope. That knowledge had flapped off, with a primeval fury replacing it. I breathed out, pushing the volume of my voice down to a conciliatory level.

'From what I understand, the root cause is more of an adult problem from the point of view that Rowan feels sad that he doesn't see Caro anymore and I gather he's been a little bit unkind to Theo in blaming him for stealing his grandparents.'

India didn't respond, so I blundered on.

'I can see why he might feel like that, but obviously Theo hasn't tried to take Rowan's place on purpose, it's just an unfortunate coincidence that they're the same age.'

'But your son pushed my son and injured him.' I could see why Caro found her difficult to deal with. She had none of her mother's warmth or charm.

A vortex of words whirled around in my head, along with the anxiety of not knowing the parenting steps required for this kind of shit. 'I've already had a word with him. He knows he's made a mistake. He'll write a letter of apology to Rowan tomorrow, but I'd also ask that you make it clear to Rowan that your family dynamics are not Theo's fault.'

India folded her arms. 'My family dynamics are none of Theo's business.'

'But Rowan thinks they are.' I was aware of the Punch and Judy cadence of our discussion, but there was no way I was backing down. None. She could plant herself there, all daughter of the manor dealing with the understairs staff, as long as she liked, but I wasn't going to serve Theo on a platter for her.

'I'd like a word with him, please.'

I glanced at Fergus, who said, 'Come on, India. I was always getting into fights at his age and Mum never bothered to run round and "have a word". We gave each other a good thump, then the next day we went back to playing football. Move on.'

It was like someone had pulled a pin on a grenade. 'Oh shut up, Fergus. What do you know about kids? And, of course, Mum never went to have a word. She was too busy drinking gin with all her oddball arty-farty cronies. Not because she'd actually given any thought to what was best for us.'

Fergus wiped his hand across his face. 'For God's sake, India. You are such a drama queen. I don't even recognise the childhood you think you had. No, Mum and Dad weren't perfect, but they were good enough. You talk about them as though we were left chewing on scraps in a dungeon, fending for ourselves. What about all the times Mum drove you back to university so you didn't have to cart all your luggage on the train? Or got up at the crack of dawn to drive you into Exeter to find somewhere to print your dissertation because the printer had broken?'

India shook her head, her eyes filling with tears. In that moment, I understood her. Her pain was real. She wasn't making up those feelings of loneliness, of being left out, of being the child no one liked as much as Fergus. To her, Caro was someone who made her feel she wasn't enough, whatever enough would look like. Everyone could argue against it as much as they wanted, but for India, that was the truth, not something she'd invented so she could feel unhappy and insecure, despite me thinking Caro was one of the kindest and most generous people I'd ever met. But because of their mother-daughter relationship, their expectations of each other had somehow, somewhere, imploded along the family fault lines, like dynamite planted in the DNA.

A bit like me with my mum. Maybe I'd done a similar thing: decided my story was that I was an unwanted child from a previous relationship left out from the new family, an inconvenient reminder of my mother's former life. I'd convinced myself that I'd learnt not to rely on anyone else because everyone let me down at some point. But listening to India and her take on their family made me wonder if my 'truth' was as solid as I'd once perceived it to be. Could it be that Mum had done her best, pulled in lots of different directions and had assumed that I could cope better than I could? That I didn't need or want her input?

I felt a wave of sadness for us both. It was amazing how some people floated along with their parents, bobbing along like ducks on a stream, sometimes wandering off a bit, then paddling back to the hub of security without any drama, without anyone taking a bit of dissent or break for freedom as an insult. And some people twisted and turned and agonised, trying to please everyone without ever pleasing themselves and, in the end, cauterised the pain of not fitting in, of not getting it right, by cutting themselves off.

'Would you like to sit down and have a drink? A cup of tea? A glass of wine?' I asked.

Fergus had puffed out his cheeks, which was probably in lieu of a throat-slitting gesture.

I stepped towards India and tentatively put my hand on her arm.

She shook me off. 'No, I just want to speak to Theo so I can get home.'

I was sorry for her, but not that sorry. 'That's not going to be possible. He's had a very traumatic time of things and we're still finding our way. He needs to trust me to have his back and I don't think letting someone he doesn't know discipline him is going to help.'

Fergus hadn't learnt his lesson. 'India, Theo's a good lad and I'm sure Rowan is as well. You coming here and making a great big bloody deal out of it is going to turn it into a right palaver. Just let it go.'

India gestured towards Fergus. 'So typical of my family. So generous and understanding with a random stranger down the street. They've always been like this. Do anything for Lou in the village, or the bloke that's fallen on hard times but actually step in and fight for their own daughter or grandson... hah. Not a chance. In our family, your bloody mother snogs your husband!'

And with that, her face crumpled and she slammed out of the door, leaving Fergus with the uncomfortable job of explaining this unexpected twist in the Campbell saga.

CARO

November 2018

I knew Gilbert was going to see her. He had that face on. The one where he tried to look all nonchalant, pretending to flick through the paper, reading out a few little snippets he thought I might be interested in – even though after four decades of marriage he hadn't yet clocked that my desire to hear about what the Chancellor might do to pensions while I was eating my yoghurt was zero. The giveaway was that he kept looking at his watch. He never wore his watch now he'd retired – 'I'm not running to anyone's timetable anymore.' But of course he was. Greedily, desperately snatching at the half an hour India afforded him for coffee, or the hour after school while the kids were snacking on their lentil crisps and carob nib cookies while listening to an audiobook in French. No doubt he had to work doubly hard to earn his place in her life since the Andy showdown. I could quite imagine India demanding that he fix a cupboard door or secure a wobbly door handle while he was there.

I wanted to make it easy for him to tell me. But on the rare occasion he did say where he was going, I couldn't resist a 'Must be wonderful to be the perfect parent who got it all right' or 'Feel free to blame all the mistakes on me.'

As he always had, Gilbert took the path of least resistance, though whether he was protecting me or saving himself, I didn't know. The result was that we remained marooned in a mute dance where I felt grateful he tried to spare my feelings but betrayed that he attempted to hide what he was up to. 'I'm just nipping down to the village to see if I can get hold of something to fix the…' and his words would run out as I waved him away, 'OK, love. See you later.'

I took myself off to my painting studio, today's frustration and pain manifesting themselves in a stark winter landscape, a lone tree on a bleak hill. I was at that point of creativity where I wasn't sure whether I'd produced a visual representation of internal angst or I'd lost myself up my own pompous, painterly backside, indulging in a view of myself as a tortured artiste seeking meaning from the world. I was just considering going the whole hog and having a gin with my mid-morning biscuit when Gilbert knocked on the door and came in.

He rarely disturbed me in the studio.

'Are you all right, love?' I asked.

He shook his head. 'Theo's been bullying Rowan.'

'Who told you that?' Maybe this was why I hadn't cut it as a mother because my hackles didn't rise, my need for vengeance on the person who'd wronged our family didn't immediately distil into action.

Gilbert went through the whole saga. I worked hard on not screwing my face up and saying, 'Really? Theo pushed Rowan over completely unprovoked?'

'Apparently India came up here last night to discuss it with Vicky and Fergus happened to be there and effectively told her to get lost.'

Fergus had always been inclined to get the bellows out and boost the flames where India was concerned – 'Oh come on, Mum. She's so dramatic.' I tended to agree, but since the whole kissing Andy debacle had come to light, Gilbert had shifted away from me, like a voter switching his support after a lifelong affiliation to one party. In the aftermath of that disastrous day, I'd explained my version of events and my reasons for dismissing what Lou had said in front of India. Gilbert assured me he believed me, but still I sensed a leaning towards India at my expense.

I tried to get to the crux of the latest drama. 'I'm guessing India doesn't want to confine the quarrel to two eight-year-old boys but wants the whole family to draw battle lines?'

Gilbert frowned. 'You could be a bit more charitable, Caro. I mean, Theo is bound to have a few issues, isn't he?'

'I think we should hear the other side of the story before we jump to any conclusions.'

Gilbert looked down and scratched at a fleck of paint on the window. 'India wants us to ask Vicky to leave.'

I slammed down my paintbrush, a dark splodge splattering into the middle of my canvas. 'For heaven's sake! The two boys have a bit of a contretemps and India wants us to fire the person who manages our business and enables us to retire properly. Not to mention makes a damn good living for us all. What is her problem? I hope you told her to get on her bike and pedal off into the sunset with that idea.'

And there he stood, my rock-steady husband, with a tear seeping down his cheek. 'She said if Vicky's not gone by the end of this school year, she'll never speak to any of us again.'

I wasn't going to notice the difference in my life. And, oddly, after all these months of trying, biding my time waiting for her to come round, there was a bit of me that welcomed it as a way of drawing a line under my pain. While I hoped, I couldn't heal.

Gilbert flicked his hands up in despair. 'You can shrug all you want, Caro, but she's still my daughter. And there are reasons why she feels the way she does. You kissing Andy won't have helped.'

There it was. It had been a long time coming. He'd never said it explicitly.

He blamed me. It was liberating to know where we all stood.

'I wondered how long it would take to be all my fault. You heard what Lou said. Even though I was drunk and sitting in a lonely sobbing heap because my own husband had gone to bed, I pushed him off straightaway. I've taken the blame as far as India is concerned because I don't want her to lose her marriage as well as her mother. But from you, I'd expected better. You could even consider feeling a bit pissed off with Andy, rather than holding me entirely responsible?'

For a man who was over six foot, Gilbert looked small, as though his internal strength had withered away and his body had folded in on itself. His words when they came sounded weary. 'Don't make me choose between you, Caro. She's still that little girl we loved. And if I don't maintain some kind of relationship, she'll stop me seeing the kids. You know what she's like. So black and white.'

I stared at him. 'I don't want to make you choose, Gil. But she's not a little girl and she's making grown-up decisions that mean I probably won't be part of her life. I can't affect that anymore and, to be honest, I'm really tired of trying. I'm not going to send Vicky packing and put her on the street with that poor little boy.'

'And you'd prioritise her over us?'

'I'm prioritising doing the right thing. And Fergus over India, because don't forget he's worked really hard to build up the business with Vicky's help and India's not going to snatch it all away from him on a whim. Plus sacking employees because a daughter who doesn't even work in the business gets a bee in her bonnet is probably on the shady side of legal.'

Gilbert opened his mouth to say more, but I put my hand up to stop him. I couldn't hear it. I couldn't spend another moment asking myself how that little girl with her serious face, the child who spent hours pressing wild flowers under the doormat to make bookmarks, stirring suet bombs for the birds for the sheer joy of seeing them outside the kitchen window, had become a woman so full of resentment that she would threaten to ban her own father from contact with his grandchildren.

Following the thread back to where it all began was like tracking a trail of breadcrumbs after a flock of crows had feasted. And now, with a moment of real clarity, I no longer had the energy to bother.

Next to the agony of loss was a surprising sense of relief.

VICKY

Winter 2018

The Rowan-Theo shitstorm dislodged the status quo. Theo had overheard India – my heart went out to him, cowering in his bed, wondering whether she was going to steam in at any moment. But finally he seemed to understand that I was on his side. That way he had of hesitating, of considering what would be the right response before he answered, gave way to a more spontaneous exchange, as though he trusted me not to disappear if he didn't say the right thing. I resisted thinking about the turmoil I'd created for this sweet boy; instead I focused my energy on convincing him he could rely on me.

I'd asked for a meeting with his teacher and explained more about our family situation, though I'd skimmed over the walking out on my son on Christmas Day and not returning for nearly six years. I fudged it with a 'Theo lived mainly with his father'. She'd still used loads of words such as 'inappropriate behaviour', 'necessity of consistency' and 'coping strategies', which made me feel she'd swallowed her teacher's handbook to 'dealing with difficult children'.

On the upside, I felt as though I'd adjusted the balance to a bit less Rowan – Goody, Theo – Baddie – than before. So when Theo came home asking me where we were moving to, I shook my head. 'I'm very happy here. I'm not planning to go anywhere else.'

Theo went very quiet. 'Are you going to send me away then?'

'What do you mean?'

'Rowan says his mum will make sure I have to move. And if you won't leave, will I have to go on my own?' As he said it, his eyes filled.

It was instinctive. I pulled him to me and he sobbed, juddering great gasps of loss that an eight-year-old should never have experienced. I stroked his hair and patted his back and at some point I moved from wondering whether he was waiting for a convenient moment to pull away from me to feeling as though I was exactly where I should be, doing what I should do. He clung to me until his body stopped shaking.

'Listen. For all sorts of reasons I can't expect you to understand, I wasn't there for you when you were little. But now, you need to be very very clear that I'm your mum.' I took a deep breath to suppress the raw emotion created by daring to define myself like that, a ferocious determination never to let Theo down again dominating the complex tangle of love and fear. 'I'm going to protect you and I will never, ever leave you again. So you can stop worrying about that.'

As I said it, I recognised that it would take years for Theo to develop that deep trust he should have been able to take for granted. My culpability made me shout, 'And you can tell Rowan that we are here to stay.' The second the words left my mouth, I had the horrible sensation of promising something that might not be within my gift since Fergus had let slip that India wanted to oust us.

Once Theo had cried himself out, I thought he'd retreat from me, embarrassed. But when I sat on the sofa, Lionel leapt up with me and Theo snuggled in next to him until I was clinging on by a buttock. Theo tickled Lionel's tummy, then he put his head on my shoulder.

I dropped a kiss onto his hair. 'We're going to be okay.'

He swivelled round. 'I know I can't move back in with Granny Barbara, but can I go and see her soon? Please?'

Given how dispassionate she'd been about forcing me to take a boy she'd looked after for eight years, I was pretty sure she wouldn't be cracking open the tea and scones for us any time soon. I gave a non-committal answer along the lines of 'Let's see how it goes', then distracted him by asking him to make us some hot chocolate.

It didn't go away. By the beginning of the spring term, school seemed to have settled down, with Rowan not such a feature in our conversations, though whether that was because things were actually improving or Theo just got better at telling me what I wanted to hear, I didn't know. The one thing that remained constant, however, was Theo's requests to see Barbara. He had a dogged persistence that was hard to resist: 'Could we go at half-term?' 'Could Fergus take me if you can't come?' 'Would she be able to come here and stay in one of the cottages?'

In the end, I phoned her, because I didn't know how to refuse Theo the one thing he'd asked for.

Her voice was different from how I remembered. Less strident, less definite about her place in the world. I explained why I was calling.

There was a pause before she responded and I braced myself for an accusation that I was trying to dump him back on her now I'd had a go at 'proper' motherhood for a few months.

She was straight to the point. 'I don't think so, Vicky, no.' She sounded as though she was yawning, barely able to muster the interest required to consider my request. As though my son loving her for eight years amounted to nothing now she'd discovered there was no shared blood.

I couldn't go back to Theo and say Barbara had refused. He was adamant he wanted to see her. Surely I could deliver an hour with the woman he'd grown up with?

I choked back the surge of anger and pleaded with her. 'Please, Barbara. He's desperate to see you. It's not a trick to get you to take him back. I want to keep him.' I couldn't believe how lame I sounded, as though we were discussing who was going to find space for a well-loved but oversized dining-room table. I still baulked at the vulnerability of telling her how much I loved my son, how glad I was she'd coerced me into facing up to motherhood, the absolute unthinkability of ever being separated from him again.

Her response was cold and clinical. 'No, a clean break is what's needed. Please don't call me again. You get on and enjoy your son now you've found him. Look forwards, Vicky, not backwards.'

The line went dead.

I stood, mouth open, knowing I'd played it all wrong, that if I'd only chosen the right words, she would have welcomed the brilliance of my idea. Instead, I'd half-promised Theo it would happen and was going to have to hurt him with the truth – Barbara didn't ever want to see him again – or lie to him and leave him with a false hope that would no doubt be dashed again at a later date. I couldn't allow that to happen.

If I took Barbara photos, if I sat opposite her and explained that he needed this connection, this sense of belonging, she would see that I loved him, that I was there out of a desire to make things right. Perhaps she'd relent. I had to give it a go.

Fergus offered to take Theo to see the Exeter Chiefs play rugby at the weekend. 'Do me a favour. Could you take him for dinner and keep him until I get back? Probably around nine o'clock this evening?'

He dipped his head. 'Got a date?'

'Not the sort you're thinking of.'

'Feel free to share.'

I pulled a face. 'You'll talk me out of it.'

Fergus rolled his eyes. 'You're not going down to reason with my sister about her latest tack of trying to chase you out of town, are you?'

I stared down at the floor. 'I don't think she'd listen to me even if I did.'

Although Fergus had dismissed her demands as entirely unlikely to succeed, the refrain of blood being thicker than water kept running around my head. I'd hinted a few times to Caro, probing to see if they'd discussed it any further, but she never took the bait.

Fergus frowned. 'Like we see her anyway. She just pisses me off. She only wants to be part of the family if she can call all of the shots. I can't be bothered with her.'

'But your mum and dad probably don't see it like that.'

Fergus shrugged, just like Caro, ending the conversation without actually finishing it. I had no choice but to learn to live with an axe dangling over my head.

'So where are you going?'

I filled him in.

'You're a glutton for punishment, aren't you?' His face grew serious. 'You won't let him go and live with her again, will you?'

'No. Definitely not.'

As his features relaxed, I was reminded again of how lucky I'd been to land with a family who weren't my family but felt like one.

I drove towards Guildford, thinking about the difference between this visit and the one before. Last time I felt on the back foot, wounded before I got there. This time I was invincible, determined to bring home the prize for my boy.

I parked in the drive. Weeds poked through the paving stones of the path. The spring sunshine showed up windows in need of a good clean. I knocked at the door. No answer. Perhaps Barbara was out golfing, though her car was here. Maybe she was in her greenhouse round the back, giving it a clean-up after the winter. I hovered by the back gate. How rude would it be to walk into the back garden unannounced? I dithered before deciding that I'd probably have to become a lot less polite before the day was over. I banged open the garden gate and called out as I went round the corner. I turned towards the greenhouse. No Barbara in her canvas hat and gardening gloves, coaxing dormant plants back into life. The French windows to the sitting room were ajar. As always, I had a catastrophic thought rush in before a rational one – would I find her stabbed to death in the hallway – or making a cup of tea in the kitchen with the radio on so she didn't hear the bell?

I jumped as I stepped towards the open doors. She was sitting in an armchair, her head resting on her chest, tucked under a blanket. Her breathing was shallow and wheezy. Her head was completely bald.

I stood, staring, trying to order my thoughts. Her head jerked up and I stifled a gasp. Barbara, but not Barbara. A skeletal Barbara, devoid of eyebrows, her skin sallow, with a yellow tinge.

'Theo's not here, is he?' She sounded strident, almost angry.

My voice trembled. 'No. I came on my own.'

Her whole body relaxed.

I wanted to say something normal, something that didn't sound horrified and shocked, but 'Sorry to barge in like this, but I needed to talk to you about Theo' no longer seemed like the right opening line.

She waved her hand at me. 'Don't stand there gawping. Come in, since you're here.'

'Are you on your own?'

'I have a carer three times a day.' She glanced at the carriage clock on the mantelpiece. 'She'll be back in an hour to check I haven't died.'

She squared her shoulders with an effort but still had a glint in her eye defying me to pity her. It made me brave.

'Is that likely?'

'Very. And soon. Pancreatic cancer. Already outlived their predictions, so don't waste your money buying me any books in a series.' She winced in pain as she laughed.

'Did you know when you started searching for me?' My voice was pleading. The old Barbara would have delighted in taunting me for my neediness.

Again, that mirthless laugh. 'It's *why* I looked for you.' She stopped, her naked face vulnerable.

I was torn between not causing her any anguish and a desire to understand before I lost my chance.

'I needed to be sure Theo would be looked after. If Clara marries again, his happiness would depend on the new husband. I knew you would have that maternal love for him.'

'But you taught him to hate me.' A sob rose in my throat.

She gestured at herself. 'And look how I've been punished. I understood what I'd taken from you when William died. William fell in love with Clara when Theo was a few months old. I was afraid you'd move away with Theo and go back to your own family if you found out. I loved Theo so much and I wanted to protect William. I couldn't bear it if he lost his son. Even though he was the one at fault.'

I realised the knowledge that William had been having an affair with Clara was a confirmation rather than a revelation. It surprised me how much it hurt even so. Another person who'd preferred someone else to me. However, I couldn't dwell on that now. There'd be plenty of time to pick at that wound.

Barbara wiped at the single tear that ran slowly down her cheek, as though her body was just a husk, with scarce resources to demonstrate the deepest grief. She closed her eyes.

My eyes darted to her chest to see if she was still breathing. There was no time to be polite. I put my hand on her arm, my fingers finding bone rather than flesh. 'Barbara, I'm sorry, but I need to know. Did you really give him back to me because he wasn't your blood relation?'

Her eyes flicked open. She struggled to focus. 'Sorry. I get so tired. No. Of course we were all devastated when we realised he wasn't William's. I was angry because I felt we'd been tricked – that's what William and I rowed about. He defended you, saying he didn't think you knew. Of course, later, after William had died,

I understood that none of that mattered, that we loved Theo for who he was. I found out my cancer was terminal shortly after that. I knew I'd have to play hardball to get you to take Theo, which is why I threatened to call social services. I didn't have a choice and I needed to sort it out while I still could.'

I should have been angry for all the hurt she'd caused. Instead, I felt sadness for all that she'd lost. And guilt. Huge guilt that because of me she'd rowed with William and he'd shot off on the motorbike in a temper. It terrified me that love was capable of turning its power into something poisonous.

'Do you want to see Theo to say goodbye?' I wanted to snatch back those words as soon as they left my mouth.

She looked at me for a long moment.

'Tell him I love him. That I always will. That I've gone to see Daddy in heaven. I'll be watching over him. It would only frighten him to see me like this.'

I breathed out, ashamed of my relief that I wouldn't have to deal with Theo's distress in front of Barbara. Lionel was much less judgemental. I stood in the sitting room, memories of William carouselling around me, in awe that I'd ever been audacious enough to believe we could survive with so much stacked against us. I wanted to reach back into my past and give myself a hug, both to congratulate me for my bravery and to commiserate for the naivety of my ambition.

Time to leave. To treasure every future moment with my son rather than mourn the ones I'd missed. I stood in front of Barbara, sifting about for a suitable goodbye.

Her head drooped, her voice, little more than a whisper. 'Try and forgive me, Vicky.'

'Forgive yourself, Barbara. Go safely.'

I stepped out, closing the French windows behind me to keep out the afternoon chill. And in the three hours it took me to drive back to Okeridge, I turned over in my mind how fear of loss makes us choose ill-judged paths, scooping those we love into tightly-tentacled strangleholds so that we suffocate them rather than set them free. And who knew precisely how much air and oxygen everyone needed? Was one person's idea of freedom another person's neglect? What were the guidelines for persevering with people who didn't appear to want us in their lives? I'd assumed Theo would have a better life without me. Had my own mum thought the same thing about me? Rather than realising that my pushing her away was a contrary desire for her to prove she did miss me, did love me, that I was important to her? In a world where there were ever more ways of communicating, the chances of crossing our wires had proliferated.

Theo and I marked the news of Barbara's death by planting tulip bulbs in the field behind our cottage. 'Tulips were her favourite flowers. They'll come up every spring and we'll feel that she's still with us.'

I never said out loud that our lives were easier without her, but I struggled to stop my internal voice from speaking ill of the dead. In the end, I made peace with the conundrum that it was possible to grieve for people you didn't like when they were alive. I mourned her for what she represented to Theo, sad that my poor boy, at eight years old had faced yet another loss in his life. I squeezed Theo's hand and listened without commenting when he recounted the good times he'd had with Barbara. Flying kites in Cornwall, poking about in rock pools, building sandcastles on the beach – all the family holidays I'd missed. Or chosen to miss. I no longer knew the truth – whether Barbara's love for Theo had been stronger than mine – or whether her desire to protect William – powered by two decades of maternal love – meant my nascent bonding with Theo couldn't compete.

On good days, I felt nothing but sadness for her. On bad days, when Theo would trot out 'Granny used to say you didn't understand love because your mum didn't love *you* and that's why you left *me*,' I'd feel a blow to my stomach, a complex rush of anger at her audacity, mixed with anxiety that she might have been right. I adopted the habit of saying, 'I can't change what I did, Theo, but I promise that I will always be there for you in the future. Always.'

And he'd slip his hand into mine and say, 'You won't leave me again, will you?'

And I'd hug him really tightly. 'Never. I am going to stay with you forever and you'll never get rid of me.'

And I really, really meant it.

CARO

June 2019

It was hard to believe it was nearly twelve months since Theo had come into our lives and two and a half years since I'd seen my grandchildren. Somehow the approaching end of the school year made me feel more melancholy than ever, particularly now the banners advertising the school fete were all over the village. I knew India would be there, manning the book stall as she always did, the choices people made in their reading altering her opinion of them forever. Theo invited me to go with them in that casual way children had, 'You'll come and watch me in the tug of war, won't you, Caro? I'm the first one at the front.'

I loved that he had no awareness, despite the argy-bargy with Rowan at school, that my presence, the mere fact of turning up, would be like throwing a match onto drought-browned grass and watching a small plume of smoke convert into a raging bushfire.

'Gilbert will come down, but I'm having to work.'

'Work? But aren't you a painter?'

I forgave him as he had only just turned nine. I also decided to educate him. 'Painting is work for me, darling. That's how I get paid. Not all jobs involve going to an office.'

His face dropped. 'Do you have to paint on my fete day? I wanted you to bring Dalí down for the best dog competition.'

'Your mum will bring Lionel. You can take lots of photos and tell me all about it afterwards.'

But in the lead-up to the fete, with Fergus helping Theo brush Lionel and Theo declaring that he couldn't leave Dalí out so he was going to enter them both, I couldn't accept that India was dictating what I did and where I went. India hadn't invited Gilbert, but he didn't feel pushed away in the same way I did, even though in the seven months since she'd started making rumblings about getting rid of Vicky, she'd only allowed him to pop round a few times for a cup of tea.

When he'd returned from India's latest offering of a one-hour slot, I'd asked, 'She wasn't still going on about Vicky, was she? I hope you set her straight?'

He'd cleared his throat in the manner I recognised as buying himself time to think. 'I said that we really needed her for the business at the moment, especially over the summer.'

'But?'

'That we'd revisit it after the holiday season.' His voice was small, weary.

'You what?'

Gilbert had sighed. I would have felt sorry for him, caught in the middle, if I hadn't experienced decades of being the bad guy while he had waltzed in with Easter eggs and Toblerones and, later, designer clothes and ridiculously expensive trainers I'd already vetoed. 'Caro, I don't think you appreciate how serious she is about this. It could be the stumbling block that kills off any chance of fixing things.'

'I think you're looking at it from the wrong angle. Leave aside for the moment that India's our daughter. Have you asked yourself whether you want a relationship with *anyone* that's built on blackmail and bullying? Because that is what this is. More complicated, I grant you, because she *is* our daughter. But unless we follow every single one of her rules – which, half the time we don't even know what they are – she'll use our grandchildren as a weapon against us. Do you really want to live like that?'

He shook his head. 'Of course I don't. I just keep hoping we'll manage to sort it all out.'

And, in that moment, I'd realised I didn't hope anymore. I accepted. With sadness, with reluctance, but still with acceptance.

He'd bent down to stroke Dalí, but I knew he was choking back tears. 'Please let me try.'

As the day drew nearer, with Fergus volunteering to be the goalie for the football stand and Theo practising his press-ups on the lawn while Lionel tried to lick his face, I railed against the role I'd been assigned. That whether I was allowed to come to an event open to everyone depended on the whim of someone who would never see the good in me anyway.

I watched Gilbert shaving, his back to me, and said, 'I thought I might pop down on Saturday.'

His razor stopped moving. 'I don't think that's a good idea.'

'Maybe not. But I'm going. I want to see Dalí and Lionel in the dog show. I won't provoke India, but she is not going to tell me what I can and can't do.'

'If it stops you going, I won't go either.'

'I'm going, Gil. I'm not frightened of my own daughter, even if you are.' And with more bravado than I felt, I said, 'I want to watch Theo in the tug of war.'

He didn't answer.

On the morning of the fete, he said, 'Are you sure you really want to do this?'

'Yes.' But I wasn't. I wasn't sure whether I was being pig-headed and picking a fight for the sake of it, or standing up to someone who loved to dictate the exact volume of the tune she wanted us to dance to.

We walked down together in silence, though there were plenty of questions echoing noisily in my head. Perhaps my inability to lie low, to button my lip, to assume anyone who disagreed with me just hadn't appreciated my dazzling point of view was at the root of everything with India. Maybe I should slink off home, pay the penance for not succeeding as a mother and accept that as my lot.

But where would it stop? Would I have to give up time with the people who did want me around on the off-chance the ones who hated me might have a problem with it?

Fergus had gone ahead with the dogs and Theo and Vicky. I saw India straightaway, on the other side of the field, with Holly, who looked as though she'd shot up half a foot and lost all that toddler plumpness, nothing like the little girl I remembered. My heart ached for everything I'd missed.

I took a deep breath. 'I'll just go and get some coffee over here if you want to go and have a chat.'

Gilbert scuttled off, as though sidestepping a toxic tide. I positioned myself so I could spy on them from behind the bunting. I peered over, Gilbert greeting Holly, her delight at seeing him, India's stony face. Gilbert trying to jolly her along, waving his hand in an overexuberant way towards the football stand and the stall where you counted how many sweets there were in the jar. He could have abseiled from the bloody church spire in a Superman costume and India would probably have stood there looking as if she was about to have a boil lanced on a buttock.

She swivelled in my direction, her face blank. I pretended not to see her, busying myself adding milk to my coffee. Then I spotted Fergus.

He sauntered over, his face open and smiley. 'You decided to come then?'

'I'm not here to cause trouble.'

'It'll be fine. Come to the football with me. Her kids are probably not allowed to do something as fun as that. She'll be rushing them home to practise their algebra in a minute.'

'You don't have to take my side, Fergie. I can be big and brave on my own.' Though actually I loved that he backed me up, even if out loud I felt the need to encourage neutrality.

A shout went up for the tug of war.

Theo ran up to me with Vicky and pulled at my hand. 'Caro! Come and watch!'

I hadn't intended to be right there at the front of the crowd, but it just turned out that way. And, directly opposite me, at the other end of the rope, was India. I tried to move away from Vicky, to distance myself just a little, so India couldn't reproach me for taunting her with my 'other' family. For one fleeting moment, I felt the urge to rush over to where she was, to hug her and say, 'Come on, this is stupid, look at your lovely kids, look how brilliantly you've done. Look how much love there is in our family. We can get past this.' I raised my eyebrows and smiled. Hope was like the dandelions on our lawn – just when we thought we'd got them all, a sneaky little seed became airborne.

India held my eyes for a second, then looked away. My courage evaporated.

I focused on Theo and Rowan on opposite sides of the rope. I made sure to shout for them equally, giving a little more volume to 'Row-an!' so India couldn't accuse me of favouring Theo. It was laughable that I used my energy for petty mind reading.

Theo's team emerged triumphant and he shot over to Vicky, red-faced and sweating, at the very moment that Rowan came scampering up to me with a huge hug. 'Nan!'

I couldn't help it. I hugged and hugged him, burying my face into his hot little neck so he couldn't see my tears.

Before I'd even had the chance to tell him how wonderfully he did, India was there with Gilbert, pulling him away. 'Rowan, let's have a go at the treasure hunt.'

But Rowan had never been any good at falling into line. 'I'm staying with Nan.'

I patted him, 'We'll catch up some other time, sweetheart. So lovely to see you though. I've thought about you so much.'

India looked at me. 'Yeah, so much that you cheer on the boy who put him in hospital.' She leaned towards Theo, 'I hope you're ashamed of what you did.'

Gilbert put a warning hand on her arm. 'India, this isn't the time or place for this.'

But what we hadn't bargained on was Vicky. She stepped forward, right up to India, who was several inches taller. 'India, I completely understand your need to defend Rowan and Theo has already apologised – written him a letter of apology in fact – but I think you'll find Rowan had his part to play as well. The boys have let it go. Look at them. They aren't even thinking about it anymore. I'm sorry it happened, but you are not going to get away with bad-mouthing us to everyone. And I will be down that school making an official complaint about you harassing us.' Her voice didn't even shake. She turned to Rowan and said, 'Well done for moving on. You've been very grown-up,' and then strutted off with Theo.

I wanted to clap. She couldn't have put India in her place better if she'd tried. India was all about 'learning from an experience', her kitchen had all sorts of fridge-magnet wisdom on various postcards – 'Setbacks are challenges in disguise'. 'It may be stormy, but the rain will eventually pass.'

Rowan's face crumpled. 'Will she really complain about us?'

But before I could come up with an answer, India grabbed his arm and flounced off, saying, 'I meant what I said. If she's not gone by the end of summer, you won't see any of us again.' She took a few steps away from us, then turned back. 'And you, we all know what sort of a mother you are. And when they're old enough, don't think I won't tell them.'

I was conscious of a few heads turning towards us and a ripple of people moving away from the 'problem' family.

'I'm sorry, I shouldn't have come,' I said to Gilbert, who looked as though he'd understood the magnitude of India's fury with me for the first time. Without meeting anyone's eye in case they knew I was the mother who'd kissed her daughter's husband, I strode away, my heart hammering. And breaking.

VICKY

June 2019

I'd watched Gilbert and Caro leave the fete, trying to judge the collateral damage to them – and, indirectly, to me. Gilbert's pace was slow, nothing like his usual energetic purpose. Caro was brisker, holding the gate and waving him through. Gilbert sank down onto a bench as though he had just enough stamina to reach it but the forward motion to go any further had deserted him. I asked Fergus if he should stay with them, but he said, 'Let Mum tell Dad what he thinks, so he can present us with her amazing idea.' He didn't look anywhere near as worried as I felt.

We started up the hill, with Fergus and Theo arguing about the best way to save a goal. I dragged behind, imagining Gilbert chewing on the arm of his glasses as he did when he was thinking, with Caro listing the for and against of keeping us here. Knowing Caro, she'd be carrying the responsibility for not only her own relationships but the tangled dynamics between everyone else. I'd often heard her say, 'I was so desperate for India not to be an only child, but my two have never had any time for each other. Chalk and cheese, they are. I don't know if I somehow set them against each other by wanting them to be close.'

Gilbert never seemed to wonder if he'd made mistakes. And Fergus dismissed India as you would a wasp at a barbecue – irritating but inconsequential.

It was ironic that so many families with members who loved less and hurt more managed to rub along perfectly well, periodically rumbling towards falling out but shrinking back from the brink with a few sharp words and a couple of weeks of sulky silence. They seemed to confine their dynamics to a surface irritation under the banner of 'Oh he's always like that/someone got out of bed on the wrong side/take no notice of your mum/dad/brother/sister', which dissipated by the time the next barbecue rolled around – nothing a beer and a snide comment about being a 'touchy bugger' couldn't fix.

Yet other families like mine and Caro's seemed to have these deeply drilled fissures ready to suck everyone into an explosive alchemy of resentment. Who knew where the initial weakness originated, bubbling under the surface for years before finally blowing us sky-high decades later? Was my mum like Caro? Had she been caught in the middle, placating, appeasing, turning her spotlight to the person who shouted loudest, who needed her more than me? Had I chosen to take it as a personal slight, as proof that I didn't matter? I thought back to my graduation. Mum's voice wavering on the phone from the hospital as she told me she couldn't make it because Emily had broken her wrist. Perhaps not just with guilt that she'd let me down. Perhaps also with disappointment that she would miss it.

I was so lost in my thoughts, I was unprepared for Theo bursting in with, 'Will India really make us leave?'

It wasn't a conversation I wanted to have in front of Fergus, so I said, 'We'll talk about it later.'

But Fergus ruffled Theo's hair and said, 'Don't be silly. Of course we're not going to get rid of you. Who would play football with me? Or give me an excuse to go on the trampoline?' Then he said, 'Anyway, I'd really miss you. And your mum, too. A bit.' He turned to me and rushed in with, 'Anyway, you can't leave, otherwise I'd have to work really hard.'

He blushed then, his freckly face taking on quite the rosy hue. And, for some reason, the blushing spread to me, like ink on blotting paper, until we were walking along in a cloud of heat, the noise of our boots loud on the lane until Theo broke the silence by demanding that Fergus show him how to do somersaults on the trampoline.

Once we got back to the farm, I sat on the wall watching Fergus bouncing about and swinging Theo round by his legs. Apparently I hadn't needed to experience the years between two and eight to realise how easily a child could break his neck, so I kept leaping to my feet, shouting, 'Careful!' and hearing them gang up on me for being such a wuss. At least it was a distraction.

I didn't share Fergus's confidence that his parents wouldn't give in to India. That visceral desire to divert unhappiness away from your child didn't follow the rules of a meritocracy. It was ironic that just when I'd stopped waking up every morning wondering whether Theo would be better off in care, I'd have to uproot both of us to yet another uncertain future. I'd manage. I'd done it before. But Theo had already discovered how precarious the world was. Two of the people closest to him had died in the last year alone.

My gaze drifted over to Fergus, who was flipping Theo over backwards. I didn't want to take him away from this. He was just starting to ask questions that made me feel as though he trusted the community set-up of Fergus, Caro and Gilbert and – I hoped – me: 'If you can't pick me up from school, Fergus could come, right?' and, more recently, 'If something happens to you, will Fergus or Caro look after me?'

I had to swallow hard at that. When I was nine, Ian hadn't been on the horizon and Mum and I were a merry band of two. It never occurred to me that something might happen to her. For me, death was something that happened in films or to people who were very old. I wished that it had been the same for Theo.

Even though I didn't want to leave Applewood Farm, I couldn't get away from the feeling that our security was at the expense of someone else's family. Caro loved Theo. Gilbert did too in his gruff way. But as long as we stayed, our presence would be a tangible barrier to rebuilding their own family. I vacillated. Selfish me argued that if we left, there was no guarantee that they'd repair things with India and I'd be giving up a flexible job where I could do the school run, make up time in the evenings, take a day off at short notice, for nothing.

But the me who'd finally understood that very little about motherhood fitted into rational boxes didn't want to be the catalyst for them losing contact with India. I did marvel, though, that a forty-year-old woman could hold us all to ransom like this.

As I watched Theo leaping over Fergus, it struck me that we all choose our own narrative. The world as we see it. India felt hard done by, no doubt about that, unable to see how much Caro and Gilbert loved her. I tried to ignore the image in my head of Theo explaining his commitment problems to a tearful girlfriend in twenty years' time: 'I know you want to get married, but my mother abandoned me when I was two and a half...' He'd never understand that I loved him so much – and had so little confidence in getting it right – that I was prepared to give him up to someone who could.

And maybe Mum had been devastated by our estrangement while I'd been convincing myself of her disinterest. Maybe she'd spent years whitewashing me from the family history to protect herself but still, reluctantly, quietly, marking all those occasions I had noted for Theo – not just the birthday itself but the fact that it would be his birthday in a week, in a month. At least I'd been able to create a picture of Theo in my mind, safe with William, growing and flourishing without me. I'd even seen that photo of him in his rugby team, his friends holding him aloft, smiling and popular. My mother didn't have that luxury. She had no idea what had happened to me. I'd kept off social media, lost touch with all my friends.

Theo running up with Fergus broke into my thoughts. 'Fergus says I must have some Olympic athletes in my family to be so bendy. Do I?'

I laughed it off. 'I won the relay race at school when I was about twelve. And before that, I was a dab hand at running with a bean bag on my head at sports day. I think it was my mum who had the sporting genes really. She was a great tennis player.'

Theo sat on the wall beside me. 'Your mum? Have you got a mum?'

'I have,' I said, wishing I hadn't started the conversation in front of Fergus.

'Can I meet her?' Theo asked.

'I haven't seen her for a long time.'

'Did she go away, like you did?'

I really wished I'd kept my mouth shut.

'No, I went on a long holiday and sort of forgot to go home again. We lost touch a bit.'

Theo stood up. 'But you said we might go on holiday this summer. We won't forget to come home, will we?' He moved away and sat next to Fergus. 'Can we still come back again?'

With great cowardice, I let Fergus make a promise that I wasn't certain we'd be able to keep.

CARO

June 2019

Gilbert didn't answer India, just allowed me to steer him off the playing field towards the duck pond, where we sat on a bench. He leaned back, raising his face to the sun. I tried not to be the woman I was, the one who demanded quick thought and immediate answers. I resolved to sit in silence for as long as it took. I concentrated on looking at the bright green of the beech trees, the ducklings paddling behind their mum, the little bits of hawthorn blossom settling on the water's surface.

Eventually, he turned to me. 'I don't know what to do.'

I sieved through his words for the blame and accusation. They weren't there.

'Could you just leave it for a while? Give her time to miss you?'

He paused. 'What if that day never comes?'

'We'll have to learn to be happy anyway. Could you do that, do you think?'

'I don't know whether I'm brave enough to try.'

That admission from a man who had never conceded that he might fail at fixing a barn, mending a tractor, even at marriage – 'I don't know what you're talking about, Caro. If you think you'd be better off with someone else, then say that. Otherwise I am who I am and you'll have to get on with it' – touched my heart. It filled me with the sort of love that gets shoved to the back of the cupboard when children arrive with their wants and needs, rediscovered decades later, slightly mildewed, a little frayed round the edges, but still a joy to behold.

I put my hand in his. We sat with nowhere to go, no one with a greater claim on our time, taking it in turns to deliver tiny squeezes of support. I thought back to forty-two years ago and the two years we were married before we had children. How we were willing to indulge each other in talking about things that didn't have a specific purpose, that weren't a stepping stone to solving a problem or making money. How we had the space to talk about a painting I might do, or a business idea Gilbert might consider, with all the tolerance, love and joy that goes with encouraging a spouse to dream big. And how abruptly all of that love poured into my husband became diverted into parenthood, primed as I was to abandon a conversation any time the kids burst in. Our communication distilled down to who was where when and who needed what, with Gilbert sitting parched and waiting for water like an African violet on a forgotten windowsill. No room for daydreaming. And how even stripping ourselves bare in order to give more to the children hadn't been enough. For India, at least.

A clear picture of Gilbert picking up India out of the crib at the hospital and cradling her close rushed into my mind – 'You're going to have a lovely life.' We were astounding in our optimism.

'Let's get us back. You and me. Then hopefully the rest will follow.'

He sighed. 'I do think Vicky will have to go, though. I can't see India ever coming round to a young lad the same age as Rowan being a big part of our lives. Even if we didn't let him in the house, we can't stop him using the grounds. It would make things very awkward with Vicky.'

I got to my feet. Theo, my little shadow to fetch the eggs, the one child I had left to spoil with Bakewell tart and meringues, who'd sit with me in my studio and natter on about his day, had returned an energy to me. He inspired me, this young boy, who'd lost so much but adapted with a resilience we could all learn from.

'I think that would finish me off, Gilbert.'

And just like that, we got up and headed for home, the connection between us cut like a call dropping out of signal in a remote area.

All afternoon, I tried to imagine Applewood without Vicky and Theo. Dalí would pine for Lionel. I watched Fergus on the trampoline out of the window. He was so good with children. Probably because he'd never had to grow up himself. At thirty-five, I'd all but given up on him finding a girlfriend. It was so long since he'd had a serious relationship, I couldn't even envisage what sort of woman would suit him. I backed away from the idea that, like India, he might find someone who didn't get on with us. I couldn't lose another child to the vagaries of in-law chemistry.

After they'd finished outside, Fergus burst into the kitchen, red-faced, throwing open the fridge door and swigging milk straight out of the carton.

'Are you all right after today?' he asked.

'Bit worried Dad will push to get rid of Vicky,' I said.

Fergus banged the plastic container down on the island. 'Vicky's not leaving, Mum. She's done a brilliant job. India is just throwing her weight around and you're letting her get away with it.'

The frustration and fear I'd been keeping locked down burst forth in a rant. 'I'm not letting her get away with anything! I'm bloody trying my best to keep everyone happy, to stop us being at each other's throats for the next twenty years, to – yes, selfishly – find a way to enjoy my grandchildren before they forget what I look like. I don't want to live like this. I'll really miss Vicky and Theo if they leave. But if you can come up with a plan of what we could do differently, then I am all big, fat, flapping ears!'

Fergus stared at me. I waited for him to burst out laughing like he usually did when I lost my temper with him. But he didn't. He stood with his hands on his hips, looked me straight in the eye and said, 'This is such a screwed-up family. No one listens to a word I say, but you're all soul-searching away the second India says boo to a goose.'

I started to protest.

'Mum, save it. You know it's true. But, on this one, you're going to listen to me.' He paused for a second and I braced myself for another damning indictment of my flaws. He bit his lip. 'Don't tell dad. Not yet anyway.'

That phrase injected a familiar dread into my heart. Fergus hitting a cricket ball through a window at school – 'It would have been a six!' Fergus borrowing Gilbert's tractor and getting it stuck in a ditch – 'It wasn't even a deep ditch!' Fergus and friends letting the chickens out when they were drunk and a fox killing them all – 'We just felt sorry for them all cooped up in that little shed.'

I tried to soften my voice. 'What, darling?'

He pinched his thumb and forefinger on the bridge of his nose. 'This is so embarrassing.'

'Ferg, nothing could be more embarrassing than Andy kissing me. And everyone knowing. And India shouting about it down at the fete.'

He grinned. 'You're right there. Okay. I'm just going to say it, even though I'm going to sound like a total knob. I don't want Vicky to leave partly because she's great at the job but—' He screwed his eyes up. 'I love her, Mum.'

Fergus never talked about women like that. Just made jokes about doing 'all right with the ladies' if I ever asked him if he'd like a girlfriend. Was I really that mother who'd spent her life saying, 'You can't hide love or a cough', who hadn't seen what was going on right under her nose?

'Are you together?'

He sat on a stool at the island and put his head on the counter. 'No. She doesn't know. She never gives any sign of noticing any man.'

'She's been hurt a lot, Ferg. Are you sure? Because you can't mess her around. She's got Theo to think about.' Disloyally, I had a flashback to when Fergus went to his prom after his A levels with Molly from the village, but I bumped into her best friend Sienna sneaking out of the annexe in the morning. Hopefully he'd grown up a lot in the intervening seventeen years.

'I'm sure. I don't know what to do about it, but I am sure.'

That was a cherry on top of the nightmare of complications if ever I saw one.

VICKY

June 2019

The very next day, before I convinced myself it didn't matter whether Theo knew his grandmother or not, I wrote to my mum. I chose a letter because I wanted her to have time to think, wanted this one possible opportunity for reconciliation not to depend on whether the pasta was boiling over or someone was ringing the doorbell or Joey and Emily were mouthing questions at her while she was on the phone. I realised with a jolt that Joey would probably have left home by now. Followed by a weird sense of missing out on seeing them grow up, even though I'd chosen to leave.

Within half an hour and a pile of crumpled-up paper later, I understood why estranged people never got back in touch, because who did have the words to transform those feelings of hurt and resentment into olive branches of compromise?

I kept it simple in the end.

Dear Mum,

This is a very difficult letter to write and I'm probably not going to do all the emotions swilling about inside of me any justice. I have a nine-year-old son of my own and becoming a mother has helped me see things differently. I'm sorry for not understanding how difficult everything was for you when you were probably bending over backwards trying to keep

everyone happy. You might not want to hear from me now,
but I hope you do.
   Love Vicky

A few paltry lines seemed pretty inadequate from someone
who'd gone on holiday to Corfu and disappeared for a decade. I
popped in a photo of Theo for persuasion and stuffed it into the
postbox when I dropped Theo off at school. I tried not to allow
the prospect of seeing India intimidate me, but it wouldn't have
taken much for me to dump Theo at the corner of the road and
skulk away. Instead I chatted about which beaches we'd try in the
summer, how I'd buy him a bodyboard.

'Will you come in too?' he asked.

I laughed. 'I'd probably sink it.' Disappointment washed across
his face. I forgot how easily he lost confidence in me. 'I'll give it
a go though. Fergus is probably brilliant at surfing. It's all about
balance. We could ask him to show us.'

And, as easily as that, Theo's face lifted. I was just praying I
could deliver on that promise, that the Campbell family dynamics
wouldn't disrupt our gilded little existence, when Rowan came
running up to Theo.

'I'm doing press-ups with my dad so we'll win the tug of war
next year.'

I attempted to diffuse the animosity by saying, 'That will
certainly help build up your muscles. It'll be a tough competition.'

But Theo wasn't in peace envoy mode. 'Fergus is taking me
surfing, so I'll have incredible balance and won't ever fall over.'

Rowan's face fell. 'My Uncle Fergus? Can I come?' he asked,
seeming to forget that he'd been goading Theo a few moments before.

Theo shrugged. 'I can ask him.'

Rowan smiled. 'That would be awesome.' And they both ran
along the street with their arms stretched out like pocket-sized
Patrick Swayze in *Point Break*.

It was no wonder that adults fell out when the dance of one-upmanship started so early, but equally I couldn't help thinking we had a lot to learn from the ability of Year Fours to move on.

I didn't dare look round to see who Rowan was with. I didn't have to. Andy appeared beside me. I rejoiced that I wasn't face-to-face with India.

'Hi,' I said, as though he'd made my morning by taking up most of the pavement.

'Oh hello, didn't see you there.'

For one dreadful moment, I wasn't sure I'd kept the words, 'My arse!' from bursting out into the atmosphere.

Thankfully he defaulted to the Britishness of how lucky we were with the weather. We caught up with Theo and Rowan, said our goodbyes and just as I was allowing the prospect of imminent escape to filter in, he said, 'I hear Theo's leaving at the end of term.'

I turned to him, my heart thudding in preparation for confrontation. 'I'm not sure where you heard that.'

I said it lightly, hating myself for wanting Andy to like me. Even though the current discord that threatened my security was down to him trying it on with Caro when she was so vulnerable, I still couldn't call him out.

He tilted his head, puzzled. 'Oh sorry, I thought it was common knowledge.'

As though my thought processes had suddenly been released from a time-delay safe, I said, still gently, as though I was correcting him on the date of sports day, 'I think you must have got the wrong end of the stick. He's not leaving.'

And like a switch flipping, Andy put his face right up to mine. 'Well, you'd better tell Caro and Gilbert that unless he does, we'll be taking out a court injunction to keep them away from us.'

I cursed myself afterwards for not arguing back. I should have spelled out the facts, even said something as banal as 'Sod off, you big bully,' but I didn't. I stood with my legs trembling until Andy whistled off along the street and turned a corner, then I sat on a bench at the bottom of the hill, trying to stop the sobs building in my chest and to chase away the self-loathing that comes from not sticking up for yourself.

On that steep walk back up to the farm, I drove myself mad working out how I could stay without ruining Caro and Gilbert's life. Maybe if I talked to India, she'd come round or maybe I'd just make it worse. Even if I left, she might serve the injunction anyway. Could that happen? Didn't she have to prove Gilbert and Caro were harassing them? Would Gilbert texting or phoning count? I didn't know how it worked. Andy was probably just seeing if he could frighten me into getting what he wanted.

More than ever, I wished I could talk to my mum. I fought against the hope that if she replied, maybe in a day, or a week, or sometime, I could. Watching the Campbell family, I'd seen that a lot of energy went into solving the problem of India. She was always in the spotlight even though Caro never saw her and there was no doubt that Caro really loved Fergus. It did make me wonder about how I viewed my own upbringing. Mentally I snapped the storybook shut. I'd read my story in the way it had appeared on the page to me. It was probably too late to rewrite the ending now.

A few days later, I got my answer. Initially, my heart dropped when I thought she'd just sent back my letter unopened. There was a line through the address, 'Return to Sender' scrawled across it. And there, with a large arrow pointing to my mum's name: 'NOT AT THIS ADDRESS'.

I stared at it. No. That couldn't be right. Hundreds of images of Mum in our little terraced house rushed into my head. Watering her spider plant and snipping off the little babies. Rinsing the soap suds off the saucepans despite Ian saying it didn't matter if you were going to dry them up with a tea towel. Hurrying up and down the stairs with washing.

What did 'Not at this address' mean? That they'd all moved? That she'd walked out like me, leaving them in the family home? I dismissed that thought. She wouldn't have left Joey and Emily. I'd taken it for granted that she'd never move. That she'd cling to that house forever because then I'd know where to find her. That somewhere, stupidly, in my unconscious, I'd expected her to be waiting for the moment that I returned, the proverbial prodigal. The shock winded me.

I sat on the floor, staring at the envelope.

Maybe because I'd used one of Applewood Farm's business envelopes and printed a label to make sure Mum wouldn't recognise my handwriting and chuck it in the bin without opening it, they'd thought it was junk mail and hoped to be taken off a mailing list.

The envelope was still sealed, but I opened it anyway, on the off-chance there was a note inside and they'd managed to stick the flap back down. Nothing. Just a few bald sentences written when I thought I could decide it was time to make up with Mum and she'd be ready and grateful. I'd allowed myself to daydream about how she might meet Theo. And now these words, probably scribbled in irritation that mail was still arriving for the old occupiers, meant I might not ever find her.

I'd have to ring. Like a school hymn etched into my memory, an automatic reflex without thought, our landline number popped into my head. Along with it, an image of me crouching in the little alcove under the stairs whispering secrets to my friends with Ian walking past multiple times, saying, 'You'll be seeing her in the morning' and tapping his watch.

I picked up the phone. My hand was trembling. When was there a good time to find out that no one knew where she'd gone? Or that they were all still there, but she didn't want to speak to me?

My heart was hammering as I tapped in the number. A pause in which the temptation to press the big red symbol and never know the next thing nearly overwhelmed me. The pause turned into a robotic voice. 'The number you have dialled has not been recognised.'

I pressed my phone into my forehead. I couldn't think straight. If they weren't living in the house any more, how would I find them? I sifted through all the different options in my mind. Directory enquiries? Johnson was a pretty common surname. Writing a letter to the new owners? Visiting them? I imagined the hideousness of explaining who I was and seeing their faces shift from curiosity to awkwardness that a chance house purchase had launched them into someone else's drama. Private investigator? How much would that cost? I wish I'd kept the details of the one Barbara had sent.

I thought backwards. I'd last had contact with Mum eight years ago. I told myself not to speculate on what could have happened. They could be anywhere. Even abroad. What if she'd died? What if that 'Not at this address' meant 'not at any address'? I did a few sums in my head. Mum was only fifty-five. Joey would be about eighteen, which made Emily sixteen. I told myself off for letting my mind run away with me. The idea that I might not find her made me want to upturn tables and chairs and hurt myself so badly that the pain would obliterate this sick, falling feeling inside me.

Fortunately before I could disappear further down that path, a couple who'd booked one of the dog-free cottages turned up with a great hairy Burmese Mountain dog, requiring all my juggling ability to allow them to stay.

Afterwards, I lost myself down the rabbit hole of Google, 192. com, and conflicting articles on how to find out if someone was dead and how to trace someone you'd lost touch with. I ended up dashing down the hill to collect Theo after cricket practice.

He was tired and moaned about me not bringing the car. I'd hoped the walk with its view over the valleys might clear my head, but by the time he'd dawdled home, I thought I might start shouting and never stop. Which didn't make it a good day for Theo to push away my home-made chilli. I'd spent ages chopping vegetables into tiny, easily disguised pieces in an effort to diversify beyond baked potatoes. The 'we had cake and crisps at cricket' obliterated my last shred of patience.

I snapped. 'Come and sit down and get some goodness inside you.'

'I don't want it.'

'Just get on and do what you're told.'

'No.'

Theo was so compliant usually. I didn't know what to do in a stand-off, especially when I was always braced for the 'You dipped in and out of motherhood, so why should you tell me what to do?' rebuttal.

'Right, well, you can go to bed then if you're not eating dinner.'

'I want to watch *Horrible Science*.'

The voice inside my head was saying, 'Let it go, it doesn't matter,' but the voice coming out of my mouth barked, 'If you don't eat your dinner, you can't.'

With that, Theo swept the plate onto the floor, all the tiny pieces of red pepper, courgette and mushroom splattering across the tiles.

'Theo! That's really naughty!'

He turned round to me. 'I wish you'd died instead of Dad.'

By a tiny frayed thread of maturity, I managed not to shout, 'He wasn't even your father!'

As I absorbed his words, the fight drained out of me. He stood, open-mouthed, as though he'd surprised himself, then dashed off into his room.

I started to cry. Maybe he really thought that. It was frightening how without the monolith of many years of parenting behind us, any discord shook our foundations.

I wanted to go to him. I wanted to rush in and tell him how much I loved him, and that it was just a bloody plate of chilli, but it represented so much – so much that he couldn't even begin to understand. Me being a better mother than my mother, me showing my love by feeding him healthy food, the one thing I knew I could do well rather than the fifty million things I cocked up.

Such as coping with his anger. I had no idea how to defuse it. I started clearing up instead, hoping the answer would come to me by the time I'd wiped all the sauce off the table legs.

I was down on my hands and knees when the doorbell went. I ignored it. I could not handle a guest complaining about a missing teaspoon right now.

'Vick?'

Fergus.

I couldn't admit how useless I was.

He knocked. 'Vicky?'

I wiped my eyes on my T-shirt and found a cheery voice. 'Just coming.'

I opened the door.

'Christ. What happened to you?'

'Another example of my perfect parenting.' I was aiming for a joke, but a wail of hopelessness escaped. I turned away.

The door clicked behind me. I knew Fergus would be taking in the whole shambolic mess, me included. I tried to pull myself together, but the tears I so rarely shed had gathered their armies to defeat me.

He put his hand on my shoulder and turned me round. I was squirming away, not wanting him to see my blotchy face that had developed its own sprinkling system. He leaned forward and pulled me towards him.

I resisted. 'I'll make your shirt all wet.'

'It'll dry.'

I stood rigidly at first, feeling ridiculous that someone I worked for had seen me in such an unhinged state. Every time I went to move, Fergus said, 'Just stay there a minute.' Gradually my shoulders dropped and the muscles in my neck relaxed. It was ages since another human being had touched me beyond a casual handshake or brief goodbye hug from the occasional guest. It was so comforting, I could have gone to sleep right there, resting against him. His hands were stroking my hair, so rhythmically that I could feel our hearts beating in time.

Eventually that woman-too-close-to-a-man embarrassment engulfed me and I drew back. 'Sorry. Mad Monday in the Cottingdale/Hall house.'

'Only mad Monday? I should move in here.' He nodded towards the main farmhouse. 'Insanity reigns every day up there.'

I flopped down onto the sofa.

He looked at me. 'Go on then. What's up?'

'I don't know where my mother's gone.' I told him about the letter. I braced myself for him saying, 'But you hadn't seen her for years anyway.'

But he didn't. He breathed out. 'You do have to deal with a lot.' He put his hands in his pockets. 'Shall I go and have a word with Theo? Man to man?'

'Yes. Yes please. Make sure he knows I love him.'

Fergus smiled. 'He knows that already. Don't be silly. Everyone has bust-ups with their parents.' He pulled a face as it dawned on him that our two families weren't great examples of making up again. 'Okay. I get it. Let me go and talk to him.'

I lay on the sofa listening to the burr of voices, the high, indignant tones from Theo, the smooth, calm rumble from Fergus. Then a spike of laughter. And, eventually, the door clicking open. Fergus emerged with his hand on Theo's shoulder.

Theo looked at the floor. 'Sorry.'

'That's okay. I'm sorry too. I'd had a difficult day and I wasn't feeling very kind. Shall I run you a bath?'

'Yes please.' He paused. 'You won't send me away, will you?'

It was instinctive. I reached down to hug him. He clung to me.

'No. Never. I love you and you're stuck with me.'

I felt the solidity of those words as they left my mouth, the ones I'd wanted to say but never been able to release. I felt Theo react, a muffled cry as though he'd yearned for those words and feared they'd never come. We held each other for a moment longer, then I dropped a kiss onto his head and sorted out his bath.

Once Theo was settled, Fergus said, 'So what's the plan?'

I explained what I thought my options were, secretly hoping he'd offer to come with me to my old house.

'Have you looked on Instagram?'

'Instagram? Mum wouldn't have been on that. She didn't even switch her mobile on if she didn't want to phone someone herself.'

'But I bet your brother is. How old is he? Eighteen? Shall we have a look?'

'I'm not on Instagram. Or any social media. I gave all that up, well, when I left Barbara's house.' I couldn't bring myself to say, 'Walked out on Theo' even though Fergus knew the whole sorry story.

He leaned forward in mock exasperation. 'You're probably the only thirty-one-year-old on the planet who doesn't have a digital footprint. But I do.'

He pulled out his phone. 'What's his name?'

'Joey Johnson.'

'Seventy-four results.'

There it was again, that feeling of wanting to know and running away from knowing. But Fergus was a man with a task. He brought the phone to me. I flicked down the photos, afraid to find the answer. 'I might not recognise him. He was only eight when I last saw him.'

Fergus scrutinised the profiles. 'Him? He looks about eighteen.'

I peered at the thumbnail of a young man in a baseball hat. 'He looks quite blonde. Joey had dark hair, a bit wavy and quite olivey skin.'

I sat next to him on the sofa, peering into pictures as he clicked on their feeds, which more often than not were either set to private or were photos of beer bottles or people making weird faces in a nightclub.

I kept shouting up to Theo to check that he hadn't drowned. I didn't know how old he'd have to be before I stopped worrying about that, but without the history of bathing him as a young child, I didn't feel I could go barging in on him naked.

'What about him?' Fergus asked.

I stared at the photo. Fergus made it bigger. 'Maybe. He's got eyes a bit like my mum.'

'And just like yours actually,' Fergus said. 'They're quite distinctive, wide-set with really dark lashes.'

I wasn't used to being noticed. I blushed and leaned away slightly in case he could feel the heat of me. 'Tap on the profile.'

It wasn't set to private. We scrolled down. Pictures of the boy with a guitar. Singing. Joey had been a musical child, but I still wasn't sure. Then one with a girl, younger than him. The spitting image of my mum. 'That's him. That's Emily, my half-sister.'

I remembered her sitting on my bed, sucking on the ear of her pink elephant. And now there she was with a barely-there skirt, doing that teenage pouty thing with a face full of make-up Mum would never have let me get away with. I told myself that it didn't mean anything except that the world had moved on in the fifteen years since I was sixteen. That probably having lost one daughter, she picked her battles with the one she had left.

A sob lodged in my throat as Fergus worked his way down the photos. I kept thinking a picture of a grave would pop up. I never would understand why people posted such personal stuff on their social media. But apart from that one picture of Emily, there was nothing to give me a clue about Mum, whether she was still living in our little village or had done a Shirley Valentine and disappeared off to Greece. That would be ironic.

'Shall I message him?' Fergus asked.

'No!' I paused. 'Not yet. Hang on. Let me think.'

I went upstairs to tell Theo to get out of the bath, hearing reassuring swishing noises from the other side of the door.

I tucked him into bed, telling him again how sorry I was for shouting. I was feeling quite smug that I'd managed to articulate how much I loved him and how good it was that we'd talked about our feelings even if we'd both been a bit angry.

He nodded and said, 'Can you ask Fergus to come up?'

Yet again, I felt wrong-footed, dismissed. I gave him a clumsy hug.

When Fergus came back from saying goodnight, I said, 'I've no idea how to bring up a child.'

He grinned, that easy way he had. 'No one has any idea. Everyone is just throwing mud at the wall and hoping some good sticks. If they're lucky, they end up with kids who aren't a danger to society.'

Despite myself, I had to laugh. 'I'd like to think I'll do a bit better than that.'

'You know what I mean though. There are so many bloody variables. Your personality, theirs, the other influences on them. India was nowhere near as uptight before Andy came along pointing out all our faults.'

I blurted out what had happened at school with Andy earlier that week. Fergus practically spat out his beer. 'I'd like to see them serve an injunction on Mum and Dad. They haven't done anything wrong. He's living in cloud cuckoo land.'

'I could make it easy for you all and just leave.' I gave a half-laugh as though I was joking.

Fergus's face grew serious. 'That's not going to happen. Mum and Dad don't want you to go and I definitely don't. You're not the problem; India is.'

I felt the anxiety I'd been carrying around all week subside. I loved Fergus's certainty about life.

He picked up his phone. 'Anyway, back to the task in hand. Shall I message?'

'I suppose it's the best chance I've got of finding her without a great long search. She could be anywhere.'

Between us, we worded a message with enough information that Joey would know it was really me – where we used to live, the fact that I'd gone to Corfu, how long it was since I'd seen them, plus my phone number. As Fergus pressed send, my body shivered with a mixture of excitement and fear.

'Come on. We should celebrate,' Fergus said. 'Champagne? I can nip home and fetch some.'

'I feel that might jinx it. He might not respond.'

'You're such a pessimist.' He sighed. 'Shall I just go home?'

I didn't want him to go. I didn't want to be left alone on phone watch with nothing to distract me. 'I've got wine. Can you find something decent on TV?'

'I've heard *Catastrophe* is quite good.'

I'd never heard of it, but I didn't want to cement his view of me as someone with no life, so I said, 'Yep, great.'

Except we then sat there sipping our rosé while the two main characters had rampant and adventurous sex.

Fergus said, 'If I'd known how much sex there was in it, I'd have watched it before,' but I could tell from the way his foot was twitching that he was as uncomfortable as me.

Eventually, after yet another shagging up against a wall, I said, 'I find this really awkward.'

He pulled a face and said, 'Do you think it's because we haven't had sex with each other that watching people who are is more embarrassing?'

The wine had slowed down my brain, so I was still processing what he was saying when he added, 'I don't mean you should have sex with me so *Catastrophe* isn't so mortifying.' Then he went red and put his head in his hands. 'Sorry, I didn't phrase that very well.'

I smiled in that clenched-teeth way you do when you can't think of how to improve an entirely cringe-making moment.

I got up. 'Right. I'm going to go into the kitchen, fetch some more wine and when I come out, I want you to have switched over to something else that isn't going to make us blush.'

When I came back, the TV was off, but Fergus was still sitting with his hands over his face. He looked at me through his fingers. 'Can I say something?' His voice muffled into his hands.

'Depends what it is. Please don't let it be anything that is going to make me more mortified than I already am.'

He opened his fingers so one eye was looking out. 'Is there any chance I could kiss you?'

My shoulders came up around my ears. 'I can't come over and sit down and start kissing you. That's so teenage. No one our age asks. It's supposed to just happen.'

He got up. 'I've been thinking for ages about how to make it *just happen*. But, oh God, never mind. Come here. I'm so crap at this.'

I couldn't look at him. I stared at his feet, as he pulled me against his chest. This was a whole new level of complication. We stood in each other's arms, his chin resting on the top of my head, my thoughts and fears of the day stilling and slowing. The solid feel of his body made me think about William in Corfu, all those years ago, the first day I met him. I saw him in my mind's eye, ringing his phone from mine so I'd have his number. That impression as I walked away from him of something special occurring, of an opportunity to guide the universe rather than letting life buffet me about.

'Look at me.'

I raised my eyes without lifting my head.

'Properly. Oh my life, you're a difficult woman.'

He put his hand under my chin but didn't dip his head to kiss me, just smiled at me, his eyes warm. He raised his eyebrows in a question. I kept my gaze steady. I couldn't put myself on the line. It seemed so long since love, lust or anything in between had been an option for me.

Gently, he touched his lips to mine. And suddenly there was that tipping point when my defences gave way to pleasure, where the delicate dance of teasing and retreating that kept us as friends stepped over a boundary where something else might be possible. It was ages since I'd kissed anyone. I could feel the thrill of it reverberating through every nerve ending, shaking them awake to enjoy the moment.

We broke off to look each other in the eye, that odd moment where everything has changed, the dice suspended on the final edge before rolling to a halt and both people assess whether the gamble has paid off.

He brushed my hair back from my face. 'I knew you'd be gorgeous. You are gorgeous.'

His phone beeped.

I pulled away. 'Could that be an alert from Instagram?'

He grimaced. 'You want me to check? Now?'

'Would you? Please?'

He walked over to his mobile, straightening his shirt and running his fingers through his hair. Just for a second, I hoped it wasn't a reply, something that we had to deal with straightaway.

He tapped the screen. 'Damn.'

Fergus stared at his phone.

'What does it say?'

He closed his eyes for a second.

'Vicky, I'm sorry.' His voice was soft, as though he could somehow reduce the impact of the words. 'She died two years ago.'

'No! Show me!'

He handed me the phone.

Hi Fergus. Bit of a surprise 2 hear from Vicky this way. Been trying to find her. I don't know how 2 say this and even if I shld be saying it here but no easy way. Mum died 2 years ago – she had a huge stroke. We've moved 2 Cheltenham now

*for Dad's work. Could you ask her 2 call me please? 07700
900713. Sorry for bad news. Joey.*

I didn't react. Just stared at the words, the detached part of my
brain wondering if all teens only ever wrote in text speak, even
for something as important as this. But that passing thought was
pushed out of the way by remembering the cavalier way I spoke
about having no contact with my mum in the early days. I was still
establishing myself as the tough girl on the block, a few years older
than Joey, and often said to anyone who asked, 'It's no different to
a parent dying when you're young, it's just that you have a choice
about whether to see them again.'

Now I understood that having a *choice* made all the difference.
Somehow, although I'd never made a plan to see Mum again, I
must have thought I would. But now I never could.

The difference between what I imagined would happen – hurtful
and hard conversations resulting in forgiveness and a potential
rebuild of a relationship – and this dead end with no possibility
of redress floored me. I didn't cry. The shock of something I'd
dismissed as an outside possibility seemed to cauterise everything.

I sank down onto the sofa.

Fergus sat next to me, leaving a respectful distance between us.
'I don't know what to say. I'm sorry. Do you want me to leave?'

'Do you want to go? I don't mind.'

'Christ, Vicky, no. I'd rather stay. You don't have to cope with
everything on your own.'

I was too tired to think what message I was giving out, whether
I was doing the damsel in distress, not being feminist enough,
sending out the wrong signals. In that moment, I wanted someone
to distract me from the sadness so deep inside me that I had an
irrational urge to claw out my eyes. The sort of sadness that might
only be improved by hurting another part of me more.

I leaned against him. 'I've made such a mess of my life. Poor Joey. He was sixteen when Mum died. Emily was fourteen. I could have helped them. Ian was hopeless with all that emotional stuff. Just brushed it all away.'

I'd spent years not talking about any of this. Not thinking about Emily's little smile when she offered me one of the jam tarts she'd made with Mum and how them baking together made me feel lonely. Pushing away the memories of Joey and how he managed to get me to play goalie in the back garden even when I had revision to do. And Mum, a rush of disconnected images, not even the ones I wanted to have, of times when she'd made me feel important or special. Just odd things, her using her little finger to scrape cake mixture off a spoon. Sorting the socks into pairs and pegging them on the line together to save time later. The saucepan without a handle that she wouldn't throw away because 'no other pan does gravy like it'.

Fergus stroked my hair. 'Just talk about her. Whatever you want to say. Whatever comes into your head.'

'It's all just a muddle. It won't mean anything to you.'

'It doesn't have to mean anything to me. Start with anything. A birthday. Christmas Day. A holiday.'

And I started to talk, smile sometimes, remembering things I didn't realise I'd ever known, with Fergus nodding and prompting, 'Was that before you left for university?' 'I could see you doing that.'

And we drank wine, toasted Mum with whisky and, sometime in the early hours, I changed into pyjamas and fell asleep on my bed, next to a fully-clothed Fergus, who murmured, 'I'm still here,' every time I stirred.

VICKY

July 2019

I couldn't read Joey's feelings towards me when we spoke on the phone. The conversation was hard-going, his reply often 'It is what it is' to my questions about how he was coping or whether Ian was managing. He'd passed his driving test three weeks earlier and offered to drive down to Devon, but I knew Mum would've worried about that. I said I'd go to Cheltenham and meet him.

As I walked towards the lake in Pittville Park, I couldn't help thinking Mum would have loved the town, with its Regency buildings and arty-farty shops full of pottery and funny signs.

I wondered what had happened to the little plaque I'd brought back from Whipsnade Zoo that said, 'Home is where Mum is.' The memory made my eyes prickle. I scanned the benches by the boating lake, looking for a young man in a red T-shirt. My heart was beating with the fear of not recognising my own brother. But there he was, unmistakably Joey, with his thick, dark hair and those small, even teeth, a smile just like Mum's.

I couldn't speak. I wanted to be the big sister, the one – though late to the party – he could rely on, when he'd been through far more than most people had to bear at his age.

He stood up as soon as he saw me, a shyness mixed with pleasure in his gait. That little boy lining up all his train carriages in front of the fire had become a man, with broad shoulders and stubble. Funny memories of him stroking next-door's ginger cat and the collection of garden snails that he kept in a box jostled to adjust to the passage of time in front of me.

As he moved towards me, I couldn't wait anymore. I ran to him, and after pausing briefly to ask if I could hug him, I pulled him to me and pressed my cheek into his shoulder, tears pouring out of me. I felt the exact moment when he let go, when he allowed himself to give in, a wheezy dry sob, then a folding into me, and we stood, hugging and crying until eventually we laughed at the absurdity of ourselves.

We sat on the bench. I kept seeing little bits of Mum darting before me. The way he moved his hands when he talked. How his face broke from serious into a big open smile in seconds. His long, slim fingers as they held out a stack of letters. 'I kept these for you. They were in Mum's wardrobe. I don't know whether you want them.' I flicked through them. Letters and cards I'd sent to her from university. A letter from Liv saying she'd lost touch with me but she'd try and find out where I was. The large rounded lettering took me straight back to all-nighters when we sat side by side, drinking coffee and cursing ourselves for leaving assignments to the very last minute. Another one from Liv with William's address. I looked at the date on that one. After Mum had died. They wouldn't have known where I was anyway. Shamefully, I felt a glimmer of relief that Mum would never know I'd left Theo. At the bottom was a batch of about twenty letters, with my name written in Mum's neat cursive, but no address.

'Have you read these?' I asked.

Joey shook his head. 'I know what's in them though.'

'Is it bad?'

'No. She used to say she couldn't talk to you, but she didn't want you to miss out, so she used to write to you on your birthday and at Christmas. She'd always take herself off for a bit. "I'm going to have a moment with Vicky," she'd say. Em and I always thought she loved you most.'

I watched a mallard skimming across the lake. 'I thought she didn't really love me at all once you two arrived.'

He picked at his thumbnail. 'She couldn't speak after her stroke, but she could hear. The only time she really reacted was when Em said she was going to look for you. But she died within a couple of days.' He breathed out. 'We didn't have much energy for anything except holding ourselves together after that.'

I turned to him. 'Do you think I caused her stroke because she was stressed about me?'

'No, I don't. It was a brain aneurysm. The doctor said it was a weakness in the blood vessel wall. They couldn't tell us what caused it. It just came out of the blue.'

I felt all the angst that had been tightening my chest dissipate. 'I'm sorry I wasn't there for you. Are you angry?'

He put his head on one side, considering. 'I'm angry that she died so young. I'm angry that Dad gets impatient with Emily because she keeps talking about Mum and Dad says it's not helpful. It's not helpful to him maybe, but Em processes stuff with words. Em is frightened that she'll forget what Mum looked like, what she used to say. Yep, I am angry. It's just really shit.'

I waited a moment. 'Do you feel angry with me though?' My voice was quiet and everything in me braced for the answer.

'I'm not angry with you, Vicky. I'm really sad for you. Feel like we all missed out on time with Mum. You because you felt left out, us because she was often upset because she'd lost contact with you. And Dad got fed up with her talking about it, so I don't think we even saw the half of it.' He shrugged. 'It is what it is.' There it was again, that phrase. I wondered if he really believed it. I wished I knew him well enough to judge.

I studied him, scanning his face for traces of Mum. The thing that broke my heart most was that at eighteen, he'd already lost his certainty about life, already knew that being a decent person, doing the right thing, didn't guarantee that the world would deliver what he deserved. I'd been so sorry for myself at his age, jealous of my siblings and their claim on Mum's attention, but I'd also had huge chunks of carefree selfishness when my most pressing thought was who was going to buy the next round of drinks. Joey was already carrying a sadness that made him different from the other boys his age.

When I'd caught up on what he was studying, which A levels Emily planned to do, I couldn't put it off any longer. I had to tell him what I'd done, what had happened with Theo. I steeled myself for his disgust, even his fury, that I'd left my son of my own free will when I was sure Mum would have done anything to stay. But his face lit up.

'I'm an uncle? That's so cool. Em will love being an aunt. She's really good with children.'

Again, I had the sense that this eighteen-year-old man-boy was so wise, so generous-spirited. He reminded me a bit of Fergus, with his bursts of youthful enthusiasm, in-between the soul-searching.

I meant to sound welcoming and confident, but my words came out with a whimper. 'Would you like to come down and meet Theo one day? Emily as well if she wants to?'

His face did that seriousness into sunshine thing. 'That would be awesome.'

When it was time to say goodbye, I hugged him. 'Thank you. Thank you for not judging me.'

'Mum wouldn't have judged you either.'

I'd been too cowardly, too entrenched in my own self-pity to find out. And now I never would. Somehow, despite the knowledge that we all die and some people sooner than others, I'd assumed she'd live long enough for me to decide that I was ready to throw some earth over the lost years and fill in the cracks.

I waved until Joey was out of sight, then strode back to the car with *carpe diem* running through my head.

CARO

July 2019

I was in my painting studio when Gilbert appeared. He didn't even knock, just burst in. 'I've had India on the phone. They're thinking about emigrating to New Zealand.'

I stopped adjusting the grey of the clouds I'd painted in the corner of an otherwise peaceful landscape and stared at him. 'New Zealand? Where has that come from?'

Gilbert suddenly looked all of his sixty-nine years. 'Says that she's always wanted to live in New Zealand, that the kids would have more space and a more outdoorsy life and the only thing holding her back was being far away from her family.'

'I've never heard her even mention New Zealand.' I scoured through my memory. 'She doesn't even like taking the dog out, let alone hiking in the mountains. I bet she hasn't climbed up to Dumpdon Hill Fort in five years, never mind chasing halfway across the world for country walks.'

Gilbert ignored my comments and carried on. 'She said she realises that it would be silly to forego the great opportunity for the children when her family aren't interested in her anyway and never prioritise what she wants.'

'But that's not true. We'd love to have a relationship with all of them. Are you sure she's serious?' I waited to feel panicked, desperate to rush round to her house, to plead with her to forgive me and offer to do anything to make amends. But in the place where love used to reside was a kind of hopelessness, a resignation. I stood still for a moment, letting my feelings wash in and out.

Gilbert sounded close to tears. 'She'd definitely looked into it. Said secondary-school teachers were in demand and they wanted to get settled while they still had time to forge a proper career out there.'

'There's a big difference between googling something and shipping your sofas to the other side of the world.' I must have sounded flippant because Gilbert smacked his hand on the work surface.

'Caro! It's all right for you, because you're six years younger than me, but how long am I going to be able to fly backwards and forwards to New Zealand? Ten, fifteen years? Don't you even care that she'll disappear and we might see her once or twice again *in our lives*? Never know what Ivy ends up doing, whether Rowan carries on with his football, what Holly looks like as a young woman?'

I put down my brush and settled onto my velvet sofa. 'We might not know these things anyway. I haven't seen any of them since the fete and look how well that went. And the last time I happened to bump into her in the village was about ten months before that. She only lives eight miles away, but she might as well be in New Zealand.' I stroked the arm of the chair, the difference in the colours as the pile swept one way then the other distracting me momentarily. 'What's brought this on? Now, I mean?' The initial numb shock of Gilbert's news was subsiding. The magnitude of what India emigrating would actually mean was sinking in, the first tremors of alarm making themselves felt.

Gilbert rubbed his eye. 'I'm not sure.' But I could tell by his face he had an inkling.

'What?'

'She says she can't forgive you for trying to steal her husband.'

'Did she say something like "I'm dead to her anyway"?' As the words left my mouth, I could almost hear India's caustic tone.

Gilbert shook his head. 'No, Caro, she didn't say that. She said the only way she thought she'd discover who she really was and what she wanted out of life was to go a long way away, get some space between us and give herself time to work out what was worth saving, if anything.' His voice caught on the last two words and my dear husband screwed up his eyes to stop the tears escaping.

I went over to him. 'Gilbert, I'm sorry. I'm sorry I've made it so difficult for us all. Could we help her compromise at all? Maybe pay the mortgage on her house for a couple of years while they see how it goes, so they don't have to burn their bridges back here straightaway?'

He lifted his head. 'Would you do that?'

'We'd have to sell up the shares we were saving for the cruise to celebrate your seventieth birthday. I can't help thinking that India associates money with love, so it could be quite a powerful peace offering.'

To me, it felt like a massive and undeserved bribe. I refused to consider Andy's satisfaction at winkling thousands of pounds out of us. If it wasn't for me rushing in to carry the can, he'd probably be running his finger down studios for one to rent as we spoke. I forced myself to think of it as the gift of stability for my grandchildren. Emotional tax avoidance.

Gilbert said, 'Of course, we'd have to even it out for Fergus, make sure he gets treated fairly when it comes to sorting out our wills.'

I had to ask. 'You don't think she's doing this because we won't get rid of Vicky, do you? Surely she wouldn't do something so drastic over what was essentially a bit of a ding-dong between two eight-year-olds?'

There was always one question it was dangerous to ask.

VICKY

July 2019

I parked up and ran out onto the field to find Fergus and Theo, who were playing a version of football that involved pushing each other over and laughing hysterically. Fergus shot over to me immediately. He stood close to me, near enough for me to feel a desire to lean into him, for my stomach to lurch a little. His hand brushed the back of my arm and I moved away. This time I had to put Theo first.

His face clouded with understanding. 'How did you get on?'

'It was very emotional.' I swallowed down the tears that welled up as I spoke.

I turned to Theo. 'I cannot tell you how excited Joey was to be an uncle. He'd love to meet you. Only if you want to, of course.'

Theo nodded. 'How old is he?'

'Eighteen. He really likes football as well. Supports Peterborough United.'

Theo didn't look like he thought that was the most impressive thing about Joey.

Fergus stepped in. 'Perhaps we could take him to see the Exeter Chiefs, see if we can convert him to rugby?'

Theo perked up. 'That would be really cool.'

Yet again, I envied Fergus's easy way with him.

'Anyway, you carry on. I'll start getting dinner.'

'Can Fergus eat with us?' Theo asked.

'It's only pasta.'

But Fergus greeted the invitation as though I'd offered him a rack of lamb covered in some fancy herby crust.

I shrugged, his little wink filling me with a disproportionate amount of joy. I walked past the back of Caro's painting studio. The huge side windows with the view over the garden were open and I could hear Gilbert speaking. I had a little 'Aw, that's nice' moment, glad that he was keeping Caro company after the turbulent times they'd had. Then I heard him say, 'I think we will have to ask her to leave. I'm not sure how we'd fare legally because she's done a really good job. And Fergus won't be happy. It's not so much Vicky, but the fact that Theo has become part of our lives, that upsets her.'

My stomach plunged. Caro's voice was quiet. I stood out of sight at the corner, my ears straining to hear her reply.

'I'm not asking her to leave. She hasn't done anything wrong and neither has Theo.'

Gilbert's voice raised slightly. 'You'd choose her over our own daughter?'

'No, but I would choose her over blackmail, over petulance, over trying to bend everyone else to her will, while never cutting anyone any slack.'

I wanted to cheer.

'You kissed her husband!'

Something toppled over and I held my breath in case one of them stormed out and found me eavesdropping. I couldn't leave now, even though I was well aware no good would come of hearing their exchange.

'It wasn't like that and you know it. In the end, you can believe what you want. I've taken the blame for it, but it's not me you should have the issue with. And it's not as simple as that anyway. Fergus loves Vicky.'

Even in my tense state, her words shot a little thrill of happiness through me.

'Wha-at? Since when? Is he going out with her?'

I searched his tone for scorn, for disapproval, for the sense that I wasn't good enough for his son. I didn't find any.

'I don't think so. I think he'd like to, though.'

'And you'd barter India and her whole family on the off-chance that Fergus might actually make a relationship work? Not sure Ladbrokes would give you great odds.'

I didn't wait to hear any more. I doubled back, walked behind the hedge and cut through the little copse to my cottage. Before I could change my mind, I typed a letter of resignation and slipped it through the farmhouse letterbox. I'd have to have a conversation with Caro and Gilbert, but at least I wouldn't have to see the initial relief on their faces first-hand. I couldn't be the cause of India sitting on a bench with her brother in ten, maybe twenty years' time, wishing that she'd done it all so differently. Even if it meant giving up the one person who made me feel as though I was enough.

VICKY

July 2019

Fergus was hanging around after Theo went to bed. I just wanted to slump onto the sofa, and not face what I had to face. I'd been mad to think I could stay at Applewood.

I carried on washing up, without offering him a beer or telling him to find something on TV. 'Thanks for looking after Theo today. You must be worn out. Go and have an early night if you're tired.'

Fergus did his usual selective hearing. 'You're the one who's had an exhausting day. Always my pleasure to spend time with Theo. You know it is.' He looked down. 'He's a lovely lad.'

I couldn't let this conversation carry on.

'Fergus. There's something I need to tell you.'

He cracked his knuckles. 'Is it going to be something I don't want to hear?'

My words fell out, stumbling and awkward. 'I'm moving away, probably to Cheltenham to be near my brother and sister. Not yet of course, not until you find a replacement.' I didn't tell him I couldn't think of anywhere else to go.

'On the strength of one meeting? You haven't even spoken to your sister yet.'

'I know it seems a bit quick, but my sister is only sixteen and Joey's away at university. I want to make amends and give her the support she needs to finish school and get to college. I hope you understand.'

Fergus was shaking his head. 'I don't, no. I thought your priority was Theo. He's settled here and happy. Think what he's been through at a much younger age. Your sister has still got her dad and her brother. Theo's had to rebuild his life completely. And he's done brilliantly.'

'I can't stay here.' I needed to finish this conversation before my resolve crumbled.

Fergus put his hands in the air. 'Is this because of me? Because of what happened, you know, the other night? Because if it is, I promise I'll never come near you again. Literally even if it kills me, I will act like you're the ugliest, smelliest woman that ever walked this planet. I'll only talk to you about work stuff. I don't know, I'll put bromide in my tea or something.'

He was so earnest while being funny that I got caught on that knife-edge between tears and laughter. I didn't quite make it to a laugh.

'You've been so good to us.'

Fergus stood up. 'You're really puzzling me now, Vicky. It all seems a bit hair-shirty to me. I get that you want to look after your brother and sister now you've found them, and that maybe their dad isn't all that great. But you could support them without actually uprooting Theo. I just don't understand why you would do that when he's starting to make such good progress.'

'I think it would be best for everyone.' I kept clearing my throat, but the sounds I was managing to produce were the polar opposite to the words I was saying.

'You don't look like you think it's best for you.'

I was digging deep for the argument that would make Fergus let me go without a massive drama when there was a knock at the door.

Fergus stormed over and flung it open.

'Dad!'

Gilbert was holding my letter.

'Fergus, could you give us a moment?'

Fergus folded his arms. 'Is this about Vicky resigning?'

Gilbert nodded. 'You know already?'

'She's just told me.'

I couldn't bear it. I wished I'd never come to Applewood Farm and caused so much unhappiness. I'd not only messed up my own family but had managed to get all the Campbells at loggerheads as well.

'Please don't fall out over me. Please. It's not worth it. Let me leave and then when the dust settles, we can talk about me coming back to work here. Or maybe I can work remotely or something, but the last thing I want is to cause a huge rift between you all.'

'She's not leaving, Dad. This is nothing to do with Vicky. It's India acting like an idiot as usual. You can run the business yourself if you're going to let India dictate who works here.'

Gilbert put his hand up. 'Hang on, you haven't even heard what I'm going to say yet.'

Fergus's face settled into a sulk.

'I've just come to say that Caro and I have had a long talk about your resignation and although you don't say so, I believe I'm right in thinking the motivation to leave is because of the conflict of interest with India?'

I suddenly felt as though I was being interviewed again. On cue, Lionel leaned against Gilbert to have his ears scratched. 'Sort of, yes, because I don't want to see you all tear yourself apart.'

Fergus butted in. 'What does Mum think? I bet she doesn't want Vicky to go.'

I scowled at Fergus. 'Let's just hear what your dad has to say.'

He rolled his eyes but stopped speaking.

Gilbert flicked an irritated glance at him. 'We've decided that it wouldn't be in the best interests of the business for you to go, and that with no guarantee of reconciliation with India, we should take the bird in the hand and let the future look after itself.' He took a big breath. 'And, of course, we've all grown to love you and Theo and we'd be really sad if you left.'

I couldn't help it. I threw my arms around his neck. Which seemed to take him by surprise at first, but then he pulled me into his arms and gave me a quick hug. He smelt of wood smoke. And there was something sturdy about him, how I'd imagined a dad might be.

'So will you stay?' Gilbert asked, clearing his throat.

I looked over at Fergus, who was still working on the transition from grumpy to joyous.

'For God's sake, Vicky, don't even dare say that you need to think about it because I'm just going to implode,' Fergus said.

'All right. All right. I'll stay. If you're sure,' I said, feeling as though I might start running round the garden in delighted circles like Lionel did when he saw me pick up his lead.

Gilbert moved towards the door. 'Right. I'm off to tell Caro. She wouldn't come in case you said no anyway and it all got a bit messy.'

I smiled and said thank you, while wondering what exactly he meant by 'messy'.

Fergus stood in the middle of the sitting room, muttering to himself. 'My family really gets up my pipes.'

'I love them. I think you're really lucky.'

Fergus pulled a face. The face of someone who'd never had to question whether or not he was loved. 'Come here. Don't argue, just come. Please.'

I walked over to him, looking at my feet.

'Is it always going to be like this? Am I always going to be the one putting myself on the line? Running the risk of looking like a complete loser, desperate for a girlfriend?'

'Are you? Desperate for a girlfriend?'

'No. I want you. And I'd like to think I could, I don't know, be good for Theo.' He kissed the top of my head.

'You're great for Theo.' I felt myself blush. 'And me.'

The next day I should have been elated. But I couldn't shake the feeling that my own happiness was at the high cost of someone else's. I managed to find out where India worked by asking Fergus about secondary schools in the area for Theo. He had stroked my face and said, 'I'm loving the long-term thinking' before warning me against Staniford School 'because you don't want India teaching him'. Deceitful yes, but I hoped he'd forgive me.

A week later, I was parked on the road opposite the staff car park. After two hours, I was about to rethink my plan when India walked towards a red Polo.

I ran over, my heart thumping. 'India!'

She stopped. 'What do you want?'

I held my hands up. 'Could we just have a quick chat?'

'I've got nothing to say to you.'

She swung round as the school door banged and another teacher headed out, laden with a huge pile of books.

'Please. Just five minutes.' I gestured towards my car. 'We could sit in there.'

I saw her glance over her shoulder, weighing up the chances of me making a scene. I hoped she was remembering that day at the school fete. I was in luck.

Her face clouded with annoyance. 'I really haven't got time for this. It's two days until the end of term and I've got plenty to do.' But she still walked over with me.

Reluctantly, she climbed into my car, her nose wrinkling at Theo's damp swimming kit discarded in the footwell.

'I need to get home, so say what you've got to say.' She folded her arms.

I turned in my seat, feeling ridiculously nervous. 'Look, I know things aren't easy for you with your family and I'm sorry that we've somehow made the situation worse.'

She did a little snort of confirmation.

I battled on. 'It's not my place to offer advice, but I haven't spoken to my mum, or my brother and sister, for ten years. I tried to get back in touch with them recently and I've found out my Mum died a couple of years ago.' I paused, willing myself not to cry. 'I'd give anything to be able to sort things out with her. I did love her and, too late, I've found out that she really loved me.' I'd read and re-read through the letters Joey had given me, bawling my eyes out at all the lost opportunities every time, especially at the phrase she often used: 'As long as you're happy, I can accept not seeing you.'

For a minute, India looked as though she was going to shrug her shoulders and say, 'And what's any of that got to do with me?' But instead she dropped her hands into her lap and said, 'I'm sorry to hear that.' We sat, just for a second, before she added, 'I think it's too far gone for me and my mum now. There's quite a lot of water under that particular bridge and it doesn't just involve me.'

I didn't comment in case it was a trap and she accused them all of gossiping to me. I could hear her now: 'I'm the last to find out anything in the family, but Vicky, she knows the ins and outs of everything. Why don't you adopt her as your daughter?'

Instead I said, 'You might not believe it, but both your parents are absolutely devastated that they don't see you and that you might move to New Zealand. They love you, India. They might have made mistakes, but they definitely love you.'

I held my breath, hoping my words were finding their way home.

Her eyes filled and she pushed open the car door. 'They've got a funny way of showing it.'

I shouted after her. 'Don't leave it too late.'

My heart ached as I watched her cross the road, racing to the safety of her car. She'd no doubt spend her drive home justifying her version of Caro and Gilbert to herself, refuting my words as the misguided ramblings of an outsider – or worse, the cuckoo in the nest – who had *no idea*.

She really believed they didn't care about her. I hoped she came to her senses before she was standing at a graveside.

At least I'd tried.

CARO

Christmas 2019

Fergus and Theo chose the biggest tree, which required a delicate balancing act on the forklift truck to get the lights right to the top. Gilbert ordered the fattest turkey, Vicky had kept half of the south-west's delivery vans in business with parcels arriving daily.

For the first time in a long time, I really looked forward to Christmas. Keeping the door open to reconcile with India in the future while accepting that we wouldn't have any contact with her in the present had allowed us to take pleasure in everything we had rather than grieving for what we didn't. Gilbert's thinking had also changed – 'She has to do what's right for her, but so do we.' He no longer seemed to be caught in the trap of resisting but longing to contact her, which, with the contrariness that was human nature, meant she occasionally rang him of her own accord. The wheels of the emigration process were grinding round so slowly, we sometimes wondered whether it was an empty threat.

In the meantime, Gilbert seemed freed from his role of the family mechanic, duty-bound to repair the faulty components. He'd started a walking group with all his mates from the village and frequently tottered home with Dalí after a hike that inevitably ended in the pub.

And today, three years after that disastrous Christmas with India, his face no longer fell into melancholy repose when he thought no one was watching. There was a brightness about him, quick to have a go on Fergus's new quad bike, eager to help check over Theo's before they shot off down the field together.

I stood next to Vicky and we clinked our champagne. 'Here's to a wonderful Christmas and a very Happy New Year.'

Her eyes glittered. I'd noticed that since she'd got together with Fergus, she seemed so much more emotional. Which really went to show that mothers only know a tiny fraction of their children. I'd always thought Fergus blundered along, dodging feelings and walking away from anything and anyone who required effort. But I had to hand it to him, I'd seen Vicky lose some of her intensity, that inclination towards abruptness in his company and he, in turn, had become far more thoughtful than I'd given him credit for. Or maybe as Gilbert had said so kindly when I'd mentioned it to him, 'Perhaps the right circumstances to showcase his qualities hadn't previously presented themselves.'

Vicky took a sip of her champagne and said, 'Thank you. Thank you so much for inviting the rest of my family to come over for Boxing Day. Ian can be a funny old stick.'

I waved my hand towards Gilbert. 'So can my husband. We'll stick them under the patio heater with a bottle of brandy if they get too cantankerous.'

She laughed. 'You're very tolerant. And Fergus is amazing with Joey and Emily.'

'That's because he's still so immature himself,' I said, then told myself off for pointing out Fergus's faults to the best woman he'd met in years. 'Well, I say that about him, but I think he's been a good influence on Theo,' I said, patting myself on the back for wading in with the big guns where it really mattered. And it was true. Fergus, Joey and Theo were a joy to watch, male energy in triplicate.

I loved it when Vicky's brother and sister came to stay. Joey became like my adopted teenage son – someone to bake for, someone whose face brightened at the offer of more roast potatoes, someone whose problems could still be solved with twenty quid

– with none of the responsibility for making sure he didn't short-circuit his brain with cocaine or whatever teenagers did for kicks these days. And although Emily had been quiet around us at first, she was actually very quick witted with a great sense of humour, reminding me of Ivy with her outbursts of giggling.

I was just thinking how much Vicky had brought to our lives in a way we could never have anticipated when I heard a shout from the driveway.

As I walked over, a tall, slim woman emerged from a battered Golf. 'Nan! Happy Christmas!'

'Ivy? What are you doing here? Happy Christmas, darling!'

She flung her arms around me. Sheer willpower stopped me clinging to her and begging her to stay forever. I didn't dare ask if India knew where she was.

Instead I said, 'I didn't know you could drive!' Then again, I didn't know much about her at all.

She looked at me under her lashes, cheekily, in a way that reminded me of Rowan. 'I've just passed my test. I made a bargain with Mum that I'd take Rowan and Holly to school if she bought me a car for Christmas. I didn't think she would because we're supposed to be moving to New Zealand. Though I don't know whether we're even going. I overheard Mum say she wasn't sure she wanted to be so far away...' She hesitated, as though weighing up whether to say the next bit. 'Now you and Granddad are getting older.'

I didn't want to be that grandmother pumping her for information, so I just laughed at that comment and said, 'Cheeky!' even though my stupid optimistic heart felt a leap of hope that India might be softening towards us. But in keeping with my newfound philosophy, I was going to enjoy the moment, not worry about stuff I probably couldn't affect anyway. I hugged Ivy to me, stunned at how old she looked with thick mascara and heavy eyeliner. She could have passed for twenty, not seventeen. Frankly, she could have been bleached and tattooed and sunbed orange and I would still have found her the most beautiful granddaughter in the world. 'Come and see Granddad, he'll be so pleased to see you.'

Gilbert lit up like shooting stars in an August sky when he saw who it was.

And there was no doubt that Ivy loved starring in her own adventure, the subterfuge, the sheer adrenaline rush of knowing that she shouldn't be here. I didn't want to encourage her to lie to India, but I'd always championed the rebellious, the non-conformist. It was gratifying to see that you could choose to reject your family but it was a bit harder to sidestep the genes.

Perhaps Ivy would be the life raft back to India. But for the moment, Ivy hadn't forgotten us and that was enough for now.

VICKY

Christmas 2019

There was one present left under the Christmas tree. An envelope, with Fergus's scruffy writing.

'It's yours,' he said.

'Shall I open it now?'

He nodded.

I wasn't so hot on the whole letters thing. Since I'd read through the bundle that Joey had brought me from Mum, I associated reading personal notes with pouring feelings into a great big urn and giving them a good churn, requiring several weeks for everything to settle down again.

'It's a good thing. I promise.' He was grinning, as though he'd had to work hard to keep the secret.

I glanced at Caro, who was nodding. 'I think you'll like it.'

I had that moment of fear in case I didn't and couldn't find the false face of gratitude.

Fergus sighed, shaking his head in mock-exasperation. 'You can open it later, if you like, when you're on your own.'

I flipped the flap open, more out of a desire not to disappoint them. I pulled out the paper inside, to find two tickets to Corfu for Theo and me.

Fergus put his arm round me. He whispered in my ear, 'Go and visit Freddie. He's still running the same bar, according to the reviews on TripAdvisor. Let Theo know his dad. I'll be jealous as all hell, but I'll be here waiting when you get back. Then we can talk next steps.' He blushed. 'Obviously, if you don't decide to stay in Corfu.'

I felt several pairs of eyes on me, including Caro's. There it was again, that mother look, not so dissimilar to Barbara's. Her face striving for neutral but etched with a determination to protect. There'd still never be any competition about who she'd save in a fire. I glanced over at Theo busy building an Airfix Spitfire with Gilbert and knew exactly how Caro felt.

I reached for his hand. 'Don't worry. We'll definitely come home.'

Home. Those words were reassuringly solid. For once, I looked forward to leaving for the joy of knowing, without a single doubt, that I'd be back.

A LETTER FROM KERRY

Dear Reader,

I want to say a huge thank you for choosing to read *The Mother I Could Have Been*. If you did enjoy it, and want to keep up to date with all my latest releases, just sign up at the following link. Your email address will never be shared and you can unsubscribe at any time.

www.bookouture.com/kerry-fisher

Families fascinate me, not least because of the tendency for everyone living in the same house to view the same event in a totally different way. My family holiday to Australia is a great example of this – while I remember surfing with my teens on Bondi Beach and climbing the Sydney Harbour Bridge, my kids love to recall my sense-of-humour failure when I left the map-reading to my husband…

I became interested in why and how people lose touch with close relatives after hearing on the radio that, in Britain, estrangement affects one in five families. Whatever the cause – a fallout over a will, a second marriage, a step-parent, in-laws or just a misunderstanding that gathers traction – it struck me that the event that breaks the camel's back is often a culmination of a thousand preceding paper cuts. Families have such a power to heal but also know which buttons to press to hurt. In my research, some people became estranged because of abuse, but very often families recounted such normal lives where there was – and still is – so much love, but no one could find a way to build a bridge.

I also wanted to explore how mothers put pressure on themselves to be perfect. I was thirty-three when I had my first baby, not twenty-two like Vicky. Despite feeling I should be mature enough to deal with any challenge a child threw my way, the reality was much harder than I'd anticipated. I floundered about, feeling as though every other mother was more competent than me. It was only much later that I understood that there are so many ways from A to B with children and most of them eventually sleep through the night/learn to read/eat broccoli – maybe not that last one...

I read a lot around the subject of women who leave their children. One of the common threads was that it wasn't that they didn't love their children, rather that they either thought someone else would do a better job or they just wanted a momentary release from feeling that they were failing, always intending to go back but never finding the right time.

I write this in every book, but it still stands: one of the biggest privileges of my job is receiving messages from people who've enjoyed my work. Sometimes readers have shared their own personal stories, occasionally for the first time in their lives. I am absolutely humbled by the raw honesty of some of these messages and the trust you put in me. Thank you.

I hope you loved *The Mother I Could Have Been* and would be very grateful if you could write a review if you did. I'd love to hear what you think, and it makes a real difference to helping new readers to discover one of my books for the first time.

I love hearing from my readers – you can get in touch on my Facebook page, through Twitter or my website. I will always do my very best to reply.

Thank you so much for reading,
Kerry Fisher

kerryfisherauthor

@KerryFSwayne

www.kerryfisherauthor.com

ACKNOWLEDGEMENTS

The Mother I Could Have Been is my seventh book and the more I understand about publishing, the more I realise how lucky I am to have the brilliant Bookouture team behind me. My editor, Jenny Geras, is an absolute joy to work with – her calmness and clarity of vision make my job so much easier (and lead to fewer words disappearing under the delete button). There are so many people behind the scenes working their Bookouture magic that I'm nervous of listing them in case I leave someone out – but I do have to mention Kim and Noelle who pull out all the stops to make sure our books reach their readership.

Thanks – as always – to my agent, Clare Wallace. Wise, kind and smart – it's a great combination. I'm also very grateful to Mary Darby and Kristina Egan at Darley Anderson who help my books on their journey into the wider world.

As always, the bloggers and FB book groups have been a force to be reckoned with – they do an amazing job in spreading the word about new books and give up so much time to read and write reviews.

Thanks to all the people on my author Facebook page – too numerous to mention individually – who helped me with random queries from whether librarians need qualifications, whether golfers play in teams and the most popular: the most irritating thing a grandparent can do while looking after a grandchild! Not only do you help me make sure my research is spot on (and if it's not, it's my fault, not yours), but I love hearing all the side anecdotes about your lives.

Finally, a huge thank you to all the readers who buy, review and recommend my books – and especially anyone who takes the time to contact me personally. Those messages are motivational gold dust.